Chris had terrifying nightmares. They went beyond a child's usual images of ghouls and ghosts, for they contained a consuming rage at his life; Chris's visions were of real death. It was like living in an imaginary town where behind every door someone was performing a murder, and at any moment a door would open and it would be time for another guest. These were dreams with frightening detail, from the dazzling flash of a stiletto to the terror Chris felt when the figures in the shadows caught him. His nightmares belonged to someone much older, who knew how much there was to dread. They should have belonged solely to Chris.

Yet they didn't.

Angela knew Chris's dreams intimately, not because the boy talked about them—he didn't—but because she had allowed Chris to share her room. On the third night, Chris's nightmares became her own, the visions terrorizing her sleep. She lay awake, wondering how anyone could have such dreams without being driven mad.

MINDBENDER

**James Cohen
& Peter Rubie**

LYNX BOOKS
New York

MINDBENDER

ISBN: 1-55802-228-7

First Printing/January 1989

This is a work of fiction. Names, characters, places, and incidents are
either the product of the authors' imagination or are used fictitiously.
Any resemblance to actual events, locales, or persons, living or dead,
is entirely coincidental.

This book is published by Lynx Books, a division of Lynx Communications, Inc., 41 Madison Avenue, New York, New York, 10010. The
name ''Lynx'' together with the logotype consisting of a stylized head
of a lynx is a trademark of Lynx Communications, Inc.

Printed in the United States of America

0 9 8 7 6 5 4 3 2 1

To Vince and Kathy O'Brien
    and
Eric, Sara, and Jenna Bergerson
        —James E. Cohen

To my parents
        —Peter Rubie

MINDBENDER

Prologue: The Power

1985

He was sitting by a box of explosives, nervous and impatient. The room was dimly lit, with only slices of light cutting through the cracks of a boarded fourth-floor window. In his hand was a revolver.

For close to an hour, he had rocked on a wooden chair, pushing the gun back and forth across the top of a small table, counting the clicks as the copper-topped bullets slid in line with the hammer. A knock on the door made him look up.

"Yeah?"

"Smack," a voice whispered.

Twenty-five dollars slipped through a mail slot.

He crossed the room, took the cash, and jammed it in a pocket. Then he went back into the shadows. Behind a small stack of boxes was a large plastic freezer bag. He opened it, took out a yellow envelope, and slid the envelope out the mail slot. With the deal finished, he again counted the cash.

More money, he thought. But what difference did it make if no one came to pick him up?

He sat down and peered into the muzzle of the revolver

as if it were a wishing well. If he had one wish, it would be to get the hell out of this room.

Where were they. . . ?

Terry Cooke massaged her forehead. With her eyes open, she saw the patches of tar and pavement that somehow made a street; closed, she could just as clearly see a nervous young man playing with a pistol in an abandoned apartment. It was like flipping the channels on a television set.

"Are these punks coming or what?" Gordon Weiss, her partner, asked. "We've got about seventy hours of overtime coming to us, and I'd like to spend mine before I die."

Gordon watched another junkie hurry away from the tenement building. He lifted a 35 mm camera with a long lens, focused on the junkie, and snapped a picture. They were in a pale yellow Ford Fairmont, parked on a side street off Avenue D in New York City. The street ran east to the first tower leg of the Manhattan Bridge. Half a block south of their car was a Chevy van with five more detectives.

Terry concentrated on the image in her head. It was strange—if she blinked her eyes, she was in the car; blink again, and she was back in the tenement, watching a middleman count his cash and wait anxiously for his friends.

There was no explanation for the phenomenon, and that was fine with Terry. She preferred not to think about it. Hell, it was nothing more than sound reasoning, she told herself. She had spent months working on this case.

While Terry sat with her eyes closed, Gordon leaned against the steering wheel and stared at his partner. He admired the way Terry dressed. Even in the casual clothes she wore for a stakeout, Terry Cooke had the groomed look of a successful thirty-one-year-old detective. She was especially impressive when sitting beside Gordon—a twenty-nine-year-old divorced guy whose dress sense stopped with designer jeans.

"Sixteen months, eight fucking explosions, and we're stuck here looking up the asshole of Manhattan," Gordon said.

Terry opened her eyes and stared at the tenement. The building had the decayed hollowness of a skull. The windows of the first three floors were sealed shut by corrugated iron and cinder blocks, and graffiti was sprayed on the walls. Above the entrance hung an oversized yellow "Condemned" sign painted on a tin sheet.

Terry rummaged in her shoulder bag for a clean tissue. She pushed aside the loose change, her tampon carrier, a bottle of children's Tylenol. . . . The tissues were squeezed between her police I.D. and a snub-nosed pistol. She tore the packet, blew her nose, and threw the crumpled ball back in her bag.

"They must be having a fire sale in there," Gordon said. "How much longer we gonna be stuck here, Terry? My toes are ready to freeze off."

"They'll be here," she said, somehow certain. The man in the apartment sold drugs and guarded a cache of explosives for a group of urban terrorists called the Democratic Liberation Party. His name was John Griffin—a detail that had suddenly come into her head.

Gordon focused his camera on a hooker, maybe seventeen or eighteen, with straggly red hair that hung past her shoulders. "Ms. Big," he said as a joke.

Terry ignored him. She couldn't shake her image of an unstable kid surrounded by drugs, guns, and explosives.

Where the hell are your friends, Griffin?

She tried concentrating harder, but the image was already disappearing—the young man, the boarded window, the long row of boxes. . . . Terry preferred not to think

3

about it. Daydreaming, that was all. She sat straighter and nudged Gordon. "Over there."

He followed her finger and focused on two men in leather jackets. They crossed the desolate street and paused by the entrance to the tenement, glancing about. The Fairmont's radio blared questions from the other watch. Terry took hold of the microphone and said, "Not yet." Gordon took more pictures.

"They're professionals," he said. "Or at least they're trying hard to be. You recognize them?"

"No," she said. "They're not D.L.P.; they're middle-aged and fat."

"You mean they're cops?" Gordon grinned.

Gordon was exactly right. "Get them out of there," she said.

Gordon pulled up his coat collar and left the car. Terry hoped he would handle the situation delicately and quickly. All he had to do was say a few words, flash his badge, and get those guys the hell away from that tenement.

She saw Gordon flash his badge and watched the two men turn away from him. Gordon grabbed the nearest man, forcing him to stand still. The second man continued inside.

"Terry?" the cops radioed from the Chevy van.

Gordon led the man to the Fairmont. Terry rolled down the window, bracing against a rush of cold air.

"D. S. Wilcox, Narcotics," the man said, rubbing his hands.

"Detective Sergeant Cooke, Intelligence. Get your partner out of my building."

"You're joking, right?" Wilcox said. "I mean, this building's the Chase Manhattan of the drug trade around here." He glanced at his watch. "In about ten minutes we're gonna bust the place. You're welcome to hang around and watch."

"You're not doing *anything* to this building," Terry answered. "It's been under my surveillance for three straight days. This is an *Intelligence* operation."

"No way," Wilcox said.

A series of shots echoed from the tenement. Gordon spun about.

Another shot.

No one waited for orders. The detectives emptied out of the van while Terry phoned for more backup and then followed the team into the tenement. They heard another volley echo from the upper levels.

Gordon rushed up the rotted staircase and stopped on the second-floor landing. He braced against a wall, pointing his revolver into a dark hallway. Wilcox continued upstairs. Someone at the far end of the hall ran into a room and slammed the door. Gordon started down the hall, but Terry pulled him back. "Fourth floor," she said.

The detectives ran upstairs, Gordon and Terry in the rear. There were more shots. Through a window came the sound of police sirens.

Two detectives stayed by the staircase, while Terry and Gordon crouched forward, their free hands rubbing the pitted surface of the wall. Terry motioned Gordon with her weapon.

"Police!" she shouted.

They had reached a doorway. *The* doorway, Terry was certain. Gordon glanced at her, took a breath, and threw himself into the room. Terry moved alongside him, then bent down to examine Wilcox's partner. He had been shot through the neck. Blood was soaking his shirt and pooling on the floor. Wilcox was nearby, buried underneath overturned boxes.

"Where's Griffin?" Gordon asked Wilcox.

Wilcox pointed to a door that had been splintered by bullets. Terry pushed it, then jumped back. The door swung slowly open, and she peered down a long dark hallway. Somewhere from the hall came the sound of whimpering. She moved carefully into an open room where the sunlight was stronger.

"Griffin?"

She saw him in the bathroom, a girl knotted in his arms, a revolver pressed into her ribs.

Terry made her way back to the entrance.

Wilcox was in shock. When Terry walked past him, he reached out and grabbed her pants leg.

"I'm *bleeding*!" Wilcox screamed.

Gordon tightened a tourniquet around Wilcox's injured leg. Wilcox wrenched back, trying to free himself.

"Hold still," Gordon said. He turned to Terry and asked, "How's the other one?"

"Dead," she said.

"Dead?" Gordon repeated. Even Wilcox froze.

Gordon leaned against the wall and hid his face in an arm, overcome by the whole damned day.

"We've got to get Griffin out of there," Terry said. "He's in the bathroom with a girl."

"Wonderful," Gordon said.

Terry rested alongside him. "He's also got a box with him."

Gordon dropped his arm and rolled to his side to stare at Terry. His eyes were bloodshot from fatigue and failure.

"What do you think it is?" he asked. "Drugs?"

She shook her head.

"I think he's got explosives," she said.

Terry made it out of the building as uniformed cops erected the last of the blue wooden barriers. An ambulance threaded its way to the door of the tenement, and both of the Narcotics detectives were carried out on stretchers.

"For Chrissakes, clear the area," a precinct lieutenant ordered. Terry slipped under a barricade and shouted to Frank Tracelli.

Tracelli sent a man up the stairs, then turned to Terry. He was head of hostage negotiations for the New York Police Department, a heavyset man in his late thirties, with a thick, graying beard. He smiled and shook Terry's hand.

"What's it like in there?" he asked.

Terry did her best to explain, but her attention was distracted by a score of newsmen closing in on the operation. A camera flash blinded her, and she shouted at the photographer. A cop shoved the journalist behind a squad car.

"It's not supposed to be like this," she said with a sigh.

Tracelli looked toward the top floor of the building. "If he's really got explosives, we'll have to clear the neighboring buildings."

"Just don't step on any loose needles," she said.

"I'll speak to the lieutenant."

Terry rested on the stoop and looked around the street. Excluding Griffin, there couldn't be a junkie or pusher within six blocks of here. With all these cops, it was now probably the safest street in the city.

She watched the reporters and photographers jostle one another for a clearer view of the tenement entrance. Seven cops—no, make that seven *detectives*—working overtime on a long weekend. Calculate the cost, then add a few zeroes for this circus. All for a gofer like John Griffin, and there was no guarantee she'd even catch him.

Tracelli returned, then used his radio to order all the officers out of the building. Terry and he climbed the stairs to the fourth floor, joining Gordon in the apartment. Terry tried sneaking a look into the bathroom.

"Get *back!*" Griffin warned.

"John Griffin?" Tracelli called out.

Silence. Gordon wiped the sweat off his hands.

"Griffin, keep calm. That's all we ask." Tracelli switched places with Terry so he could edge closer. There was a noise, and the girl dropped to her knees. If Terry had been next to the door instead of Tracelli, she could have shot Griffin. Now, Griffin had pulled his hostage deeper into the bathroom.

"He's near a window," Gordon whispered. "Maybe we could get him from the street?" He went to the radio as Tracelli moved carefully into the room. It was cluttered with stacks of paper, boxes, and maps.

"We can't get anywhere if you don't talk, John," Tracelli said.

There was no answer, only sobs from the girl. Terry touched Tracelli and inched forward. She could see the toilet, the sink, and the edge of a tub. She caught a glimpse of Griffin and the girl pressed underneath the shower head. She stopped just inside his view, for the first time seeing him completely in person. She simply stared at him, not quite sure what to think, aware of only one thing.

He was just as she had imagined.

Griffin sobbed louder and beat the wall with his gun. Terry moved closer. In the tub, near Griffin's feet, was a cardboard box. "Leave me alone! You can't make me! Oh, God—"

Terry glanced at Tracelli. A litany began to pour from Griffin's mouth.

"I don't want to, I don't want to, I don't want to . . ."

Terry went back to Tracelli.

"What do I do now?" she asked.

"Anything you want," he said.

"Don't screw around."

Tracelli grinned, more from nerves than humor. "Listen to him. He's not talking to you, he's talking to the air. He hasn't heard a word anyone's said."

Terry listened.

". . . I don't want to, I don't want to, I don't want to . . ."

"The guy's *wacked*," Tracelli said.

The girl screamed, and Terry heard them tumble in the bathtub.

"No," Griffin shouted, "I don't want to kill her. You can't make me!"

"John," she said to Griffin, "you've got to—"

"Leave me alone! Get him off!"

Gordon moved to join her, but Terry waved him back. She shoved her revolver in her belt, near the small of her back, then stepped forward.

"Let go of the girl."

"He won't let me," Griffin said.

"Who, John?"

The girl sobbed, and Griffin stiffened. He leaned into the light, and Terry could see Griffin's cheeks squeeze together, as if an invisible hand were pinching his face and lifting the skin. He jerked his head violently up and down, in a pitiful imitation of a nod. There was more determination in his voice. "I've got to kill her," he decided.

Terry watched, terrified. It made no sense. Nor was it just Griffin; Terry couldn't explain her own actions. This was Tracelli's job, not hers. What was she doing here?

"You're hearing voices, John," she said quietly. "Don't listen to them. Listen to *my* voice."

Terry pushed away from the bathroom wall. She could see Griffin clearly now; he was a young man—unshaven, exhausted, his eyes red from tears. His revolver was pressed into the girl's throat. The dripping shower head had soaked both of them.

"No, no, no . . . ." He shook his head as if to clear it. Water spun off his hair. The girl lay slouched against him.

She walked deeper into the bathroom. Griffin held the girl tighter and pointed his gun at the box. Terry waited. Control yourself, she thought. Control *him*.

"It's over now, John. You can give me the gun."

Terry stopped talking. She watched Griffin's finger tighten on the trigger. One squeeze would blow them all away. Terry stared at the muzzle, transfixed by the thing. His eyes, catch his eyes, she remembered. That was the trick.

"John?"

He looked at her. An amazing look. Griffin was shaking like a drug addict, but his eyes belonged to someone else— a cardsharp, watching her coolly, waiting for her to play out the hand.

"What do you want?" she asked quietly.

Griffin's arm opened. The girl fell to the floor and lay still. Then he looked at Terry, and with both hands pointed his gun at her head. He was trembling horribly, his knuckles turning white.

"No!" Terry screamed. She flinched and heard Gordon shout from the hallway. She was convinced it was the last thing she would ever hear.

When she opened her eyes, Griffin was on his knees, weeping, his head bowed. Terry found the strength to rest a hand on his shoulder. With her other hand, she bent down and retrieved the gun.

He looked up at her. "I didn't want to," he said. "He couldn't make me do it."

While Gordon and Tracelli handcuffed Griffin, Terry threw up in the sink.

Bill Reed, the lieutenant in charge of the Intelligence division, was waiting in the lobby as Griffin was hustled downstairs.

"You look terrible," he told Terry, and together they walked outside. Camera bulbs flashed in their faces, but Griffin kept his head low until he was pressed into the back seat of a patrol car.

Reed hated publicity. His job was avoiding the news, not making it. "What a mess."

"I'm sorry, Bill."

"Let's just get out of here."

Reed left Terry standing by the Fairmont. She watched Gordon help the hostage into the back of another squad car and then come running back.

"Come on," he said, his voice low. Like Reed, he was uncomfortable with the crowd. "We've got a ton of paper work."

"Not yet." She looked back toward Griffin. "I got some questions to ask him."

"We'll do our talking later," Gordon said wearily.

Terry ignored him. She went to the patrol car and pulled Griffin onto the street. Behind her, photographers nagged for just one more shot. Terry didn't oblige. Someone else demanded her attention—a man leaning against a medical van, a camera raised to his eye. An odd tingling sensation ran across her face, stopping at the tip of her chin. The tingling grabbed hold of her chin and tilted it to the side, the way an artist would gently move the head of a model.

Terry pointed Griffin toward the van, put an arm about him, and waited. She didn't move until the camera flashed.

"Terry?" Gordon shouted. More photographers pushed at him. He was furious, and two cops had to keep him from breaking the camera. "Terry?" He raised an arm to block his eyes. "What the fuck are you doing?"

A moment ago, she had felt compelled to stand absolutely still. Now, she couldn't remember why. Her face showed the confusion.

"I still have to talk with him," she said.

"You can talk *later*," he insisted. "Let's just get the hell out."

"But there's something else."

Gordon looked around. "You want to tell me about it?"

Terry didn't answer, nor did Gordon expect her to. She usually told him nothing. He figured she didn't trust him as a cop, or as a person. Either way, Gordon wasn't happy.

"Then see you tomorrow," he said, walking away.

Terry watched him leave; instead of following, she returned to the patrol car and climbed in the back seat with Griffin.

"Let's go," she told the cop in front. The driver turned the ignition, flicked on the roof lights, then inched through the traffic. More photographers pressed against the windows, but Griffin sagged to his knees. Terry stared at her suspect and wondered what had compelled her to sit beside him. Gordon was right; there was no rush to talk with Griffin. In fact, at the moment she couldn't think of anything she wanted to do less. All the same, she *had* to ride with him back to the precinct. There was unfinished business.

"What a mob," the driver said.

Terry bent closer to Griffin. "John?" she whispered.

Griffin didn't reply. He seemed asleep.

"Griffin, wake up." She touched his shoulder. Griffin mumbled and fell back.

"Come on," she said. Terry pushed him hard against the car door. He grunted.

"What the hell's happening back there?" asked the driver.

Griffin began heaving, as if to vomit.

The driver glanced nervously in the mirror. "Hey, detective, do me a favor. Don't let him stink it up, all right?"

Griffin kept heaving. The driver leaned to the side and turned around. "Stick his head out the window," he said. Griffin retched again.

The cop stopped the car. Griffin was alone and still gagging in the back seat.

"Detective?" the driver called. He rolled down the side window. "Hey! What about your prisoner?"

Terry ran back into the crowd. Past the bystanders, around the barricades . . . It seemed to take forever. "Lieutenant!" she shouted. She pushed aside a reporter. The lieutenant was before camera lights, giving an interview. "Where's the bomb squad?"

"In the apartment."

Terry rushed inside. Cops were everywhere. When she recognized a member of the bomb squad, she pointed toward the upper stories.

"The *fifth* floor," she said. They reached the top flight of the building. More cops checked the hallways; one tested the window to a fire escape. *"No!"* she shouted.

The window was forced up.

Seconds later there came the flash and thunder of an explosion. Then the roof collapsed in a fog of dust and plaster.

A picture of the explosion would be on the front page of all the New York dailies. Only one photographer at the scene missed the incident—the cameraman who had been standing near the medical van, taking an unusual interest in Terry Cooke. All he had was a portrait of the detective, her head tilted against the blue police lights.

But that was the shot he had wanted.

Chris Easton left the scene as soon as Terry entered the patrol car. He had anticipated the explosion; he had seen the setup while sifting through John Griffin's mind. But Chris was bored with taking pictures of explosions. He seemed to have spent half his life doing that.

How much more interesting to *cause* explosions.

Chris surprised himself with the thought. That was one of the problems with his mind probing; if he did it too long, he was often left with an imprint, a reflection of a person's thoughts or personality. A year ago, he had wondered if his mind was just a collage of ideas and memories from other people. Now, he no longer cared.

"Terry Cooke," he said aloud. She was strong, very strong, even though she didn't know it. He hadn't met a person like her since his visit to a P.L.O. camp in Syria. The power in her was seductive.

Then again, the power was always seductive.

PART ONE

CHRIS EASTON

One

OCTOBER, 1960: STEPNEY, EAST LONDON, ENGLAND

Devonport Street was just one of many quiet side streets that connected the main roads running east–west through the city. Apart from schoolchildren on bicycles, there was little traffic—except perhaps on Saturdays, when noisy soccer fans wearing colorful scarves and shaking rattles used it as a shortcut to a game. A terraced row of grimy, identical red-brick Greater London council houses lined both sides of the street, which was bordered by a small public house at one end and an Asian grocery shop at the other. The Conservative Prime Minister, Harold Macmillan, had recently declared that the "winds of change" were blowing through apartheid South Africa, but that didn't affect the people of Devonport Street. Asians were still "wogs," and Pakistanis the butt of most jokes. Conversation usually centered on the local news and a radio soap opera called "Mrs. Dale's Diary."

Behind the council houses was a network of laundry lines, heavy with clothes that snapped stiffly in the wind. The small backyards were separated by five-foot-high slat fences. A dirt track ran between two of the yards, leading to a chain-link fence with a splintered sign: PROPERTY OF

BRITISH RAIL. KEEP OUT. TRESPASSERS WILL BE PROSE-CUTED. The path continued through a hole in the fence and up a railway embankment.

Mrs. Ivy Aspel closed the kitchen window, killing an autumn wind that had blown out the pilot light of her new gas oven.

"Did you hear all that nonsense last night?" she asked.

"No," said her neighbor. Mrs. Elsie Lipson reached for a biscuit from a tin and waited for more gossip.

Mrs. Aspel covered the teapot with a hand-knitted cozy and turned up her favorite show, "Music While You Work," on a transistor radio. She found two clean cups and carried them from the sink to the kitchen table.

"Bleedin' hell, ducks," said Mrs. Aspel. "I don't know how you missed it. There were these awful screams, must've been eleven, twelve o'clock. Didn't you hear it?"

"You know me, dear," Mrs. Lipson said. "Sleep like the dead once I go. What happened?"

Mrs. Aspel looked astonished. "It was like Paddington Station with the Old Bill around here. Lights flashing, people banging on the door." She paused, then, with a shade of pride, whispered, "I called 'em, you know." She sat back, waiting.

"Who, dear?"

"The rozzers."

"Well, I never did," said Mrs. Lipson. "What for?"

"Live and let live's my motto, you know that. But my Eddie was snoring like a tractor, and I couldn't wake him for love nor money, and I could hear all these screams coming from number twenty-five. Didn't know what to do, did I?"

"How could you?" Mrs. Lipson agreed.

Mrs. Aspel looked about the kitchen, as if her words were dangerous. "It's not the first time. Anyway, about a half hour later, the rozzers turned up, didn't they?"

"Bloody typical," Mrs. Lipson said.

"Don't I know, dear," said Mrs. Aspel. "I looked through the curtains—just peeked like to have a quick gander. There was two police cars and an ambulance, all their lights flashing and everything. They wanted me to make a statement, but I told 'em I don't want to get involved, do I? Done my bit."

"Oh, yes, dear. I know what you mean."

"I seen them take a body out." She lowered her voice. "If you ask me, it was her."

"Well, I never did," said Mrs. Lipson, astonished. "Who'd have thought?"

"I never got a good look at who the Old Bill nicked, but it must've been him. If you want my opinion, he did for her."

Mrs. Lipson sipped her tea and had another biscuit.

"Don't surprise me, dear," Mrs. Lipson said firmly. "He was always a dark horse. Never used to see him, did we? She led him a right dog's life as well, and that's a fact. Our bedroom's right next to theirs. Me and Bert used to lie in bed half the night listening to him screaming at her to stop tormenting him. It was *pitiful*. Clear as day you could hear them going at it."

"And she was such a small woman, too," said Mrs. Aspel.

"Fragile," agreed Mrs. Lipson. "How'd he do it?"

The question disgusted Mrs. Aspel. "Now, dear, let's not get gory." Mrs. Lipson nodded quickly. " 'Sides, all I could see was a little bit of blood on the stretcher."

"Oh, my Gawd," Mrs. Lipson groaned.

"Axed her," said Mrs. Aspel. "I saw one of the rozzers carrying it out of the house."

"Dreadful."

They were silent for a moment, while Mrs. Aspel poured two fresh cups of tea. Mrs. Lipson liberally spooned sugar into her mid-morning "cuppa."

"What about the little boy?" Mrs. Lipson finally asked.

"What about him?"

"Shove him in a home, I suppose."

"Four years old and with parents carrying on like that," Mrs. Aspel sympathized. "You know he used to drink, don't you?"

"Who? The kid?"

"No, you daft 'app'orth, the *husband*."

"He never used to go down the pub, 'cause Eddie's always down there and he never seen him."

"He used to drink by himself, in the shed at the bottom of the garden."

"Oh, that's nasty," Mrs. Lipson said, wincing.

"I tell you, I used to see him go in there, carrying a bottle, you know, if I was dusting the windowsill or something, and just happened, you know—by chance, like—to glance outside. 'Course, he didn't always turn the light on, but when he did I could see right through the window into his potting shed. 'Sides, I knew he was there even when it was off, 'cause his cigarettes glowed."

"Fancy that." Mrs. Lipson leaned back, still thinking of the child. "I thought they treated little Chris something rotten—beat him and stuff like that. He was always screaming and crying. Used to drive Bert mental. Then he'd get the hump with me."

"I once saw him with a terrible bruise on his face," said Mrs. Aspel, still thinking of the husband. "Fell down the stairs, *she* said. But I knew right enough what the truth of it was. Not that it matters much, does it? Can you imagine me beating Eddie up like that? He'd kill me!"

"Poor little bleeder was always covered in bruises," said Mrs. Lipson, thinking of the child. "But you can't get involved, can you?"

"Terrible woman," said Mrs. Aspel.

"Poor little bugger." Mrs. Lipson sighed.

She glanced out the window as a train rattled in the distance.

"Probably better off where he is now anyway," finished Mrs. Lipson.

Mrs. Aspel looked at her, confused. "Who, dear? The husband?"

Mrs. Lipson gazed at Mrs. Appel, as if the question were absurd.

"The boy, of course." Both women became quiet. Nothing in the neighborhood made any sense these days.

Honestly, now. Mrs. Easton hadn't been *that* bad. Had she?

Christopher Easton was what the social workers called "a disturbed child," but it was really the people around Chris who became disturbed.

In early May, a farmer from Wiltshire read a magazine story about the brutal murder at 25 Devonport Street. The boy had already been in care of the local authorities for eight months when the farmer volunteered to let Chris Easton stay on his farm. How much nicer for a five-year-old to grow up with green hills and fresh air, rather than behind the walls of a city institution.

Chris stayed less than a week with his first foster family. The farmer returned to the Council Home, his face livid from embarrassment, and explained that he and his wife had changed their minds. When the administrators asked why, the farmer refused to answer. Only when pressed did he belligerently say, "Chris kept us from sleeping. All right?"

When Chris was sent to a second family and then returned under similarly vague circumstances, the administration decided to put him in the custody of Angela O'Dowd, an intern who specialized with problem children. It was Angela who discovered that Chris's problems with his foster parents had nothing to do with temper tantrums; the problem was in his dreams.

Chris had terrifying nightmares. They went beyond a

child's usual images of ghouls and ghosts, for they contained a consuming rage at his life; Chris's visions were of real death. It was like living in an imaginary town where behind every door someone was performing a murder, and at any moment a door would open and it would be time for another guest. These were dreams with frightening detail, from the dazzling flash of a stiletto to the terror Chris felt when the figures in the shadows caught him. His nightmares belonged to someone much older, who knew how much there was to dread. They should have belonged solely to Chris.

Yet they didn't.

Angela knew Chris's dreams intimately, not because the boy talked about them—he didn't—but because she had allowed Chris to share her room. On the third night, Chris's nightmares became her own, the visions terrorizing her sleep. She lay awake, wondering how anyone could have such dreams without being driven mad.

There was a knock on her door, and then it slowly opened.

"Angela?" Chris called, looking in shyly.

She stared at Chris, wondering if the dreams were driving the boy mad. But all she saw was a five-year-old child. The nightmares were no more his fault than hers. She wished she didn't have the dreams, and selfishly she wished that at the very least he could keep them to himself.

She suffered for a week before begging off the assignment. When the administrator asked for an explanation, Angela found it impossible to tell the truth and simply said Chris needed time alone.

But even after she had separated herself from Chris, the nightmares still haunted her, as if they were now her possessions. Not even quitting her job and moving far from the Home—and Chris—helped her escape. And the vision that most haunted her was of an axe burying its head deep into a sleeping woman, blood erupting in a fountain . . .

It was enough finally to lead her to Davenport Street, the source of her bad dreams.

"I'm looking for number twenty-five," she asked a passing teen-ager. He pointed across the street. Angela walked slowly toward the Eastons' former home.

From a distance, the building was just one of many identical council houses. As she drew closer, she noticed the litter on the front steps. Crabgrass poked through the concrete path, and a dusty film coated the cracked windows.

It was no longer a home for people.

Angela rang the doorbell. The sound echoed through the empty rooms.

"Help you?" shouted a woman from a neighboring house. Angela looked up. Mrs. Aspel peered down from a bedroom window.

"I was just ringing the bell," Angela said.

"No one living there, dear." Mrs. Aspel leaned farther out the window. "What are you, some bloody Sunday reporter? I suppose it makes a difference if you get paid to be foolish."

Angela didn't understand. Mrs. Aspel smiled to herself.

"Try the handle, ducks."

Angela turned the knob. "It's not locked."

"You're a bright one, ain't you?" said Mrs. Aspel. "Place ain't been locked for a year. No need. No one daft enough to go inside."

"I just wanted to take a look around," said Angela. "I know the boy."

"You just go away," Mrs. Aspel snapped. "Bugger off before I phone the Old Bill. And I will, too; you mark my words. You've no right nosing around other people's property. You just leave them alone. What you're doing is breaking and entering, that's what that is."

"Get stuffed," Angela muttered.

Mrs. Aspel ducked back into her bedroom.

Angela opened the door. The electricity had been turned off, and the only light came from a setting sun that filled the open doorway and glowed against the dusty windows. There was just enough light for Angela to find her way to the staircase, where her hand rested against a greenish mildew that grew on the damp walls. At least there was no furniture to trip over. Everything had been removed, leaving only pieces of plaster that had broken away from the ceiling. The entire house was warping and falling apart.

Where had it happened? Angela wondered.

She walked to the kitchen and found the back door. Through a dirty glass pane, she could see Mr. Easton's garden, swallowed by weeds. When Angela walked outside, she saw the cellar door.

The news accounts of the murder came back to her. Mr. Easton, attacking his sleeping wife with an axe, splitting her like a log.

Tools, she thought. A man finds an axe in a tool room.

She stood at the brink of the cellar, daring to lower a foot into the darkness. When nothing attacked her, she protected her head and walked deeper into the shadows, waiting for her eyes to adjust to the gloom. A dim shaft of light came from a cellar window. To her left was the outline of a long shelf. She slid her hand along the shelf, feeling the thick dust and pine shavings, and came across a cold, forgotten hammer. She grabbed it, relieved to have a weapon.

Angela was still holding the hammer when she heard footsteps in the kitchen.

It wasn't the police. They were the steps of someone who knew the house. The longer Angela listened, the more acute her hearing became. With the footsteps came the faint sound of water rinsing down a sink and the clink of dishes. The hollow humming of a woman floated into the cellar.

Angela heard the quiet moan of a man. She felt his warm breath on her shoulder, and the press of sharp steel in her back.

Angela screamed, turning quickly and throwing the hammer. She jerked her hands above her head, waiting for the axe to come down. When nothing happened, she ran up the steps and into the weeds. She stood shaking, her face pale and drawn.

Nothing attacked. Angela expected Mr. Easton to come chasing after her, or to see Mrs. Easton—now a rotting corpse—waving politely from the kitchen window. But the nightmare had disappeared the moment she threw the hammer. She plucked up enough courage to approach the cellar a last time. She closed the door and locked it.

A torch beam flashed into the garden. "Someone back there?"

A policeman walked out the back door as Angela rushed up the steps. She barreled into him.

"Where's the fire, then, darling?" he asked. He led her through the house and out the front door. Mrs. Aspel was by her window, waiting for them.

"Warned you," she crowed.

"Leave it out, love, will yer?" the patrolman shouted back.

"Bad enough I got to hear them fighting every night," Mrs. Aspel said. "Now you go and get them crazy all over again."

"Oi!" shouted the cop. "Give it a rest. Mind it, know what I mean?"

"I went down to the basement," Angela told the officer.

Mrs. Aspel laughed sharply. "You're bleeding lucky, girl. You didn't see nothing in the cellar. You should have gone upstairs. That's where he done her in."

"I'm warning you—" the policeman growled.

Mrs. Aspel retreated, slamming the window. The officer grinned and turned back to Angela.

"You all right?"

Angela couldn't trust herself to speak. The officer led her away from the council house to his panda car.

Two

JUNE, 1972: FULHAM, WEST LONDON

At fifteen, Chris became fascinated with photography.

Photography demanded an understanding of shape and color, shadow and light. With a camera, one could freeze a moment, then sculpt it into a mood. It was more immediate than painting or drawing. A painter creates an entire world with a touch of reality; a photographer, however, has to overcome reality to create an entirely new world.

This fascinated Chris. The principles of photography helped him understand how to work his "magic trick"—sinking into other people's minds and learning exactly what they thought, saw, heard, and felt . . . It was as if he momentarily became that other person.

He uncovered this skill when he was eight and playing a game of hide-and-seek. When it was Chris's turn to seek out his playmates, he found that all he had to do was think about each one, and he was soon looking through their eyes and reading their thoughts.

Never was this ability more important than when he had grown old enough to choose his own foster parents. He needed a pair that would do more than provide food and shelter; he would also need freedom to test his place in the world. Chris used his trick to discern in an instant whether a prospective set of foster parents could provide such freedom. He sifted through the minds of five couples before finding a father and mother sufficiently tame to leave Chris to his own devices. Then, as if to confirm his judgment, his parents greeted him with a welcome home present—Chris's first camera.

He could not have asked for a better gift.

Just as a photographer manipulated real images, so Chris came to see memories as real images preserved in people's heads. With the right concentration, Chris discovered he could change these images—blurring a face, highlighting a happy thought, melting a frozen memory of guilt. He nurtured a power that allowed him to move freely through someone's mind. With a few gentle adjustments, he could dramatically change people.

Yes. Photography was not only a fine hobby, but it was also good practice. It taught him how to look at the world.

Chris sat in a small playground and focused his camera on a mother and her baby. Not bad. Full frame, vertical. If he cropped the edges, the picture could be a mother and child alone in a forest. The little playground would expand forever. Quiet, peaceful isolation, welcome but unsettling. Who knew what hid beyond the edges of the frame?

Mother and child, by a swing set. The mother lifted her child, Chris lifted his camera, and . . . click . . . a horizontal picture of steel bars and brick walls. Unless . . . click, click . . . Chris shortened the focus, blurring the brick walls into a brown haze and the playground into a floating island. A slower speed on the shutter and everything dropped into a gritty darkness. No more playground, no more walls; no children, no mothers, no noise, no life . . . click, click, click . . . Only outlines lost to a false night.

Chris put the camera back in its case and leaned forward.

He focused on the mother, reaching out and then reaching in, forcing himself through her skin and into her eyes. He settled inside her and saw the world exactly as the mother saw it. The playground, the swings, her child . . . And there was something more. Chris wasn't just sharing her eyes; so long as he inhabited her body, he shared her senses. When the mother brushed back her child's hair, Chris's fingers felt the boy's hair. When she lit a cigarette, his blood raced with the intoxication of nicotine.

Her mind resembled a gallery of pictures. Memories floated and projected like holographs in a vast circle—at least this was how memories often appeared to Chris. Sometimes they were no more than remnants of thoughts. Chris had been inside many people's heads in the last few months, ever since his success with the woman who guarded the booth at the movie house. Only occasionally could someone block his entry—a mystery that baffled Chris. Was it because he needed more practice . . . yes, yes, click, click . . . or because some people could lock him out? The only way to find out was to keep on trying. . . . Click. So he probed with an insatiable curiosity, driven by the desire to know everything he could about his own life and other people's.

Through the mother's eyes he glimpsed his own thin figure sitting on a park bench. The afternoon was slipping by unnoticed. Children played in the sandbox and on the slides and swings. In another corner of the yard, teen-aged girls circled together with their younger brothers and sisters. Chris recognized one of the girls as Simon O'Keefe's sister, Moira. Together, the mother and he watched Moira, sharing Chris's infatuation.

Chris thought a great deal about his friendship with Moira, almost as much as he thought about his strange ability. They were the two things in his teen-aged life that most excited and frightened him.

Chris wondered what would happen if Moira knew of his feelings. He became angry each time she talked about a boyfriend or discussed leaving London for some distant university. She didn't seem to care what he felt. Chris, after all, was younger than Moira; not one of the boys that could win or betray her affection.

Not fair, he thought.

Chris slipped out of the mother's mind and back into his own body. He grabbed his camera and walked quickly away, still wrestling with his feelings.

Moira should love me, he kept thinking.

No, he thought again. Moira *will* love me.

He left the playground and headed home, undecided what to do.

As for the mother, she picked up her child and cradled the youngster, all the time nagged by a single thought: Who is Moira O'Keefe?

Simon warned his sister about Chris.

"He's a nutter," he told her. "What d'you want to hang around a creepy fucker like that for?"

"Oh, stop it," she said. She threw a dress on the bed and went into the bathroom.

"He ain't got no real friends," Simon said. "All he does is hang around and drool. It's disgusting."

"He doesn't drool."

"Comes close to it." Simon hunched up on the bed and began drooling. Moira slammed the bathroom door. He laughed, even though he meant what he said. Simon had an instinct for people, and it warned him that Chris was destined to mess up someone's life. He cared for his sister and he didn't want that someone to be her.

Simon picked up Moira's blue lace dress and rubbed it. A daring dress, one that would cling to every part of her body—her thighs, her breasts . . .

"Simon?" Moira called.

Simon started. He had been fondling the dress, thinking embarrassing thoughts about his sister.

"What?"

"Get my dress, will you?"

Simon bundled the dress and opened the bathroom door without knocking.

"Oi! You born in a barn?" she shouted. Simon caught a hurried glimpse of her just before a wet sponge hit him in the face. "Just leave it on the knob—outside."

"Sorry." He ducked out. An arm reached around and grabbed the dress. "You ain't got much to look at anyway. What's your problem?"

"Bugger off!"

It was wrong of Moira to yell at Simon. He was only there to warn her. He crept closer to the bathroom door, lightly testing the knob. Locked. He could hear Moira humming to herself, and he imagined the warm shower running over her body.

Simon shook his head. Peeking on your own sister; definitely sick.

Still, perhaps he could look through the keyhole.

But Simon forgot the idea as soon as Chris slipped out of his thoughts.

Chris rested against a tree and looked up at the steamy bathroom window. This was the closest he had come to touching Moira. He hadn't yet entered her mind. Somehow it seemed a violation. But entering Simon's? Chris had no such qualms. Someone had to fill the vacuum.

Besides, for the first time he was seeing a real use for

his power. He had used it to hold Moira's dress, to be with her at home, to see her as a lover. Perhaps this was the point of it all—to bring Moira and him together.

To make them real lovers.

Click.

"Congratulations," Chris called out. He came into the cloakroom and pushed his way through straggling groups of teen-agers.

Moira turned at the familiar voice and stopped gossiping with her friend, Stephanie. Chris pressed awkwardly between them.

"Heard you're off to Nottingham University," he said.

"That's right," said Moira. Stephanie made a face behind Chris's back, and Moira did her best not to laugh.

"When you leaving?" Chris asked.

"Oh, not until the end of August."

"Can't wait to meet all those university types, can you, Moira?" Stephanie asked pointedly.

Moira smirked while Chris glared at Stephanie. For the life of him, he had no idea why Stephanie and Moira were so inseparable.

"Steph's just jealous 'cause she's not coming with me, that's all," Moira told Chris.

"Oh, I'm not jealous," said Stephanie. Moira laughed. Stephanie pressed Chris and Moira together. "I'll just leave you two alone, then."

"Very funny," said Moira. Chris struggled for a smile.

"See you tonight, M," Stephanie said, laughing.

"Right," Moira called after her. "See you tonight."

Stephanie turned on her heels and waved good-bye, disappearing into the hallway. Moira collected several books, growing uncomfortable without her friend. Chris leaned against the gray-metal lockers. He treasured any moment Moira and he could be together, alone.

"I'm so *glad* to be getting out of this place," Moira said expansively.

"Aren't you the lucky one, then," Chris said. "Some of us have to come back next year." With a casual, dramatic tone, he added, "I'm thinking about leaving, myself."

"Simon said the same thing, and our dad went mental."

Chris hated it when Moira talked about Simon. It was a reminder that Chris and Simon were both sixteen. Moira would never let him grow up. Chris would always be like some ignored little brother.

A bell rang in the corridor. Moira closed her locker and began walking quickly away. Chris jogged after her.

"Can I see you tonight?" he asked.

"Can't," she replied.

"How 'bout tomorrow?"

"Sorry." Moira rushed off.

It's that bloody Stephanie, Chris thought. He stood alone in the corridor, red-faced and sick of Stephanie's interference.

After school he went straight home, took a bath, and dressed in his best clothes. Stephanie was not going to get in the way tonight. He needed to be with Moira. He vowed that nothing would get in his way.

Chris sat on a weather-beaten wooden bench. Two other young men were standing by the curb, laughing and talking together, keeping an eye out for the red double decker. They were heading for the hurly-burly of Soho—at least, two of them were. Chris had other plans. He stretched back on the bench and watched the cars as their passing headlights brightened Ealing Common.

The bus wheezed to a stop, and the two young men hopped on board, heading for the upper deck. As the bus pulled away, Chris tossed aside the front section of his paper and thumbed through the entertainment guide. Where to take Moira, he thought. To the pictures? Could he get into a pub?

He looked across the street. Her house was about a hundred yards away. If he focused his mind, Chris could hear Moira and Stephanie arguing. Moira was saying they should go out to celebrate her scholarship, while Stephanie moaned she felt sick.

Chris smiled and flexed his mental muscles. Stephanie again cringed with cramps.

"Oooooh! I'm really sorry, M."

The front door opened, and Stephanie stepped outside, holding both arms across her stomach. A lamp in the living room made her an odd silhouette, although as far as Chris was concerned, Stephanie had always been oddly shaped.

"My stomach's killing me," Stephanie moaned again.

"I thought it was your head," said Moira.

"It *is*," said Stephanie. "It's both."

Moira snorted. "Well, better see the doctor, then, hadn't you?"

"I said I'm sorry."

The pain overwhelmed Stephanie and she limped off. Moira slammed the door, leaving Stephanie in the dark. Stephanie walked slowly down the street, taking a breath against a streetlight.

"Hello, Steph," said Chris.

Stephanie looked to her side, but if she saw Chris, she didn't say a word. She waved to a bus that pulled up at the stop, and crawled up the steps of the double decker.

Chris walked to a nearby telephone kiosk and dialed Moira's number, praying Simon didn't answer.

She answered on the fifth ring.

"Just thought I'd phone up for a chat," he said. "See if you've changed your mind—maybe wanted to go out and do something."

There was a long silence.

"Where are you?" she asked.

"Phone box down the street."

Moira put down the receiver and went to the window. Chris waved. She returned to the phone.

"You got more brass . . ."

Chris was quiet, waiting. Moira finally laughed.

"All right. I'll be down in a minute."

"Okay," he said, and hung up.

Chris walked toward the house and waited. The lights in Moira's bedroom flicked off. She shouted something to her parents and they shouted back, but Chris couldn't make it out. When Moira finally emerged, Chris could barely believe it.

"Steph's got a bug or something," Moira said. She stopped alongside him. Chris leaned toward her, smelling her perfume.

"That's too bad," he answered.

"What do you want to do, then?"

Chris didn't know. He wanted to do whatever she'd like. He was afraid his ideas would bore her.

"Might as well go and have a drink somewhere," Moira suggested.

"If you want."

"Unless that's a problem," she added, remembering Chris's age.

"No problem."

They walked toward Chiswick, following a line of lamp posts. Chris occasionally brushed her arm, but more often they walked separately. Moira talked about her plans for the university. She told him about the courses she planned to take and the flat she would be sharing. Chris listened, throwing in a few remarks that made Moira laugh. Sometimes when she laughed, he didn't know what was funny. It struck him that Moira was so delighted at moving away

34

that nothing could break her spirits. This made him all the more melancholy.

"This place is okay," Moira said breezily. She opened the door to a pub. Chris followed, pressing through a warm crowd. "You find a table while I use the phone," Moira said, flitting away.

Chris obeyed. He found a corner table where they could be relatively alone: a romantic spot in the shadow of the jukebox. It gave him a brief thrill to think that the barmaid might mistake him for Moira's boyfriend. He left his coat on a chair and stepped up to the bar.

"Two beers," he ordered.

The barmaid glanced at him from under her teased blond hair. The boy was obviously under age. "You'll get me in trouble," she said.

Chris thought hard, his jaw jutting forward. The barmaid clutched the wet counter.

"What was that again?" she asked nervously.

"Two pints."

When Chris returned with the beers, Moira was at the table. The drinks surprised her.

"How'd you manage that?" she asked.

He took a sip and wiped his mouth with the back of a hand.

"It's all in how you ask, that's all."

"God, what a drag Steph got sick." Moira took a long sip. "We were going to get drunk together. When Steph gets drunk, she's hilarious."

"What are you like?"

Moira shrugged. "Sleepy." She uttered a marvelous laugh, and Chris took another long pull on his pint. "Well, I won't sleep tonight. I spoke to Penny, and she's phoning Andrew. I've always fancied Andrew. Penny's been promising to fix me up for months."

"Great," Chris murmured.

Moira grabbed his arm and shook him lightly. "Don't be

35

such a miserable bugger. Here, go and get us another round. I'll pay.''

Chris swallowed the last of his pint.

''I'll pay,'' he said, rising. The beer made him feel bloated. The evening was already turning sour. Moira touched his arm, and he looked down at her.

''You should get to know Penny better,'' she said with sisterly concern.

Chris looked about the pub, expecting Moira's friends to pounce on them at any moment.

''She likes you. She told me.''

''That's nice.''

He moved toward the bar.

Moira's friends *were* close; Chris could feel it. Maybe around the corner, ready to take her away. Then she would forget him and leave Ealing Common, and Chris would always remember this evening as a lost opportunity: the night he had Moira and let her go.

He paid for two more pints of lukewarm bitter and put the frothy beakers on their table. Moira checked her watch.

''So you want me to fix you up?'' she asked.

''What?''

''With Penny. You want me to fix you up with her?''

He looked about the room, taking a gulp of beer, feeling giddy.

''Let's go,'' he said, slapping down his half-finished pint.

''We can't. We're waiting for Penny and—''

''I want to *leave*.''

Moira's smile froze. Then her mouth opened slightly. For the first time, Chris began to think for her.

''Let's go outside,'' he said quietly.

She nodded, less in agreement than to show understanding. Once outside, Chris rubbed his head, uncertain if he had done the right thing. He glanced at Moira and felt embarrassed. "I just needed some fresh air. That place was getting to me."

"I hated it."

Until tonight, the pub had been one of her favorites. Now, she felt differently about a lot of things—the bar, her friends, Stephanie, Chris. . . . Confusing thoughts. Feelings and ideas that chased and battled one another.

Chris led her off the street to the common. Then he stopped her, whispering, "I love you."

Moira's head ached. She didn't want to hear this. She didn't want to be near Chris, but something inside her insisted that she did. A faint voice told her that being with Chris was the most important thing in her life, and if she left him now, she would regret it the rest of her life.

The two teen-agers paused in the deep shadow of an amble.

"It's nice out, ain't it?" he asked. They looked out on the pond. Moira turned and stared into Chris's eyes. All her thoughts and feelings came from him.

"I don't want you to go away," Chris said. "I want us to stay together." He watched her. Even in the gloom, he could sense her fear and confusion. "You'll see I'm right. I'll help you."

A chilly breeze swept past them, and with it went her doubts and fears. In their place, Chris left a hollow passion, and in her memories, he made her boyfriends look like him.

Moira's eyes became dull. She pressed closer to Chris. They kissed. When Chris pulled away, Moira waited for him to come back. He smiled, leading her by the hand into the bushes.

"I love you, Moira," he said again.

"I love you, too," she said.

He leaned her against a tree and began unbuttoning her blouse. "I'll always love you," he promised.

She let Chris lower her to the ground. He unfastened her bra and kissed her breasts. She held tightly to his hair.

"Moira," he whispered.

"Yes?"

He pushed up her skirt and looked down at her. Her eyes were tightly closed, and she was lost in Chris's fantasy, unable to distinguish the real Chris from the thousand images floating in her head.

"Yes?" she said again, feeling as though she was drowning.

Then Chris possessed her completely.

Three

Would Moira tell?

Chris hated himself every time the question entered his head. He loved Moira. How could he have gone into her head like that? "Stupid," he told himself aloud. "Stupid, stupid, stupid . . ."

Could Moira tell?

Chris leaned against a phone kiosk, wishing he had the nerve to call her. Pedestrians passed a few feet away, oblivious to his torment. Moira—dear God, what had he done?

" 'Ere, Sy, look at that!"

Chris turned to see Simon O'Keefe and a gang of cronies sauntering down Chiswick High Street. Simon was the first to reach Chris. In a low, harsh voice he said, "I wanna word with you."

Simon's friends circled Chris and made a shield. A bus approached, almost stopped, then continued down the street. Simon jabbed a finger into Chris's shoulder. "You're not in a 'urry, are you?"

He wrapped an arm about Chris and led him into an alley. Once out of sight, Simon shoved him against a row of trash cans. The other teen-agers again provided a barrier, and watched for the police.

"You bastard," Simon said. He rubbed his fist. "I'm gonna rip your fucking heart out!"

Chris struggled to his feet, only to have Simon flat-palm him between the overturned cans. Chris didn't block the blow. He knew there was only one sure way to protect himself; he looked into Simon's eyes, and for a moment Simon hesitated. No one could hurt Chris—not unless he let them.

Moira, Chris thought.

Simon's anger returned. Chris hauled himself to his feet. Simon punched him in the stomach, doubling him over.

Chris dropped onto the ground, gasping for breath, rolling into a protective ball.

A loud voice inside told Chris to protect himself—to turn Simon's brain to mush, to do anything. Just get the hell out of this.

"You bastard!" Simon gasped. "Fuck with my sister, will yer?"

He kicked Chris in the temple, and Chris's head cracked into a slat fence. Blood sprayed onto his shirt. When Simon saw this, he kicked harder. If Chris ever had a chance of running away, it had gone. Pain flared through his body. Another blow to his head made his thoughts scatter. Nothing made sense anymore, and nothing could save him.

Kicked to death in a gutter, surrounded by garbage. This is what I deserve, Chris thought.

"Hop it, Simon. Quick! It's the Old Bill. Leave him, or we'll all get nicked!"

Simon's mouth pressed against Chris's ear. "Next time you're dead, mate."

Everything grew peaceful. There was nothing but the rushing sounds of the street echoing through the alley. One moment, he heard the chorus of a pop song, then kids screaming. . . .

". . . mate."

The word echoed in his head, and Chris panicked. Oh, *Christ*, not Simon again.

"You all right, mate?"

Chris rolled over and looked into a policeman's face. It was outrageously large. The hair was graying at the temples beneath the cap. From behind the officer came another voice.

"Gang fight by the look of it, Sarge."

Chris flexed his jaw. His left cheek was swollen and had partially closed the eye. His hair was spiky from blood and dirt.

"What happened? Come on, son, you're not dead yet. You know the 'hooligoons' who just ran out of here?"

The sergeant crouched down, carefully examining the youth. "They take anything?"

Chris's head throbbed harshly. The constable returned from the panda car.

"Ambulance is on its way, Sarge. How is he?"

The sergeant studied both sides of Chris, still not certain what to make of him. "Bit of a needle match, eh, son? That's my feeling about it. What do you say?"

"I don't want an ambulance," Chris muttered. "I'm fine."

"You don't look it." The sergeant paused. "What's your name, then?" he asked.

Chris reached for the fence and pulled himself up. It flexed under his weight. The sergeant stood up with him and offered a hand, but Chris pushed it away. "I don't need your help."

The sergeant stepped back. "Fine. You want to talk in the station or the hospital, don't make no difference to me," he said. "Maybe you'll be able to remember a few faces before they give someone else a good kicking."

"It's all done now," said Chris. He wavered forward, running his palms along the fence. "Never saw 'em before."

The sergeant rested a hand on Chris's shoulder.

"Leave me alone," Chris said, shrugging it away.

"Let's get you in the car," said the sergeant.

"You gonna charge me?" The fury in Chris's voice surprised the officers. The sergeant weighed matters.

"Don't see why," he said at last. He glanced at his partner, who shrugged.

"He's the one who got a smacking," the constable said.

"Right," Chris said. He closed his eyes and followed the sound of playing children. Finally, Chris and the policemen stood patiently by the car, the officers expecting Chris to collapse and the ambulance to arrive. Neither happened.

The constable leaned on the car roof and said, "Can't stay here all bloody day, Sarge."

"Where you going, son?" the sergeant asked. Chris waved him away. Where to go? he thought. Even with his head clearer, the streets made no sense. Lines of pavement stretching endlessly. School? No. Where to go? One street seemed as good as another.

"All right, Jack, let's write it up," the sergeant told his partner. They were climbing back in the car when Chris touched the sergeant's sleeve.

"Broadmoor."

"What?"

"Just point the way," Chris said, standing straighter.

The sergeant and constable again exchanged glances, and the constable chuckled. The sergeant sighed and opened the back door. "Come on," he told Chris. "Hop in. We'll get you to the bus station."

Two years earlier, Chris had traced his natural father, but the idea of actually visiting him scared Chris. His father, after all, had killed his mother. Broadmoor was now his father's home.

Broadmoor was a Victorian prison hospital of faded red bricks, its outer walls embedded with broken glass. For over a hundred years, it had served as the final buffer between the sane and criminally insane.

As he stood outside the imposing building, Chris imagined the streets filling with madmen, ravaging until there would be no reason left in the world. Without a rational world, who dared say Chris was irrational? Or abnormal?

He walked through a wooden side door and checked in with a prison officer. A second officer escorted Chris along one side of a quadrangle, through another locked door, and into the hospital itself. Once inside, a male nurse took over the escort and Chris followed him down a pale, echoing corridor. Finally, the nurse said, "I've been here eight years. You're his first visitor. I mean, besides the usual priests and docs. Didn't even know he *had* a son."

"You do now," said Chris.

A matron in a cubicle off the ward entrance looked up from sorting pills and charting medical schedules. Beside her sat a prison officer.

"Easton," said Chris's escort.

The officer left his seat and led Chris into a sparsely furnished room that echoed faint noises from the building. Twenty minutes passed. Finally, he was brought into a room with a wooden table and two chairs. The prison officer settled comfortably on a chair in the far corner, reading the *Sun* beneath a dim stream of light that filtered through a small, barred window.

They were in the room less than a minute before Chris's father shuffled in. The thin, balding man never looked directly at his son; instead, he sat heavily on the edge of a chair and rested his wrinkled, curled hands on the table.

Chris didn't say a word. None of this seemed real. The worn murderer was a disappointment. He was too old and the life had been stolen from his body. The thought of going into his father's mind—so clever an idea earlier— was now repugnant.

He watched his father's hands. Which one had brought down the axe?

His father looked up.

"So," said the old man, "you're the boy." He studied Chris. "I can see it." He rubbed his nose and blundered about his robe for a tissue. He settled for a sleeve. "You growed up."

Chris dipped his head.

"You keeping well, then?"

"All right," said Chris. "How about you?"

"Fair to middlin'. Got a snout?"

Chris looked quickly at the jailer.

"He don't mind," his father said.

The officer nodded agreeably and Chris lit the cigarettes.

His father chewed on the smoke. "What do you want, then?" he asked.

Chris felt embarrassed.

"I wanted to see you," he said.

Chris's father took another deep drag on the cigarette. "Well?"

"I wanted to see what you're like."

"You mean, see the man who killed your mother?"

Chris didn't answer. He watched his father lean away from the table and mutter under his breath. Chris tried listening, but the old man wasn't talking with him. The officer caught Chris's eye and reassuringly patted the air.

"So, you're little Chris," his father said at last. "You was tiny last time I saw you."

Chris touched his father's arm. The old man relaxed.

"I'm a trustee now. They let me wander about, work in the library. Reckon I'm too old to cause any bother. I couldn't hurt anyone anyway. Not the way your mother gets on at me."

"Mum?" Chris asked.

"She's a strong one. Don't let me do nothing. Don't let me—" He stopped, his jaw dropping and his eyes rolling back. Chris leaned closer, glancing at the jailer. The man shrugged and returned to his paper.

"He'll be back in a second," the officer said. "Just drifts off now and then."

Chris waited, feeling somehow cheated. As promised, his father took a long yawn and looked down at his hands. The cigarette had burned down to the filter.

"You all right?" Chris asked him.

His father studied him. "I killed her, you know," he whispered. "She won't let me forget it."

Chris played with a coat sleeve.

"You're like her," said his father. "I can tell."

"No," Chris said loudly. The prison officer looked up for a moment, then ignored them.

His father leaned closer and nodded. "You got it."

"I *ain't*."

"Oh, my Gawd," muttered the old man.

"Is that why you killed her?" Chris asked. "Did she hurt you? Did she make you do things?"

The old man's face again went blank. His eyes rolled up and his face darkened.

"Hey!" Chris shook his father's arm. The officer looked up. This time, he dropped his paper and came over.

"He's choking," the guard said. He pushed Chris aside

44

and leaned Chris's father back in the chair, loosening his collar. The old man gagged on air, lost to his trance. The officer shook him, then glanced at Chris. "Get the bloody nurse!"

Chris didn't move.

"Go *on*, son."

Chris still didn't move. The officer spun around and shook him.

"Damm it! Get the bloody nurse!"

Chris didn't hear him, didn't feel anything. The officer looked carefully at the boy. "Jesus Christ!" he cursed. The kid was staring off in a trance. The officer turned back to the old man, who still gasped for breath.

As for Chris, he was no longer in his body. He was deep inside his father's thoughts, and he was terrified.

He wanted to help his father. He went in expecting to be surrounded by the blood and gore that must exist in the memories of an axe murderer. Once inside, however, Chris saw much more. His father's mind was like a gallery that had been trashed by vandals. Images crumpled; thoughts melted like hot wax; grotesque, forgotten moments were torn away like strips of skin.

Someone else had been here. Someone else had been inside his father's mind and destroyed it.

His mother.

Her face was all over. Mother as wife. Mother as nurse. Mother as judge. Even as Chris watched, the old man's fresh memories congealed and slowly dissolved. In their place came the familiar scrawl of his mother's blue eyes and haunting smile. Her power amazed Chris. How could she still be alive? How could she control his father so completely? Forget Broadmoor. This was the real punishment.

"Get out."

The voice echoed out of the darkness; a whisper that, anywhere else, Chris would have mistaken as a hollow wind. The gallery shivered and Chris panicked, losing focus. The memories of Chris had now almost completely disappeared. Chris felt his own face. His cheeks were damp. Dripping. Instead of changing his father, Chris was being changed.

"Get out."

His mother came out of the memories. Young, naked, scarred, somehow alive inside his father—a home warm and secure, where no axe could cut her. Chris stumbled back. Even as she ordered him to leave, she was taking possession of him; carving herself into her son's head, adding to her modest retreat. The flesh streamed off Chris's face. He understood what was happening. She was reaching into Chris the way he reached into other people. Chris looked into her eyes and screamed. His mother touched him. . . .

"I think I got him breathing," said the prison officer.

Chris was leaning heavily on the table. His father awoke from his trance.

"Keep your eye on him," the officer told Chris. "I'll get the nurse." Then he hurried away.

The old man stared about the room and spat on the floor.

"Christ, I've got a headache," he complained. He tried standing, but fell back in the chair. He looked again at Chris, trying to make sense of whatever memories remained of his son. Chris imagined his mother working furiously to destroy the images; probably destroying his father in the process.

The old man's forehead wrinkled.

"Who are you?"

"No one special," Chris answered.

His father did not understand, but his confusion slipped away as the questions disappeared from his thoughts.

"Where's Henry?" he asked.

Chris left to find the officer.

* * *

There was no going home. How could Chris go back to his friends and foster parents? He was too dangerous, his strange gift too powerful—almost out of control. No, he had to be on his own. There was just one last thing to do.

It was a clear night, marred only by a string of streetlights that followed the curve of the road. Chris wandered through the spills of yellow light until he thought it wise to slip into the shadows of the common. Finally, he looked up at Moira's window.

The bedroom light was off and the house was quiet. He closed his eyes and joined the household, finding his way up the stairs and sneaking into her bedroom.

Moira rolled restlessly in bed, still feverish. Memories were making her sick; she was having nightmares of an evening in the park, when she had agreed to give herself to Chris Easton. Agreed? Yes. She had wanted to make love with him. She wanted him now, desperately, and she wanted him dead.

Chris had never meant to cause Moira such anguish. He returned to her mind, looking for the terrible images that haunted her. Once he found them, he altered the nightmare, filling Moira with calmer dreams. There were no more memories of the outrage in the park, only of sitting alone, by the pond, unafraid. Chris pressed himself deep into her past, becoming the forgotten friend of her younger brother.

Memories gone, memories replaced. When he opened his eyes, Chris was crying. He knew they would never meet again.

Chris walked away from the house, aware of another secret. It was a secret he saw in Moira, in his father . . . even in his mother, as she lived like a parasite inside her husband.

This strange, mysterious power—the ability to go inside

47

people's heads and change the way they thought—could drive a person insane.

Four

A LDERSHOT, ENGLAND, 1974

It was in Aldershot that Chris became a professional photographer.

Aldershot was a military town, about an hour's drive away from London. It had a curious mix of civilians and prestigious British army regiments, many of which had seen service abroad and in Northern Ireland.

Chris had gone to Aldershot when he was seventeen, with no idea what to do, except perhaps to disappear. For nearly two months he lived by taking pictures of tourists and working the pubs. At first, he swore never to use his damned power again. The more Chris thought about it, the more he realized his little game was an invasion, a violation of his victims' private thoughts and feelings. He had no right idly browsing through someone's mind and altering it.

But he couldn't help himself. His personality was changing. There were subtle shifts that a parent might excuse as just growing up, but deep down Chris knew better. For the first time, Chris realized that each time he entered someone's thoughts, a part of his own mind was reconstructed. At first, this had happened in small, entertaining ways. But the more he played, the more he found himself drawn to more interesting minds, more dangerous thoughts. He began to follow police cars, burglars, "skinheads," ambulance men, "squaddies," trying his luck on each.

Chris trained his thoughts on controlling his power. He made his few pounds, scrounged his meals, drank his pints, and allowed each day to come and go. His only lasting possession was the camera, which he carried almost everywhere. Click. That was the end of it. He was determined nothing like Moira would ever happen again. He was ashamed just to think of it.

Chris's friend Duffy and he had been drinking pints in a pub. For the better part of the evening, Duffy watched the women while Chris sat on a stool, his Polaroid and an old Canon on the counter. Occasionally, he would make a round of the young couples at the tables, but Chris preferred picking and choosing his customers from the bar. He was feeling bored, and watched a man and woman sitting in a far corner, a package by their feet.

Chris picked up the Polaroid and wandered over to the table.

"Right, nice smile, then," he said with false brightness.

They looked up at him, surprised.

Chris tapped the camera. "Put your arm 'round her," he said.

"Get lost," the man replied.

It was Chris's habit to take a picture regardless of the answer. Often, he got something for the effort.

"Leave us alone," the man threatened.

"No trouble, squire," Chris said. "Just doing me job." He glanced down at the package, and then he understood.

He retreated quickly to the bar.

"Here," said Duffy. "Look at the 'brains' on that bird over there.'

Chris pushed Duffy aside and hopped over the bar. Using the counter as a steady level, he focused on the distant couple.

They left their seats . . . click, pressing through the crowd . . . click, click. The package stayed under the table, blocked from view, but not if Chris focused carefully and . . . click, click, click.

"Duffy, get the gov'ner!"

"What for?" Duffy had a curious smile on his face. "He'll go barmy if he catches you back there."

"Get the bloody gov'ner," Chris insisted.

"Fuck you!" Duffy laughed.

"Don't prat about. Do what I tell you."

Duffy shook his head and wandered off, but Chris didn't trust him. He scanned the crowded bar, wondering whether to shout a warning. It would be hopeless. No one would pay him any attention. Besides, how could he warn them without explaining how he knew?

Duffy became lost in a haze of cigarette smoke. Chris followed him, protecting his camera as he pushed his way to the phone near the back door. He found Duffy outside by the trash cans, dragging on a cigarette.

"Where is he?" Chris demanded.

"I looked, Chris. Honest."

Chris turned back to the pub. "The rozzers," he began, but the rest of his words were lost to a deafening "whump," then a flash filled with flying shards of glass and wood. The force of the explosion heaved them both into the street. A billow of dark smoke rolled slowly into the sky.

Chris crawled along the pavement, protecting his eyes from the blowing cinders, then steadied himself behind a lamp post and uncapped the lens on his Canon.

Click, click, click, click . . .

50

It was instinct. Picture after picture of people stumbling free of the fire. Pictures of the doorway collapsing, of people locked and lost inside the inferno, of the fire engines and ambulances as they arrived, of rescuers weeping as they carried out the maimed and picked up pieces of the dead in large black plastic bags.

"Jesus Christ!" Duffy sobbed. "Jesus Christ!"

. . . Click, click, click . . .

Chris crouched beside his friend.

"My fault," Duffy kept repeating. Chris searched his own pockets for money. He gave Duffy a five-pound note. Duffy looked up, confused.

"Get me a couple of rolls," Chris said.

"What?"

"I need more film."

"More film?" Duffy repeated stupidly. The sound of ambulances grew louder.

"I'm running out of film. Go on."

Chris helped Duffy to his feet, shaking him hard, finally losing his temper.

"Film, Duffy—get me the bleeding film!"

The film proved invaluable. The Provisional I.R.A.'s bombing became international news, and Chris's photographs of the bombers and the explosion were published around the world. After meeting Reuters's London-desk editor-in-chief, Chris became the agency's youngest photojournalist. He stayed with Reuters less than a year, then left London to visit Mozambique as a freelance photographer. He arrived shortly before the withdrawal of the Portuguese army—photos that were sold and being published as he boarded a flight to Ethiopia. There, Chris photographed the fall of Emperor Haile Selassie.

Such work kept Chris busy. While his name was never known to the general public, by the time he was nineteen he had secured his place in the profession with a series of famous shots capturing the assassination of Bangladesh President Sheik Mujibar Rahman. The composition and clarity of each shot, even the lighting, astounded everyone. As his reputation grew, everyone wanted to know—how did he do it?

Chris kept his secret. After all these years, he had finally resolved the safest, surest way to use his power: not to change or control events, merely to warn him how they were taking shape, and when it was time to escape. His power was the perfect informant. All information was accurate, all escapes foolproof. Even if he was cornered by a killer, where was the danger? A quick step into the killer's head, a momentary freeze . . . Danger without peril. Danger for the thrill of it.

The rescue of the Entebbe hostages. The Soweto riots. The evacuation of Cambodia—half a million dead. Chris saw it all before the age of twenty-one. By the time he teamed up with Murray Hunt, a stringer for Reuters and *Paris Match*, Chris was the youngest seasoned photographer on the circuit.

Murray and he had been assigned to cover some fighting in a P.L.O. enclave. Sitting outside a hill tavern in Jerusalem one warm evening, Murray listened grim-faced while Chris counted off the mayhem he had experienced. By the time Chris finished, Murray was in awe.

"Incredible," he said. Chris smiled.

Murray didn't return it. "Hasn't any of this affected you?"

"Me?" Chris scoffed. "Water off a duck's back, mate."

"No one brushes off stuff like that," Murray said.

"I do."

But Chris was lying. Sometimes he felt the changes; more commonly, Murray was the first to notice them, such as the time Chris spent a week secretly digging through the mind of a reputed arms smuggler who was left-handed. One day, Murray expressed surprise upon seeing Chris sign a check with his left hand. He said he didn't know Chris was ambidextrous. Chris also expressed surprise; all his life he had been right-handed.

Chris's philosophy toward life was also changing, becoming more radical with each story they covered. At first, Murray could argue with Chris, and Chris would sometimes admit the flaws in his own logic as Murray pointed them out—something that was easy to do because Chris's philosophies were often a patchwork of resonant revolutionary slogans. Eventually, however, Murray gave up this battle. Chris became so dogmatic that Murray had no idea where to begin arguing. Besides, Murray figured it was war fatigue. What harm was there in babbling nonsense?

Murray didn't become seriously concerned until their story in the Cordilliera Dariense, Nicaragua. They had gone deep into the jungle to interview the head of a rebel camp, only to find the camp had been massacred. The two journalists were alone, exhausted, and knee deep in dead guerrillas, when Murray heard the sharp reports of automatic weapons.

"Hear that?" asked Murray.

"It's the bleedin' army," Chris answered.

"They'll go fucking crazy if they find out journalists have been here," Murray said nervously. Chris had been washing his face in a pool of water, but now they both listened carefully. Behind the gunfire came the thud of grenades. They could also hear a soldier shouting and the chopping blades of a helicopter, both hidden beyond the trees.

"They're coming this way," Chris said.

Murray watched the woods. "We better get out of here," he said. Chris tucked away his camera and tied up the army bag. "Here," he said, tossing Murray the canteen.

Murray caught it and hushed him. They heard the sound

of snapping branches. He put his finger to his lips and hunched closer to Chris. "Son-of-a-bitch," he whispered.

Murray watched as Chris approached the trail. He was like a dog catching on to a scent, only Murray had no idea what Chris would do once he had sniffed out the enemy. Chris was often like this, but this time he looked more like an animal on the hunt than one looking for a place to hide.

A bullet ricocheted off a tree, leaving a white scar a foot above Murray's head.

"Shit!" Murray moaned.

Chris peered around the tree. Forward snipers—two of them. He sank into the mind of the closest soldier.

New target, Chris thought, and pointed the first sniper toward his comrade.

Murray crawled up to Chris and grabbed his arm. "Which way do we go now?" he whispered urgently. Chris shrugged him off, searching for the second sniper. Changing things in this one's head was a tougher job.

New target, he suggested. Chris saw the first soldier through the second man's eyes. The snipers faced each other, weapons pointed, the rifle bolts clicking back, the triggers squeezed.

Two shots, almost together. Murray winced. After a moment he looked up cautiously. Chris moved at a crouch to the edge of the trail. "You're crazy!" Murray hissed.

Silence. The sound of the helicopter had disappeared. Gradually the birds began to chatter again.

"Come on," said Chris. He stood and slung his bag over his shoulder.

"Get your ass *down*, you stupid jerk!" Murray called, his voice hoarse.

Chris walked several feet down the trail and stopped, turning back. "You staying here all bloody day, or what?" he asked.

Murray crawled forward, straining for the sound of the

54

soldiers. ''I don't think this is a good idea,'' he said, nonetheless walking quickly alongside Chris. ''You're going to get us both killed.''

''Not today, me old cocker,'' Chris said quietly.

Murray stopped one last time, listening. All he could hear now were the sounds of the jungle. Something wasn't right. Chris had judged the impotence of a previously deadly situation instantly, and there was no logical explanation for how he had known when it was safe to move.

A night mist was falling, dropping quickly like hazy gray ash.

''Let's get back to the road,'' said Chris.

By the next morning, a noon deadline delayed Murray's curiosity, and then two more late-breaking stories put the subject of Chris's behavior on hold.

It was just as well. When Murray reviewed the incidents in his mind, he always reached the same illogical, uncomfortable conclusion. There had been two soldiers in the woods. Chris had moved closer to them, and then there were two shots, followed by silence. In that kind of situation, silence only meant death.

Two soldiers, two shots, two deaths. Despite himself, Murray could not escape the conclusion that Chris had been responsible.

''Must be a perfectly logical answer,'' Murray muttered to himself on more than one occasion. But he never had the nerve to ask Chris outright. After a while, it just seemed wrong to mention it—like asking a magician how a trick worked. One either figured it out oneself or simply enjoyed the mystery.

Besides, Murray thought, what does it matter?

Five

B EIRUT, LEBANON, 1980.

Three years in the Middle East.
Three years of focusing and photographing.
Three years of probing, listening, and learning.
The time passed quickly for Chris.

Jets and helicopters passed with the clouds, sweeping
the mountaintops and sprinkling the land with air-to-
ground missiles. Mortars rose and fell with the wind, each
explosion more blinding than the sun, scattering fragments
through the cities and hills. And constantly, above it all,
the sun glared through a haze of grimy heat. Predictable
weather. A perfect climate for Chris Easton.

The Middle East was where militarists planned and terrorists surprised. Where shoppers and bombers shared the
late-afternoon traffic. Where barking dogs, shouting children, and the whining sounds of Arabic pop music mingled with the chatter of automatic weapons. The throbbing
thump of mortars played a constant counterpoint to the
hiss of incoming rockets. It was a region of shifting fron-
tiers, where Chris could spend every day testing his own
boundaries, pushing his power to its limits, relying more
and more on his strange ability.

Every Lebanese mind Chris entered—every Syrian, every Israeli—fought Chris with a mental vigor he could find nowhere else. Not in Cambodia, Nicaragua, or South Africa. Chris reached into the minds of the soldiers and saw a common soul. Every day brought him closer to that soul—but he had yet to touch it.

Then he met Francine.

Her full name was Francine Montrelle—thirty-seven years old and a writer who had published several acclaimed profiles of the world's more colorful political leaders. She was always stylishly dressed, even in loaned army fatigues. Francine was intense, with a thin, dark-eyed face and wiry black hair streaked with gray.

She had been sent to Lebanon by her editor, Murray Hunt. Murray had left the Middle East in favor of a safer, quieter job behind an editorial desk of a New York City-based news magazine. He had opted for the change after one too many mortars nearly left him a nervous wreck. He had tried taking Chris out with him, Murray had explained to Francine, but Chris had refused, saying it would be like walking away from people trapped in a burning building. Murray thought Chris had just forgotten what it was like to live in a normal, relatively peaceful world.

Still, as long as Chris was in Lebanon, Murray could think of no better story potential than teaming his best writer with his best photographer. Francine agreed, not only because of the story, but to work with Chris Easton. The chance to follow Chris onto the battlefield was irresistible. So Francine went to Beirut, writing to Chris first as an introduction, presuming he would be waiting for her at the airport. Or at least the hotel?

Chris could not be found. At the hotel, Francine checked for messages. Nothing.

She waited in the bar. The tepid atmosphere became heavier, and Francine responded curtly to the men who squeezed onto the neighboring seats. Most of the people in the room were journalists, some of whom she recognized; at the moment, however, she had no desire to speak with them. She was, frankly, irritated by Chris's cavalier, irresponsible attitude. Despite her better judgment, her anger grew. She surveyed the room once more, noticing some men in pale suits. They sat in the corner sipping anise and speaking French. Probably from the nearby French embassy. How absurd, wearing suits in such heat.

"Francine Montrelle?"

She turned from the bar. The man before her wore a dark khaki shirt, olive shorts, and army boots. A dusty *kaffiyeh*—a veil of blue cloth to protect him from dust—masked his face. Over his shoulder hung a satchel and a camera. Several rolls of film were taped to the strap. He pulled away the kaffiyeh.

"Chris Easton?"

"Would have got here sooner," he said, "but I just found out you was coming. You settled in all right?"

"Just about." She stared at his dirty clothes.

"I've been up in the hills."

"How nice for you," Francine answered dryly. "I assume you know why I'm here?"

"Sorry." Chris smiled.

"You at least got my letter?"

"No."

Francine was not certain what to say. "Maybe we should get acquainted now." She sighed, extending a hand.

"Fine." Chris ignored her hand. "Follow me."

Francine paid for her drink and followed Chris outside. It was two o'clock, and too early for any fierce fighting, he explained to her. They walked between the battle-scarred buildings, almost sauntering along the street. All the time, Francine watched her escort, aware of how well he suited the landscape. He had become a subject fit for his own photographs.

A dog barked somewhere, and flies gathered around the

58

two journalists. Francine pushed back her sunglasses and grabbed Chris's arm. "Are you telling me you haven't been to your apartment yet?" she asked.

"That's right."

"So you didn't get my letter. And you didn't get Murray's phone calls, so—?"

Chris continued walking. Francine hurried after him. A baby was shrieking in a nearby building, and loud voices in Arabic rose up, then faded away under the distorted sounds of a radio. "Yes?" Chris asked.

"So how did you know I was coming?"

"I heard you," he said.

"How?"

"Arab mysticism." He turned his back on her once more. The oppressive heat made serious thinking impossible, so Francine resigned herself to the mystery. She followed Chris down a narrow alley and into the basement of a corner building. The top story had been demolished by shelling, and piles of rubble still laid on the sidewalk.

Chris opened the door and reached for a light switch. A single bulb glowed in the basement shelter. A rolled bed mat and a clothes sack were tucked in one corner of the room, and a nearby alcove served as Chris's darkroom. Several rolls of developed film were clipped to a cord that drooped from the door and led to a wall patched with prints. Aside from these details, the room was bare. It reminded Francine of a cool, dark prison cell.

"I must smell like a horse," he said. She didn't argue.

"So what's been happening?" she asked him. "When do we leave?"

"Hang on a minute, darlin'. I ain't even changed me bleedin' knickers yet."

Francine's irritation grew as she watched Chris potter about. "It's not my fault if you can't be bothered to find out about your assignments," she finally said.

"Oi," Chris said. "I've been out in the hills for two

weeks. I'm hot, sweaty, and tired, so don't start any trouble, all right?''

Francine didn't answer. A few moments later, Chris added, ''I'll tell you what. I'll show you the Nahr al Yamuk. How about that?''

''Where is it?'' she asked.

''It runs past the Golan Heights,'' Chris said. He dumped his bags on the bed. ''With a bit of luck we won't have to leave the river until we pass Rafid. Then if all goes well we can head east into the desert toward Tibne.''

Francine stood at the doorway, refusing to leave the sunlight. Chris reached into the alcove, opened a water pouch, and washed himself.

''I've already got a ride to Mishmar Hayarden,'' he said. ''We'll have to hitch a lift with the Syrians the rest of the way.''

He picked up a *jellaba*—a one-piece robe many Arab men of the desert wore—and used it as a towel on his naked body. He turned to face Francine. She refused to lose her smile, but it tightened.

''I'm supposed to write about Lebanon,'' she said, ''not Syria.''

''Well, I'm going to Syria. There's a P.L.O. camp I want to visit about forty-five klicks up the Nahr al Yamuk.''

''What's so special about it?''

''The leader is a very powerful *mullah*. You might call him the godfather of 'em all.''

''Very catchy.''

''His blokes slaughtered a school bus full of children in Holon a couple of weeks ago,'' Chris explained. ''You probably heard about it.''

''Murray showed me your pictures.''

''They also set off a chain of bombs in downtown Tel Aviv that killed fifty-odd Israelis and some Arabs.''

''But we can't get into Syria.''

"Why not?"

"It's dangerous."

Chris laughed, brushing his wet hair back with his fingers.

"Don't you worry about that, darlin'. I'll make it safe for you." He waved her closer.

"I'm just fine where I am, thank you," she replied curtly.

Chris fanned himself. "This is how you keep cool in the desert," he said. "Lets the skin breathe."

"Stop by the hotel when you've finished your breathing exercises, all right?"

"Half an hour," he said. "Go straight back. Don't let anyone stop you. If they do, use my name."

"Are you *that* famous around here?"

"Just use it, all right?"

Francine saw Chris an hour later, after he had changed into army pants and a shirt. A crowd of merchants and children were escaping the nearby sounds of a tank. Chris walked through them. Francine noticed they ran around him, but never near him.

Despite the shaky start to their friendship, they drew closer during the next few days. She had never met anyone like Chris Easton. He neither imposed upon her nor discouraged her. Being a war correspondent meant walking a deadly edge that had always scared Francine, but she enjoyed the feeling.

She believed Chris would help her understand why.

The Nahr al Yamuk was a Syrian river near Lebanon, used as an arms route by the P.L.O. Late at night, when Israeli reconnaissance planes stopped soaring across the Syrian border, small groups of men—their faces covered and their backs laden with rifles and surface-to-air rocket launchers—escorted their supplies downriver. The river

61

gave them access to Israel or Lebanon through the Golan Heights. Three years earlier, in late 1980, nearly all the camps had been flushed off the river by the Israelis. One camp, however, had survived, continuing to send supplies and soldiers, building a reputation for random kidnappings and killings. The P.L.O. "freedom fighters" fought not only for a homeland, but to satisfy their mullah. They were soldiers with nothing to lose but their lives. Success was all that mattered, and the mullah's soldiers brought him great satisfaction.

"Imshee, imshee," ordered a young Arab. The rear flaps of the Syrian army truck opened. He waved his AK-47 as Chris and Francine jumped down from the tail gate into the reddish-dusk light of the desert. The Arab stuck his rifle in Chris's face and shouted at him again. Chris pushed the barrel aside and picked up his bag, slinging it over his shoulder. Francine and he followed the soldier down the embankment and dropped their packs, resting by the banks of the Nahr al Yamuk. Another soldier slid down the embankment, his new Russian rifle pointed steadily at the two journalists. Only his eyes were visible; his face, like everyone else's, was covered by a grubby kaffiyeh. Above him stood a ragged line of support, at ease while unarmed men loaded several trucks with squat, oblong boxes. It was hard to be sure, but there seemed no other woman in the enclave.

"We're here to see your commander," Francine told the two soldiers. The men ignored her. Instead, one of them ordered the journalists to squat in the water. Francine followed Chris's example. They waited for the mullah to appear. Chris tried entering the thoughts of the Palestinians to learn more about them. He was surprised by the unified way they all seemed to shut him out.

"Americans?" someone called. A long shadow crossed the riverbank.

Francine twisted about, squinting up into the sun. She

62

saw the silhouette of a large man. He walked forward, dressed in a jellaba that seemed to blend into the cliff. He picked his way slowly down a path while a team of soldiers guarded him. When he walked fully into view, Francine saw he was in his early forties. He overwhelmed her with his calm sense of order and control. Here was a man whose world contained no pity or reason. The mullah's brows furrowed, curious about the Westerners who had invaded his privacy.

Chris took a deep breath. He tried entering the soldiers' minds, but they had been sealed. It was like touching a massive brick wall that stretched endlessly in every direction. It was frustrating. His only chance was to find a forgotten crack big enough to squeeze through. But there was no such weakness. The men were fighting machines, free of the doubts and conscience that inhibited action, be it the execution of an Israeli soldier or the massacre of children. The only things to escape the wall were the threads of thought keeping the body in touch with the mind. When Chris touched one of them, he felt a numbness, as if he were in shock from an electrical charge.

The thought occurred to him that he had disturbed an alarm.

The mullah pointed at Francine, scratching his graying beard. "No, not quite American," he said.

"I'm half American," she said. "On my father's side." She paused. "I want to write about this strong camp and its great mullah."

"A story about me?" The mullah sounded amused.

"Yes."

"And about my soldiers?"

"I understand you've been . . . uh . . . very effective against the Israelis."

The mullah grinned. "You are a reporter, yes? For which magazine?"

She told him. The mullah showed no interest, until he looked at Chris.

"You," he said. Chris looked back coldly. "You are not American."

"He's English," Francine explained.

"I'm her photographer."

The mullah nodded slowly and tried entering Chris's thoughts. Instinctively, Chris resisted. Never before had someone attempted such a thing. Now he realized just how disturbing the process could be—the tingling about the forehead, as if ants were crawling under his skin; the prodding of an invisible hand, somehow riffling Chris's thoughts and merging with him. It was a much more physical experience than he had ever imagined. Chris surprised the mullah by pushing the thought probes away—and his secret was out. What Chris knew about the mullah, the mullah knew about him.

The mullah returned to Francine.

"You shouldn't have come here," he said. "I don't like you or your friend."

"I thought it was time someone tried to tell your side of the story."

"You miss the point," the mullah said patiently. "It is only worth my while to speak with you if I am assured of your sympathies. Is that not so?"

Chris immediately recognized the look on the mullah's face. It was the same one that crossed his own face when he slipped into someone's thoughts.

Francine grasped her shoulder bag.

"I am very busy, as you can see," the mullah went on. "We are in the middle of some important activities."

"I have an open mind," said Francine.

"Both of you?"

Francine did not know what was happening, but she understood there was something going on between Chris and the mullah. If Chris didn't watch his step, they'd be leaving feet first. What the hell was he doing?

After a long pause, the mullah announced loudly, "Come. Join me." He shouted at his soldiers, who quickly lifted the packs and helped Chris and Francine out of the water. "It is cooler in the tents," the mullah added. He strode up the bank and away from them, speaking in Arabic.

They followed, with Chris deliberately walking slowly, trying to test his senses and see if the mullah had changed him. They were joined in the tent by two lieutenants, young men who frowned at Francine with open distrust. Everyone sat in a rough circle, with Francine's tape recorder in the center. Chris placed his camera back in his sack and again focused his attention. Still nothing. It was as if all the minds in the camp had been sealed.

"Where would you like to begin?" asked the mullah. Francine wasn't sure. "Let us begin with the Israeli acts of terror," the mullah suggested.

"Yes," said Francine.

The mullah began his story, entrancing Francine, possessing her, writing his own article. Chris watched the flickering RECORD light of the cassette machine. As the photographer, he was not expected to listen. He used his freedom to concentrate on the challenge posed by the mullah's unbreakable servants. The same questions came back to Chris: Who was the source of the power? Was it the mullah? Were the Arabs somehow able to reflect Chris's power back at him? Or was there another force, some form of collective power?

As he considered the questions, Chris noticed a shadow resting against the tent wall. He stretched his back and walked toward the open fold of the tent wall. The mullah glanced at Chris. "Do not wander far," he warned.

Chris stood for a moment in the cool evening air. No

matter how the mullah scrambled Francine's thoughts, Chris was certain he could repair the damage.

He walked into the fading sunlight, his eyes scanning the truck, the river, and the blue mountains on the far horizon. He finally traced the source of the evening shadow he had seen on the tent wall.

The old man calmly returned Chris's interest.

The old man rose and, turning from the tent, walked slowly to his own shelter—a taut goat skin stretched between the barren branches of a tree. Chris studied the man. The Arab was crippled by age and the desert: a fragile sight, as brittle as the tree that shaded him. Skin flaked the corners of his mouth.

How old was he? Eighty? One hundred eighty? Immortality seemed possible for this fellow, Chris thought admiringly.

Chris sat on a rock, gazing at the river, reaching for the old man's mind.

The old man was waiting for him.

See through my eyes, he invited Chris.

Chris accepted the invitation. He watched himself sitting tiredly on a rock, his neck burned by the sun. Past his own figure was the trucks, and, beyond that, the river. Inside the trucks were bullets, grenades, mortars, rocket launchers, AK-47's, some M-16's, automatic sidearms. . . .

See through my heart, said the old man.

War exploded around Chris, plunging him into a desert on fire. The flames licked the clouds, charring them into a black fog. A poison filled the old man.

Touch my soul, he said.

Chris was filled with a strong feeling of revenge—and a desire for a homeland. He experienced an endless battle, centuries old. Chris had never known so much passion and anger.

Join me.

Chris hesitated. *Give to the teacher,* he thought. *Join him; let him take me—take from him.*

Yes, join me, the old man insisted.

Yes, thought Chris. Through the old man's eyes, Chris calmly watched his own body rise from the rock. It walked to one of the unattended trucks, reached inside the cab, and withdrew a knife. As he held it up to his face, the last rays of sunlight flashed on the blade.

Join me.

Chris opened his shirt and pressed the pointed tip of the knife against his stomach. For a moment, it lifted with his breath, but when he pressed down on it, the knife drew blood.

Brief pain, then immortality, the old man assured Chris.

It would be so easy. One quick motion with the knife. He wouldn't even have to do the work—the old man was in control. Chris struggled for survival, feeling sweat break out on his face.

Join me. Join me.

A trickle of blood dripped onto the sand. The knife tip had made a painless wound. Another inch, and he would quickly bleed to death.

Chris could feel the old man working—sinking deeper into Chris's thoughts, feeding off of his willpower, his psychic strength. If their paths had crossed a year earlier, or perhaps even a month earlier, Chris would have died, and the mullah would enjoy the power of Chris's youth.

But another thought entered Chris's head, one he stole from the mullah. He was stealing ideas, feelings, emotions more quickly now, and this one brought an end to the mullah's feast. The knife dropped, and Chris collapsed to his knees. The full terror of what he'd almost done struck home. He moaned, rubbing his wound. The old man gazed at him, a trace of surprise in his eyes. Chris looked back and forced a smile. He had almost been swallowed by the old man, but he had beaten him. It was odd; the old man would have killed him; at the same time, it was the old man's thoughts that saved Chris—that had explained to him the reason for his power.

A flicker of a smile crossed the old Arab's face. They were equals—in talent, strength, and passion—joined by the battlefield. Except Chris, at twenty-seven, already had the power of this ancient mystic. What else might Chris do? What would his power be like in another week, another year?

At midnight, with the road cleared for travel, the mullah accompanied Chris and Francine to a Jeep, assuring them of safe passage to the Syrian border. Chris knew better. He was a threat. The old man could not permit someone as powerful as Chris to leave the camp and oppose his will. Besides, as long as Chris retained his independence, he could free Francine of the mullah's influence.

Two men—a driver and an armed escort—climbed into the Jeep, kaffiyehs hiding their faces. They were like the other soldiers; Chris couldn't begin to enter their minds. He felt defenseless.

"I look forward to reading your story," the mullah told Francine.

Francine smiled. "I wish you great success," she replied.

The mullah stepped away from the Jeep, and they began their journey south, never drifting more than a hundred yards from the river. All the time Chris prepared himself. Francine and he shared the back seat, with Chris immediately behind the driver. The escort would have to turn for an attack. Chris watched him closely.

They drove for over an hour. The shielded beams of their headlights skipped off the rear of a truck. It was an uneventful trip, though the escort continually looked out his side of the open Jeep, suspicious of the night, afraid an Israeli jet would bring an end to their sacred mission.

"Here, Francine," Chris whispered. He leaned toward her and gently shook an arm.

Francine was asleep. Chris nudged her again, but she had been exhausted by the mullah. Instead, he turned to the driver.

"How much farther?" he asked in Arabic.

The driver shrugged. Chris watched the escort carefully. *Soon,* he thought.

The distance between the Jeep and the convoy lengthened. There came a subtle turn in the road and their Jeep followed a path toward the river, away from the trucks.

"Where are we going?" Chris asked.

He kept attacking their mental barriers, but without success. He heard the telltale click of a safety catch being released. The escort twisted about, his rifle in his hand, faceless in the night. The gun metal shined from a sliver of moon.

Chris jumped forward. He tried knocking the weapon away by toppling across them. The first bullet struck him in the thigh. The driver struggled to shake Chris off, but Chris held tightly, heaving him away from the steering wheel. The Jeep veered into a bank. "Francine!" Chris shouted.

Chris twisted and the escort fired again, hitting the driver. A third shot shattered Chris's shoulder blade. Chris shoved the driver on top of the escort.

"Francine!"

A burning pain seared his back. A knife had plunged into his muscle and was being tugged slowly downward. Francine was holding onto the haft.

Chris kicked her away. The length of the rifle hampered the escort's efforts to aim at Chris. The Jeep continued to veer back and forth, again heaving into the air.

Chris cried out as he crashed against the front windshield, then bounced back into the driver. Francine dropped on top of him and the escort fired another shot.

Chris knew he had no chance of changing the Arabs' minds. They had been sealed by the mullah and the old man. But there were still the threads that tied the mind to the body, synapses that flickered with lights that flashed on and off. Without these threads, there could be no connection between thought and action. The soldiers would be locked helplessly within themselves, unable to move.

Chris clipped the threads.

The Jeep finally rolled to a stop, its front wheels hanging off the road. The driver and escort were slumped in their seats.

Chris turned, still numb from the shock of his wounds. Francine was slumped awkwardly on the floor, a spreading chest wound staining her shirt.

"Oh, Christ!" Chris moaned. He dumped the Arabs out of the Jeep and tried staunching Francine's wound. He slid behind the driver's wheel and used his good arm to steer them back toward the border. The road was partially covered by sand, and countless times they drifted into the desert, only somehow to rediscover their way and draw closer to the Lebanese border. Then the darkness completely swallowed him. *Am I dying?* he wondered. He heard jabbering voices, then saw lights and a host of images that slowly focused into faces. Doctors and nurses . . . the sanitized security of an Israeli hospital.

"Francine," he murmured.

A doctor looked down at him. Chris closed his eyes. He didn't need to enter the doctor's mind for an answer. Francine was dead.

Was this worth the trip? Was Francine's life worth the knowledge he had gained?

He wished he could say no, but in his heart Chris knew it was all worthwhile. He would do anything to test his limits, to break them. The power was grabbing hold of him. Soon, it might take control.

70

All thanks to the mullah and the old man.

Before this encounter, Chris was slowly being overwhelmed by the killing and maiming he witnessed almost every day. His mind was in a desperate struggle for reason, and the endless rage inside his own head, repressed since his childhood and partly responsible for those early nightmares, was slowly destroying him. But the mullah had set his thoughts to rest. He'd put the world's violence into the context of centuries, not daily headlines. More important, something in the mullah had explained to Chris that his role was not to be on the sidelines, but on the battlefield.

There was a time when such a thought would have frightened Chris.

Not anymore.

Six

PARIS, FRANCE, LATE FALL, 1984.

Murray's Concorde flight landed at Charles de Gaulle Airport some four hours after leaving New York. His secretary, Shirley, had booked him into the Georges V, a luxury hotel close to the Louvre museum. It had all the comforts he now enjoyed and expected: marble floors and thick carpets, brass rails and crystal chandeliers. Three years ago, Murray would have felt out of place there. Now he walked to the check-in desk with self-assurance.

"Hunt," he said. "Any messages?"

"No, monsieur." The clerk beckoned for a bellboy. Murray filled out the visitor's form, reminding himself that he had no reason to expect Chris to call. During the last few months, Chris had changed for the worse. His behavior, his word—nothing could be trusted.

It wasn't just the violence of the Middle East, although Chris's pictures had become unbearably graphic. The problem was the spirit of the photographs—random images that were less a record of a struggle than a celebration of murder. Week after week, roll after roll, Chris had tried to make sense out of the senseless.

Murray went to his room on the top floor and opened a window that gave him a view of Tour St. Denise.

On the other hand, he thought, it was silly getting angry at his friend. Chris wasn't well. Hell, that was the whole reason Murray had gotten Chris out of Israel. Recuperation, mental and physical. Paris and quiet.

Murray sat on his bed, rubbing his forehead, trying to remember the name of Chris's hotel. It was a small place, tucked away in the poor Latin Quarter. Chris still enjoyed that kind of hotel.

What was it called now? Something outlandish: La Villa d'Or? La Ville de Merde? He settled on the first and dialed an outside line. It was a while before the concierge answered the phone. No, monsieur, Easton was not in at the moment. Who could say if he'd be in today? A message? Murray could imagine the concierge shrugging. Why not?

Murray hung up and called the clinic where Chris had been receiving therapy. A nurse politely took his message, mentioning that Monsieur Easton hadn't attended for several weeks. She suggested Murray leave a message at Chris's hotel.

It was almost six hours before a bellboy paged Murray at the bar, handing him a message.

"*Merci,*" Murray said, tipping him. Murray read the message and wandered outside. A doorman hailed a taxi for him.

A brief squall had cleaned the city, and the granite streets glistened beneath the glowing streetlights. Murray relaxed in the back seat, doing his best to enjoy the early fall weather. It was worth enjoying while he could; he didn't expect his visit with Chris to be a treat.

The driver rolled down his window, letting the blustery night air whisk through his car. Outside, the trees bent with the wind, showering the boulevard with leaves. Inside the taxi, Murray pressed his face to the side window, idly watching the passing street life. He noticed a vendor guarding his umbrellas on a corner. They drove past the Louvre. Nearby, a lolling *gendarme* waited for a *camionette* to pick him up and deposit him elsewhere in the district.

The taxi parked beside a small café with a faint coffee aroma and only a few customers. Chris sat just inside the door, at a table near the window where Murray could see him from the taxicab. Chris was stirring a drink and, as always, was preoccupied with some distant thoughts. Murray could also see his own reflection in the glass. He realized how much hair he had lost since last seeing Chris, and how his stomach overlapped his belt. Growing older, Murray thought wistfully. It had been even more of a trial for his friend. Certainly Chris had always looked older, but before it had been in his attitude. Now, the years were in his bones. Chris was hunched over the table, his spine bent and contorted like an old man's. He was withering.

Murray entered the café. "Hello, Chris." Murray extended a hand. Chris uncoiled.

"Well, me old mate, this is a nice surprise." They

shook hands. "You're looking fat and forty. Life must be agreeing with you."

"Thanks." Murray settled in the booth.

Chris finished his *cinquante-et-un* and raised his glass, calling for two more Pernods. Murray watched Chris.

"So," Murray said at last, "how you doing?"

"Fine."

"How's therapy?"

Chris ran a hand through his close-cropped hair. "You mean you come all this way from New York, and you don't know?"

"I'm concerned about you, Chris."

"If you're really worried, get me back to work. Send me to Beirut, where I belong."

There was another silence. Murray sipped his drink, wondering how honest he could be. Finally, he said, "Your pictures suck, Chris."

"Really?"

"Yes, really. They're unusable."

"Why's that, then? Offend some sensibilities, do they?"

"They offend *everyone's* sensibilities. Face it, nobody wants to use you."

Chris rose abruptly and moved to the bar. Murray bit his tongue. He was ready for a shouting match, a few exotic curses, a soaking in beer. He'd be able to handle anything but a brawl. Murray sensed the violence just below the surface, and it made him extremely uneasy.

Chris returned with their drinks, set them on the table, and sat back. He stared out the window, once again lost in thought.

"You want to talk about it?" Murray asked quietly.

"Nothing to talk about." Chris sipped his drink.

"Give it a try."

"What about? The photos?"

"Or Francine. The Middle East. Yourself. Anything you want."

"Anything, eh?" The thought amused Chris.

"Something bothering you, Chris?"

"Yes, mate. *Boredom*."

"I thought you'd like Paris in the fall."

"It's a nice place to spend a dirty weekend." Chris finished the Pernod and waved his empty glass. "I've been here for a sodding month."

Murray rested a hand on Chris's arm. "Slow down, all right?"

Chris shrugged it off.

"Look," said Murray, "stop feeling so sorry for yourself and come back to the States with me."

Chris gave a short, derisive laugh.

"Work on my magazine," Murray persisted. "We need a new photo editor. I'd like you to take the job."

"Tuck me behind a desk, eh?"

"Not at all. There's plenty of interesting work in New York."

"I like the Middle East."

"The place is killing you."

"Not me, mate." Chris turned away. Finally, he added, "What happened to Francine wasn't my fault."

"I never said it was. But she was too good a reporter to lose. I don't want the same thing to happen to you. It's a matter of time, Chris, can't you see that?"

Chris tried to remember precisely what had happened. He reached back, finding only a muddle of memories. The power was all he truly remembered. "Psychic" power, a book had labeled it—psi. The ability to read people's thoughts, start fires, mind travel . . . Except the books he'd read made a big deal about men and women who bent spoons and performed tricks that didn't even hint at Chris's power. Worse, there was a hidden tone to the books, as if the reader and the author secretly knew the whole business was a scam. But Chris knew it wasn't. He wondered what he could do with his power. He'd never find out in Paris, that was for sure.

"I did all I could for her," Chris said.

"I'm sure you did."

Chris shrewdly studied his friend. After a moment, he leaned forward and patted Murray's wrist. "You're all right, mate."

"Thank you."

"Straight-up. You're about my only real friend. Don't know how you stand it. I'm grateful for your help, you know that. But New York?" He shook his head. "What am I gonna do there?"

"You'd love it."

"I'd go *crazy* there." Chris wiped his face, struggling for the right words. "I'm not the same, Murray."

"Neither am I. So what? None of us is Peter Pan, for Christ's sake. We all change as we get older. Most of us mellow out. But you—"

"You couldn't possibly understand."

"Look at you," Murray went on. "You're so juiced on mayhem you'll only be happy when you're dead in some godforsaken ditch. I've known 'Nam vets with the same problem. You're an adrenaline addict."

"Hazards of the job, mate. Anyway, I don't just get juiced on it, I create it." Chris rose with his empty glass and crossed to the bar.

Murray turned to watch him. "So make a little in New York."

Chris leaned on the counter and laughed at his friend. "You don't know what you're saying."

"You've got to get out of that war zone, Chris. As a friend, as an employer, I want you out. It's in your own best interest. Christ! What more do you want? New York, a great job, good company . . ."

"You make a fair argument." Chris smiled, dropping bills carelessly on the wet counter.

"A great argument," Murray said.

Chris lifted a fresh glass of liquor. "Maybe," he said. He looked out the window, trying to imagine the big American city. What would he do in such a place? What could he find? Perhaps such a city would strengthen his power and broaden the adventure.

"Maybe," Chris said again. He toasted Murray and smiled. "You may live to regret this one, me old mate."

Chris arrived in New York two weeks later. A chauffeured limousine carried him to a midtown hotel with an expensive air reminiscent of Murray's hotel in Paris. Even French accents haunted the lobby.

"Easton," Chris said.

The uniformed clerk was quick, efficient, and courteous. Within minutes, Chris and his luggage were transported to a fortieth-floor room that overlooked Park Avenue. According to Murray, the room was a little present until Chris settled into the city. Here was a chance to enjoy the good life, with a private bar and gourmet room service. Chris was in his room less than ten minutes before Murray called, just to make sure everything was all right.

"Everything's great," Chris lied.

Murray didn't pick up on it. Who wouldn't enjoy the high life, particularly at the company's expense? Chris agreed with Murray, no matter what his friend said. Weather? Great. Trip? Terrific. Dinner? Just fine.

All the time, Chris stood by the window, staring west. The lights were what attracted him. The glimpse of a tar rooftop, blackened by the smoke of a century-old furnace. From his location on the fortieth floor, he could see a marquee of a naked neon woman, thrusting into the air. Tourists and con artists; hustlers and muggers; children and junkies; money and danger.

Home.

"Look," Murray was saying, "relax tonight, okay? Then stop by the office tomorrow morning."

"Sure," said Chris.

"And don't worry about being late. Come in whenever you like. Jet lag, right? No one's fresh after Paris."

"Thanks, Murray."

"No problem. I'm just glad you're here, Chris."

Chris hung up and pulled the curtains. He looked across the room and saw an ashtray. He leaned forward, concentrating.

The ashtray remained still.

He fell back on his bed and closed his eyes. He couldn't quite grasp the key to his power. The answer was outside, waiting for him. Chris could sense it. All he had to do was walk the streets and find it. A little bit of Lebanon alive in the United States.

After Beirut, New York should be a piece of cake.

Murray sat behind his desk, worrying about a board meeting and a luncheon with the publisher, preoccupied with putting the magazine "to bed." It was the beginnings of a terrible press day, not made any better by his new photo editor.

It had been a month since Chris had taken over the photo editor's desk, and he had barely grasped his responsibilities. To some extent it didn't matter; much of the work was easily delegated. But it wasn't just the desk work that Chris had abandoned. His photographs were still tinged with the vicious eye that had finally made his war photography unusable. Murray had hoped that Paris, and then New York, would calm his friend. Instead, Chris's taste for the macabre was maturing. The latest fiasco was on Murray's desk—a photo spread, supposedly on immigration in the city. The idea was to mix Chris's pictures with an article about the renovation of the Statue of Liberty. A simple piece of Americana.

Murray examined the photographs Chris had handed him. Junkies, needles, and rubber tubes. Whores, half undressed in cheap polyester. Smog pumping out of a smokestack and polluting the neighborhood. Poisoned rats floating in the East River.

Chris sat in a corner of Murray's plush office, his eyes hidden by sunglasses. He wore a khaki shirt, tan pants, and army boots—clothes more suited to the desert, not a December afternoon in New York. Murray cleared his throat.

"This isn't what I expected, Chris."

"Sorry."

Chris sounded far from it. Murray studied his friend for a moment. Chris's cheeks were drawn and his skin was gray.

"It's not that I don't like them. They're just not what I wanted." Murray smiled weakly. "I was hoping your apartment on Riverside would broaden your tastes. You know—a view of the Hudson, park at your doorstep . . ."

Chris didn't answer. The apartment Murray had found was a marvel of taste and comfort. Chris, however, had a secret second address—a small efficiency on Thirty-first Street. A fifty-dollar-a-week room with a bed, hot plate, and noisy neighbors, where Chris could experiment unhindered.

"I guess it's not working out."

"Of course it is," Murray said. "We've just got to find you the right job, that's all."

"Something that *moves*."

"You're getting past it, Chris. Time you gave all that up."

"What are you on about?"

"You, Chris."

"I'm your *friend*, Murray, not your bleedin' brother."

"It's unhealthy."

"But it's *my* health," Chris said, standing up. "I'm not happy, Murray."

"I know."

Murray wiped his face with his hands, feeling weary. He glanced at his watch. It was only eleven in the morning.

"Christ! What's the matter with you?" Chris demanded.

Murray was unable to voice his fears. Chris waited patiently. It would have been easy to push Murray along with one little mental suggestion, but he had yet to enter Murray's head and wouldn't try now. A man didn't do that to a friend.

"I have an idea," Murray said at last. He opened a desk drawer and handed Chris a file. Chris scanned several sheets of paper. "Possible photo jobs," Murray explained. "Just some ideas. Why don't you take a look and see if there's anything you like?"

"Fine."

"Good." Murray leaned back, relaxing. "You really are fucking crazy."

Chris smiled back. "All cameramen are. Didn't you know that?"

"Conversations like this, in the middle of a deadline, give me heartburn."

"I'd better go."

"You'd better," Murray said with a chuckle.

Murray's secretary grinned pleasantly at Chris as he left the office. Chris perched on a chair and riffled through the assignments, looking for a spread that would take him into the city's dark corners.

He threw the first sheet on the floor. Garbage. Some silly-ass story about a coal strike in Pennsylvania.

The second idea was just as bad. Gentrification in Harlem. Who the hell cared? The world wasn't getting richer; most of it was getting poorer. That was the whole point.

The sixth sheet was close. Kidnapped children, desperate parents. Not bad.

Chris dumped the assignments on Shirley's desk and left. Murray was cheating him, damn it. The story was in this city. It was waiting for him; he could feel it. He visited Trevor Osgood, the news editor.

"Murray sent me down for an assignment," Chris said.

"What kind of an assignment?" Osgood asked.

"A *live* one." Chris reached across the desk and liberated Osgood's work diary.

"Make yourself at home," Osgood muttered. He leaned back in his chair, waiting.

Chris tapped a page. "This one," he said. "Tell me about it." He turned the diary around.

Osgood put on his glasses and pushed aside Chris's finger.

"That's Tom's story."

"It sounds interesting," Chris said.

Osgood shrugged. "Haven't read it yet."

"Does it have a photographer?"

"You should know."

Chris waited, his impatience tapping on Osgood's skull. The news editor twisted uncomfortably.

"No. No photographer. We were just going to use some mug shots."

Chris stood up. "Tell Tom he's got one now."

"Wait a minute—Murray didn't say anything to me about any of this."

"Just tell Tom to stop by my office. I want to get going on this thing."

"Don't try and bulldoze me, Chris."

Chris silenced Osgood, slipping in and out of his thoughts with practiced efficiency. "Just tell him," Chris finished. He tore the page out of Osgood's diary: "Inside New York Terrorism—Profile."

When Tom came by, Chris swept through the reporter's thoughts. It didn't take long. The Democratic Liberation Party—whoever the hell they were—plus something more. Some hush-hush detective team tracking them down, and a woman cop leading the hunt. Detective Sergeant Theresa Cooke.

Chris felt his excitement rise. He sensed her presence already.

"Pull over here," Chris ordered.

Tom parked their car a block from the crowded street. At the nearest corner, police officers checked I.D.'s. Chris reached in the back seat for his Pentax and then mingled with the mob. Tom kept pace.

This was it; Chris could feel it. His mind darted in different directions, collecting information, searching for the source of his excitement. He found her talking with a police lieutenant. Something about a hostage, explosives, and a fool named Griffin.

Chris sat on the bumper of a medical van. He closed his eyes and, in his mind, made his way up the tenement stairs. He listened to the patter of the cops as he moved toward Griffin. Down a hallway, through a desolate living room.

And there he was. Crying. Chris had seen punks like Griffin throughout the world. They always ended up desperate, alone, and dangerous.

Chris reached into Griffin's mind and they began to share thoughts. He touched nerves and shared sensations. The cold dripping water from the shower head tapped on Chris as well as Griffin. Finally, Chris went to Griffin's eyes, so they could share sight.

Terry Cooke was now in the adjoining room, scared of Griffin, worrying about the hostage. She called to Griffin, then argued with another officer. Chris was delighted. Would she come forward?

He reached outside Griffin, touching Terry and making a suggestion.

Terry walked toward the bathroom, just shy of Griffin's view.

"You don't want to do this, John."

Chris watched, fascinated. He knew her secret. He felt her reach into Griffin's mind, struggling to pacify the turmoil Chris had created; she was crowding into Griffin, Chris thought. Terry Cooke was like a blind woman feeling her way through a cluttered room, instinctively avoiding obstacles. She was Chris years ago, before he understood what psi was all about.

"You've never killed anyone before today, John."

Chris smiled to himself, again allowing Terry to fumble through Griffin's mind. She was speaking without thinking, picking up thoughts and ideas that she stole from Griffin.

"No," Griffin groaned.

He beat the butt of his gun against the wall, sobbing loudly, trying to slip away from Chris. For a moment, he succeeded. The last thing Chris expected was for Griffin to find the strength to repel him. Chris clawed back, and Griffin contorted with pain.

"Leave me alone!" Griffin sobbed.

Then Terry stepped into the bathroom, and Chris saw her clearly. She almost knew. He could see it in her face. There was something strange about Griffin, and she'd been able to sense it. Chris felt unmasked. For a moment he thought Terry was looking at *him*, not at Griffin.

Cock the gun, he ordered Griffin.

Griffin pulled back the hammer.

"Let the girl go, John."

Griffin struggled to answer Terry, but Chris fought him.

Griffin kept sobbing, "He won't let me." Griffin leaned into the light.

"You're hearing voices," Terry said. "Don't listen to them."

"I can't stop him."

"Listen to *my* voice."

She moved closer. Her scent thrilled Chris. It was as thrilling as Griffin's finger on the trigger.

"No, no, no . . ." Griffin kept shaking his head, trying to clear it. Chris kept control. Griffin and he looked down at a box of explosives.

Point the gun at the box, he ordered.

Terror burst out of Terry, through Griffin, and into Chris. Terry was struggling, trying to find a way to stop Griffin.

"John?"

Chris relaxed, and Terry took hold. The gun no longer pointed at the explosives, nor at the hostage. Griffin's arm hung to his side, the weapon barely caught between his fingers. When his other arm relaxed, the hostage fell to the floor.

Chris was enjoying the game. He was intrigued by this detective.

Point the gun, he ordered.

Griffin flinched, jerking his arm up. Chris wanted one last look of fear from Terry Cooke. A warning, that was all. To make her understand. As they got to know each other better, he would be the boss.

"No, John!" Terry screamed.

Griffin screamed with pain. Chris screamed, too. A powerful tide tore through him—Terry's terror washed Chris out of Griffin and almost carried him into limbo.

Chris opened his eyes. He saw the reporters crowd closer to the tenement. He felt giddy, and it took a moment to recover his senses. All he could think of was Terry Cooke.

"Inside!" someone shouted.

Chris rubbed his head, barely making sense of what was happening. From professional instinct he started taking pictures. When Terry Cooke and Griffin left the building, Chris kept to the shadows, afraid she might glance his way. Afraid she might somehow recognize him. Still, he dared to slip into her thoughts again.

Terry heard him. Or, rather, she succumbed to Chris, reaching into the patrol car, putting an arm around Griffin, and posing. The camera bulb flashed.

"Chris?"

He glanced at Tom, barely recognizing the reporter.

"I'm heading back to the office. Coming?"

"No."

"What do I tell Osgood?"

Chris rewound his film and gave it to Tom. "Get that developed." Chris paused. "Tell him I'm on to a story."

"Really? What?"

Chris ignored Tom and walked away from the police barricades. Somewhere down the block, in the shadows, a taxi waited. In it was a man called Larry. It had all been in Griffin's head.

Chris tapped on a side window.

"Huh?" asked the cabby.

Chris surprised him. The cabby had been parked, his lights off, just out of sight from the police. Chris opened the back door and slipped inside.

"I'm off duty," Larry said unpleasantly. Chris grinned. He looked into the cabby's mind and found the address.

"Uptown. The Clover Pub," he said.

Larry looked sharply back at him. Chris calmed him, taking control.

"I know all about you, Larry," he said. "I want to join you."

Larry listened.

"Old friends," Chris went on.

Larry struggled, but Chris held him. "Right?"

"Right," Larry finally agreed.

Chris leaned back in the seat. "The Clover, then."

"Sure . . ." Larry glanced in the mirror, struggling to remember. "Sure . . . Chris?"

"Right." Larry turned the ignition and drove away from the commotion. "Been a long time."

"Too long," Chris answered.

"We can use you."

Chris rolled down the window and leaned out as they drove quickly up Eighth Avenue. He enjoyed the cold wind on his face.

"We'll see," he said.

PART TWO

TERRY COOKE

Seven

Chilling air blew through what was left of the outside wall and ceiling, making a swirl of dust that swept the length of the barren hallway. Terry blinked when the wind brushed across her face, then closed her eyes.

She was imagining a ride in a taxi—heading north on Eighth Avenue, traveling too fast but not really minding. In her lap was a camera. Her attention drifted between the passing streets and the quiet cabby. She tapped the Plexiglas window guarding the cabby's head.

"Faster," she said. Her voice was different—a man's voice. The back of her hands were thick with hair.

The cabby turned the corner.

With the instincts of a cop, she looked for the cabby's license, but it wasn't on the dashboard. She wanted the cabby's name, or a glimpse in the rearview mirror. . . . Anything to figure out where she was, or, for that matter, *who* she was.

The taxi disappeared as dust filled her lungs.

Terry coughed violently and once again saw the shattered fifth floor of the tenement. She struggled for a breath of clean air. Was there a fire? She rolled to her side, terrified that the dust was smoke and that the floor was ready to collapse. No fire, she thought. Just an explosion—remember?

She closed her eyes, feeling giddy, recalling the officer who had forced open the window. It was all so logical—hiding explosives in the pigeon coop, where no junkie or bumbling arm of the law could reach it—at least not without getting the arm blown off. The trip wire had been attached to the window. Then came the deafening explosion from the ceiling, smothering her and everyone else on the floor. Fire? There was no fire, she remembered. Just as there was no cabby.

She tried bending her knees. She could move her legs without pain, but the movement exhausted her. Instead of risking further injury, Terry relaxed against the fallen brick and plaster. She stared up at the shards of plaster and wooden struts swinging from the edges of a tremendous hole. At least the hole brought fresh air.

She tried taking a deep breath, but again she coughed. Shit! Why couldn't she breathe?

With great care, Terry brushed the pieces of wood, plaster, and brick from her lap. She played doctor and carefully probed her body for deep cuts, but there was nothing but sore muscles. The same couldn't be said for her head, which was damp with blood. She wiped her forehead with a sleeve and worried about stitches scarring her face. A silly thought. She was lucky to be alive.

Now she had to get out of the building. What if there was another bomb? She pushed off more debris and tried sitting up, but she felt too weak and fell back. Her head throbbed. Christ! she thought. I can't get up, and my head's bleeding, and I can't breathe, and what if there's a fire, and what if—

"Keep still," said a voice.

Hands tightened about her waist and hoisted her into the air. She rolled her eyes like a drunk and fought the strong grip.

"I said keep still," the voice repeated.

She relaxed, and the paramedics laid her gently on a stretcher.

"Explosion," she said. When no one answered, she wondered if it was all part of her imagination—her damned "feelings" conjuring up voices to lead her into more danger. It was enough to make her laugh, which she did. She stopped when the world turned at a slant.

"Try not to bounce her."

Despite the caution, Terry bounced with every step. She was suddenly overwhelmed by the face of Bill Reed. His hand touched her forehead, and she closed her eyes. She didn't open them again until a new wind carried the smell of soot and gasoline. It jolted her awake because she was terrified they were back on the roof. But she couldn't be on the roof—there were too many people.

"Where?" she asked.

No one heard. Her mouth had been covered by an oxygen mask. Maybe she was on the moon. Lots of space out there. Did the moon have a kaleidoscope of colors? Flashing bulbs and blinking red lights, blue overcoats and white uniforms . . . ?

Twenty minutes after the explosion, Terry Cooke was being treated in St. Vincent's emergency room. At first the doctors mistook her sleep for something more serious. It was, in fact, sleep borne of shock and exhaustion. She was lifted onto a table for more probing and X rays. Finally, she was taken to a quiet room and told to wait for the test results. She slept until there was a knock on the door and someone entered the room. Terry raised her head, and Gordon leaned forward. Without a word he felt her forehead, then his own. When Terry tried pushing his hand away, he moved down to her wrist and checked her pulse.

"Stop it, Gordon."

Gordon didn't free her wrist until he had finished the examination. Satisfied, he settled in a chair.

"This wasn't how I planned to spend my day," he said at last. A nurse popped into the room, also took her pulse, then disappeared. Terry caught sight of a policeman standing guard in the corridor.

"Well, what the hell happened?" he asked.

She rolled away from him, burying her head in a pillow. A doctor entered the room, and Gordon was ordered out. The doctor was a young man with a loose white jacket and a tired smile.

"You're a lucky woman," he said.

Terry grinned. Only a doctor could say such a thing to a patient who felt so weak.

"How do you feel?"

"Great," she lied.

"Seem fine to me, too, considering." His fingers pressed into a sore rib, and she winced.

"It should hurt. You've got a slight fracture and some abrasions." He ran a finger along a cut on her forehead.

"Do I need stitches?"

"Don't see why," he said.

"That's it?"

He sat at the bottom of the bed and massaged one of her ankles. "This hurt?"

"A little."

"It probably will for a few days." He shined a penlight into each eye. "Feel sick, giddy—anything like that?"

"Not anymore."

"And you know where you are?"

"Of course."

"Name? Where you live?"

Terry told him everything he wanted to know. The doctor leaned back in his chair. "No signs of concussion. Follow my finger, will you?"

He passed a finger before her eyes and checked her focus.

"Not bad, though I'm sure you've felt better."

She didn't answer. He began jotting notes on a chart. "I'm going to sign you up for a bed. Spend the night here, and if everything checks out, we'll set you free tomorrow. How's that?"

"I'm going home," she said. There was a clock on the wall above the door. Five after five. *My God! Is that all?* It felt like three in the morning. If she could get out of the hospital by six, she could still make it home for dinner.

"We'll see. You rest here, in any event."

"What about the others?"

"Just get some rest. I'll be back in a half hour to check on you."

At six-thirty, Terry was taken by wheelchair to the lobby, where she insisted on hobbling out of the building. Gordon ran ahead and opened the car door. Terry eased into the passenger's seat and closed the door. Her bruises had stiffened, making movement barely possible.

Gordon turned the ignition key, warmed the engine, and drove slowly out of the lot. It was sleeting, and the last thing they wanted was an accident. "Crazy weather," he said.

Terry pressed her cheek against the side window and watched the exhaust curl up from the cars. When the red brake lights glowed, icy raindrops on the windscreen made the smoky scene appear like an Impressionist oil painting.

"Artie's gonna hit the roof," said Terry.

"Wonder why," Gordon said dryly.

They crossed the University Heights Bridge and headed into the Bronx. Terry lived in a house on Morris Street, not far from Fordham University. It was a long street, pleasant and safe. Gordon parked the car some ten feet from Terry's front door. She didn't move, even when he turned off the ignition and opened his door.

"Let's just sit here a few minutes," she said.

Gordon climbed back in. Terry collected her thoughts, not at all anxious to face her family. Artie's fussing, she knew, would be the last straw.

"You want to talk about it?" Gordon asked.

Terry didn't answer for a moment, then asked, "How many people got hurt?"

He gave her the total like a sports wrap-up. "Three cops injured, two cops dead, two arrests." Now it was his turn.

"Why the hell did you go back into that building?" he asked.

"Why do you think?" she responded. "The place was booby-trapped."

"How come no one else knew anything about it?"

Terry glared at him. "Griffin told me about it."

"I heard he was busy throwing up."

"What's that supposed to mean?"

"How could he tell you about the bomb, Terry?"

"Gordon, this is the stupidest—" She turned away. "If he was throwing up, he couldn't have told me, could he?"

"Exactly."

"Ask Griffin if you don't believe me."

"Stop bullshitting," he said. "You're keeping things from me, and we both know it."

They were angry, and it took a moment's silence to realize it. Her turn to make up, Terry decided. She touched his arm. "I'm tired," she said. "Can we talk about this tomorrow?"

He tried looking agreeable. "I just want you to tell me what's going on."

"I will. I swear it."

He studied her, no longer sold on her promises. "Sooner or later you'll find it's not so bright keeping things to yourself. Maybe after some punk's got you in a corner, and I can't help because I don't know what's going on.''

Terry didn't take the bait.

''You want to go in?'' Gordon asked at last.

Terry was silent as they climbed the steps to her front door. Her encounter with Griffin had definitely changed her. She needed desperately to sort her thoughts and feelings before she was swallowed by her family. What bothered Terry wasn't just surviving the explosion or evading Griffin's bullets; it was the look in Griffin's eyes just before he dropped the gun. The detachment, the indifference. Even now, she could swear the eyes belonged to someone else. For a moment, she had felt the force of an uncompromising power—as if the owner of those eyes possessed everyone in the room. What happened to Griffin and her *had* to happen. It had all been predestined. Controlled.

''You don't want to go back to the car, do you?'' Gordon asked.

Terry shook her head and opened the door. Gordon immediately headed for the kitchen. Terry turned to the den, where Sean and Jennifer were watching television.

''I'm home,'' she called, and Jennifer ran into her arms. More than maternal instinct motivated Terry now; she carried Jennifer into the kitchen, using the girl as a shield against Artie's panic.

''Jesus Christ, Terry!'' Artie said. Terry hugged her daughter tighter. She warded off Jennifer's hands as they reached for the cut on her forehead, then waited for Gordon to take a beer and go into the den. Reluctantly, she let Jennifer follow him.

''These things happen, Artie,'' she said. She looked hard at him. At the moment, it was her career—not her marriage—that mattered most.

Artie didn't say a word. Instead, he crossed the kitchen and hugged her. Terry swallowed a touch of pride and rested against her husband. She tried to relax in his arms, remembering that this was the man she loved, the father of her children. She waited for him to become the man who would insist that her job was too dangerous and her life too selfish.

Artie just hugged her. Terry didn't know if his silence stemmed from love or fear of an argument. Either way, she appreciated it. Finally, he drew back and said, "I heard about it from the TV."

"Didn't Gordon phone you?"

"He didn't tell me anything. He said you weren't really hurt."

"He told you the truth."

"I should have brought you home myself." Artie reached for the cut on her forehead. Terry caught his hand and kissed it.

"Do Sean and Jenny know?" she asked.

"I think so. Sean's been pretty good, keeping Jenny company most of the day."

"I should go and see him," she said.

Artie pressed down on Terry's hand to keep her in the kitchen. "In a minute."

Terry waited with dying patience as Artie checked her pulse and felt her glands. She was sick to death of jabbing fingers.

"Let me get you something," he offered.

"Whiskey."

He was bringing her the drink when Gordon appeared at the kitchen door with Sean and Jennifer. This time, the children were more reserved. If they hadn't already heard about the explosion, Gordon had obviously told them. Jennifer stayed close to her brother, even when Terry held out her arms.

"You really get blown up?" Sean finally asked.

Terry laughed. "Yes." To Jennifer, she added, "Just like Tom and Jerry."

"Really?"

"It's all right," Terry said. She hugged Jennifer again, then reached out to Sean.

Eleven-thirty. The children were asleep, Gordon was on his way to see his girl friend Sharon, and Terry was in the bedroom. Artie finished straightening up the kitchen, then began outlining the next day's work. He was an architect, and he always made certain that when he faced the draft table in the morning, he knew precisely where to begin his project.

"Terry, do you need anything?"

She didn't answer. Artie went into their room expecting to find her in bed, probably asleep. Instead, she was in the bathroom, sitting on the edge of the bathtub, staring in a mirror.

"You okay?"

She didn't reply. Artie shrugged and went to bed.

Terry undressed and found her way across the room. She crawled under the covers. Artie began rubbing her shoulders. "Gordon said he'll pick you up at nine tomorrow."

"Good."

Terry enjoyed the massage while thinking of Gordon—picking her up for work, sharing dinner, worrying about her sleep. She was involved with two men, whether she liked it or not. Responsible for both of them. Not a lover's triangle, but a triangle nonetheless. She wondered if Gordon and Artie ever discussed the odd friendship. She wondered if Gordon and Artie even considered themselves friends.

Terry rolled toward Artie and tucked a blanket over his shoulder. "I can't make any sense out of it," she said. "When I left for work this morning—actually, as soon as I woke up—I knew something was going to happen today."

Artie held her hand, not knowing what to say. Terry was unable to make sense of her own thoughts.

"When I walked into that bathroom in the tenement, there was me, this guy Griffin, and a girl. The three of us, and that's all. Except there was another person. I could feel him there."

"You mean hiding?"

"No, I mean right *there*. Griffin knew it, too."

"Gordon said he's a junkie."

"Maybe. But that doesn't explain what *I* felt."

Artie kissed her. "He really scared you, didn't he? More than the explosion, I mean."

They listened to the rain beat gently against the window. She rested against Artie's chest. Artie fell asleep with an arm around Terry, his head slumped against the bed board. She lay still, her eyes wide open as her afternoon nightmares reappeared and then slowly vanished.

In their place, she saw herself as a child. A baby, younger than Jennifer, barely able to walk. It was a stifling day, with the fans blowing and the windows wide open. Terry heard her mother in the bathroom washing clothes, music from a radio blowing into the living room on a breeze.

She blinked, and found herself outside her crib, climbing up the sofa, following. . . .

After all these years, it was still only "something." Sometimes she remembered it as a butterfly, at other times as a hand guiding her forward, or just the distant sound of children coming from a playground. Whatever the shape, Terry delighted in it. Wanted it. Crawled up the sofa to touch it, followed the hand or butterfly to the edge of the third-story window, and then reached out.

She remembered the rush of air; the strange childish sense of exhilaration. She even remembered her mother's distant screams.

The fall should have killed her. Would she have died if

she had struck concrete instead of grass? Had her mother's screams somehow cushioned the fall?

The rain became heavier and shook the windows. Terry watched the darkness, expecting a mysterious hand to reach out and once again guide her over the edge—this time, without her mother's protection.

Terry hugged Artie tightly. Strange, the cop wife seeking protection with her architect husband. Still, there was safety in her family. A security that pushed the world away for a night, a day. If only it could somehow ward off the look in Griffin's eyes.

Eight

"'The Democratic Liberation Party,' " read Gordon. "Originally, the Democratic Freedom Party; founded in 1979 by Mark Schneider, currently believed to be in Nicaragua. Organized to protest university defense contracts at Princeton. Schneider was arrested the same year for unruly conduct, again for breaking and entering the Princeton Club, once again for chaining himself to the United Nations fence . . ."

Gordon paused, flipping through pages. "The name changes from the Democratic Freedom Party to the Freedom Party. Schneider and friends go underground. Friends include Jamie Lieberman, José Sanchez, Fran Alvarado, Samuel T. Brown. Brown is arrested for possession of illegal firearms, Alvarado is charged with possession of a stolen car. Brown is convicted of grand larceny. Schneider is arrested and joins Brown in Attica.

"Schneider and Brown escape prison. Brown is caught in the La Guardia Airport cafeteria. Schneider, however, manages to rejoin his colleagues and demands Brown's release. Shortly after this, bombs explode on the campuses of Princeton and New York universities. The explosives are tagged to a Tennessee manufacturer, and the purchaser is a Douglas Moore. There are four more explosions in the city—always early in the morning, never serious damage—before a town house on Jane Street explodes. Into the night stumble Alvarado and Ms. Lieberman, who are taken to a hospital, patched up, and charged with unlawful possession of explosives. Beneath what's left of the house are the bodies of Douglas Moore and José Sanchez."

Griffin sniffled and rubbed his nose. Terry sat opposite him and his attorney, watching them both. There was no longer a look of fear in Griffin's face, nor the cool detachment in his eyes. Just the confusion remained.

"Little is heard of the Party until early January eighty-two, when it emerges as the Democratic Liberation Party, claiming credit for an explosion at the suburban offices of AGM Oil in Stamford, Connecticut. There are four more explosions: two in New York, one in Chicago, and one in Anahiem, California, outside Disneyland." Gordon glanced at Griffin. "Four phone calls are received—three from our friend Schneider, the last one from a woman. A woman," Gordon told the attorney, "that we're sure your client can identify for us."

Terry took the file from Gordon's hands. There was a brief, uncomfortable silence as she reviewed the pages and dropped several photographs on the table. They were pictures of Griffin entering and leaving the tenement building.

"John?" she asked. Griffin looked up—neither at Terry nor away from her. Terry leaned in front of him. "What sort of habit you got, John?"

Griffin shook his head. Tests had shown there were no drugs in his blood or urine at the time of his arrest.

From his seat at the end of the table, Gordon said, "You don't expect us to believe you just sell the stuff."

Griffin edged uncomfortably about. The attorney looked down at a blank note pad, embarrassed. Griffin wasn't paying attention to anyone. They couldn't tell if this was Griffin's normal behavior, or if there was something wrong with him. Except for a drifting grin or shrug, Griffin wasn't listening. For a change of pace, he began chewing a ragged fingernail.

"You'd better answer the question," the attorney told him.

"Yeah," he mumbled. "Sometimes, you know, I used the stuff."

"And sold it?"

"Yeah."

"Into the *camera*," Gordon said, pointing to a high corner of the room.

"*Yeah*," Griffin said louder. The attorney poured another cup of coffee. Griffin took the cup in both hands and sipped. The attorney poured a second cup.

"All right," Terry said. She handed Griffin a copy of his sheet: a date-by-date story of his life, from his tenth-grade stutter to his drug dealings prior to the arrest. Born 1962 in South Plainfield, New Jersey. Father a lawyer at Comrich-Gleason; mother a housewife. Two older sisters. Honor student at Thomas Jefferson High School, attended Princeton University, class of 1980. "According to the campus police, you sold grass and coke," Terry said.

"Paying the bills, man," Griffin answered.

"You did your business out of the campus bookstore, didn't you?"

"Excuse me?" asked the attorney.

"He met Schneider there before he disappeared," Gordon explained.

"Yeah," Griffin said.

Terry moved closer. "You remember a girl named Susan Monroe?"

Griffin dug a finger into a corner of his eye and scratched. Gordon reached into a stack of files and slid out a thin one.

" 'Susan Monroe,' " he read aloud. "She said that at the end of 1979, you spent your days in the bookstore and your nights at 1265 Edgewood Drive. She thought you were seeing another woman."

"Bitch was always full of shit," Griffin said.

"Schneider lived there, didn't he?"

Griffin began giggling. "What you asking me for? You already know this crap, don't you?"

"Who else lived there?" Terry asked.

"Lots of people."

"Did the woman?"

"A couple of them."

"You know the one I mean. What's her name?"

Griffin slouched toward Terry. "Lots of names . . ."

Gordon threw a pencil at the table. "Come on, you little shit. Answer the question."

Griffin kept giggling and scratching. He was now drawing blood from the corner of his eye. "There were lots of people," he said. "Lots of faces. Can't remember all their names now."

"Lots of fun?" asked Terry.

Griffin smiled and nodded.

"Lots of sex?"

He nodded again.

"Lots of drugs?"

"Lots."

"Lots of guns?" Gordon asked.

Griffin laughed.

"Where are the guns now, John?" Terry asked.

Griffin shrugged.

"Are they with the woman?"

"They're at home."

"Home? Where you live?"

"Yeah."

"Where's that?"

"The building," he said.

"You mean the one that blew up?"

Griffin giggled. Gordon wiped his face and turned to Terry as if she were the only person in the room.

"We've been all over that place," he said. "He's the only one who was living there. I'm telling you, the others didn't take him anywhere."

She didn't need his impatience, not in front of Griffin. She used her eyes to guide Gordon out the door. Gordon obliged, slamming it as he left. The attorney put a hand on Griffin and smiled encouragingly.

"He's doing his best," the attorney assured Terry.

She rose from her seat and asked Griffin if he wanted coffee or tea. He asked for both. While Griffin took alternate sips from his drinks, Terry moved behind him. Her thumbs brushed against the back of his neck. At first Griffin was oblivious to her touch, but as Terry continued to stand behind him, Griffin lifted his head, rolling his eyes in a hapless effort to see her.

Terry whispered close to his ear. "Who is Meagan, John?"

"Meagan?"

"What's her last name?"

"I don't know," he said.

"But Meagan is the woman, isn't she?"

Griffin didn't answer, and Terry squeezed his shoulder.

"Who are Meagan's friends?"

"I—" He shook his head, unable to make sense of his own thoughts. Terry stared harder at the back of his head, her fingers tightening about his neck. "I can't remember right now."

"Harry? Was someone called Harry?"

Griffin shook his head. Terry concentrated harder.

"Larry?" Griffin asked. Terry waited. "Larry—" He couldn't finish his thought. "I can't remember."

Terry leaned over him, almost resting her chin on the top of his head. "Do you remember shooting the policemen?"

"Yeah."

"Why did you shoot them, John?"

"It was an accident."

Terry nodded. "The girl in the shower, John. Who's she?"

"Dunno."

"Do you remember what happened yesterday?"

"Yeah."

"You had a box of explosives. Who gave it to you?"

"Larry," he said. "He takes care of all that."

Terry focused her thoughts on Griffin. "You said someone was forcing you to hold the girl hostage. You didn't want to kill her, but someone was making you do it. Was it Larry?"

He shook his head.

"Meagan?"

"No."

"Who was it?"

"I don't know his name."

"Where are Meagan and Larry?"

"I don't know—"

"Where does Meagan live?"

"I don't know."

104

"Where does Larry live? Where does he get his explosives?"

"I can't remember. . . . I don't know."

"Inwood," she whispered. "What's in Inwood?"

Griffin closed his eyes, thinking hard. "Inwood," he repeated stupidly. He began to sweat and sucked hard on the ragged fingernail.

"*Where* in Inwood?"

The attorney shook Griffin's wrist. "Tell her, John."

He looked at his attorney, and the attorney jumped back. Never before had he seen a man's eyes so wide open. The lids were drawn tautly back, the pupils so wide they had squeezed away the irises. Black balls with white edges, kept together by a web of blood-red veins.

"A bar," he told the attorney. "Irish."

"Where, John?" Terry persisted. "Where's the bar?"

"Bar?"

"Who's Larry? Where does he get his explosives?"

Griffin drooped over the table. Terry slid her hands off his shoulders and closed her eyes. The attorney patted his pockets for cigarettes and asked Terry if she smoked. She said no and walked into a far corner of the room.

"John?" she murmured.

Griffin was beyond lights and voices.

"Who made you do it?"

Griffin's words came gurgling out. The attorney shook him, and Griffin drooled over his shirt. Terry looked away from Griffin.

For a moment, she had slipped away from the stationhouse. Instead, she was in a bed, the sun pouring through a closed window. The daydream was so real that she could taste the dusty air of the bedroom. There was a lingering odor like the musky smell of sweat and sex. It was a flicker of a daydream—one she forgot almost as it happened—but the little details fought for her attention. The clothes over a chair—jeans, a shirt and belt, a watch. A woman, kissing an ear. Terry heard herself whispering in a man's voice. She lost all sense of her sex. In her dream, she felt strange and masculine; she sensed the presence of a man more powerful than any other she had known. As his arms touched the woman on the bed, Terry felt as if her arms were wrapping around herself. Indeed, Terry and the man and the girl were one. With this came a brief, confusing passion she hadn't felt since falling in love with Artie.

"Sorry he wasn't more help," said the attorney. He rose and put his papers in his briefcase.

Terry looked at him, then at Griffin. "He did fine."

She opened the door and waved for a uniformed cop. Griffin was lifted out of his seat and led back to a holding cell. Not even the walk could bring him fully around. "It's a beginning, anyway," Terry said. "He gave us names and an address."

"An address?"

"Yeah."

They shook hands and left the small room—Terry reporting to Bill Reed, the attorney returning to Griffin. Something had happened that the attorney hadn't seen; or something had been said that he hadn't heard. Either way, it didn't make sense.

On the other hand, did he really want to know?

"You see this?" Reed asked.

He reached across his desk and tossed Terry a news magazine. On the cover was a picture of her in front of the tenement. It was an odd picture: a chummy photo of her with an arm around Griffin. The newspapers had settled for the usual action shots—police wrestling with the suspect and evacuating the neighborhood. In this picture, Terry was almost posing. She even had Griffin's head propped up, making certain the photographer caught his good side.

"You two good friends?" Reed asked snidely.

106

Terry rarely relaxed before a superior. She heard the criticism in his voice. Criticism, she knew, required either submission or challenge. "The place was a zoo," she said. "I can't be held responsible for that."

She dropped the magazine in a trash can and wandered over to the window. Reed rolled his chair around the desk and straightened his creaseless suit. At times, he had the appearance of a male model.

"So where are we?" he asked.

"We've got a couple of names and an address. I want to go uptown with Gordon and take a look around."

"What for?"

"Check out a couple of things."

Terry's evasiveness irritated Reed. Fortunately, he had grown to trust her instincts. She relied more on them than any other cop he knew—but it worked, and that was what counted for Reed.

"Tell me something," he said finally. "Is this as much of a cock-up as it looks?"

Reed didn't expect an answer. They both knew the truth.

He lit a cigar and put the D.L.P. in its proper perspective. In the worldwide network of terrorists, the D.L.P. was probably insignificant. Reed knew this from personal experience. As part of his training, he had spent several months on attachment to a special S.A.S. unit of the British army in Belfast. He had learned a number of things about terrorists that had been useful during the Patty Hearst affair. A good half of his time was spent shuttling from New York to Washington, D.C., where the F.B.I., the Defense Department, the Secret Service, and he compared files on terrorist activities. Though the urban terrorists of the United States hadn't yet emerged as a potent political force, Reed gave it a year, maybe two, before Americans began thinking of these people the same way as in Germany, France, Ireland, or Italy.

He tried to imagine the D.L.P. as the group that would

give the United States its first Munich massacre. He just couldn't see it. Unless, of course, they became closely linked with a murderous fanatic, or joined the European terrorist network. What happened when American terrorism became a profession, much as in Europe? The marines sent their men to Quantico for combat training, the Red Brigade sent terrorists to be trained in Libya, Iran, and the Soviet Union. What happened when this training became based at home? So called right-wing "survival camps" were already springing up in the South. Right wing, left wing—it made no difference in the end. Weapons, transportation, guerrilla training, tactical theory would all suddenly become much more accessible, and not just for existing terrorist organizations. That meant anything from assassinating politicians to holding hostage some small town in Idaho or Nebraska.

"Gordon said those narcotics officers took you by surprise."

"We had coordination with the precinct."

"Not enough, apparently," Reed said.

"Everything was by the book. Those guys screwed up, not us."

"Why did you let them go in?"

"We didn't know who they were!"

"I don't like what happened yesterday."

"I'm not exactly ecstatic about it."

He looked sharply at her. "The precinct commander's got a dead cop to remind him which of his men screwed up, and I know who's responsible on *my* side."

"There was nothing I could do."

"I can't accept that." Reed had finally lost his temper, which was something he rarely did. He leaned forward, trying to collect his thoughts. "Terry, when you were in the building, why did you follow Griffin into the bathroom?"

"We had a serious situation. He had a box full of explosives and the girl. He was nervous, I admit, but that's nothing new under the circumstances.''

''What made you think you could do a better job than Frank Tracelli?''

She paused, trying to answer the same question she had asked herself yesterday. ''I knew Griffin didn't want to kill her. If he fired at all, it would have been out of panic. I wanted to make absolutely certain no one panicked. Besides, he wasn't behaving like one of Frank's suicides.''

Reed was silent, and Terry knew she had given the wrong answer.

''Bill—''

''Terry, you're an experienced officer with a brilliant record, but you weren't thinking. You put your life in danger, as well as everyone else's there.''

Terry didn't argue. She could see there was no winning.

''If you're going to continue this investigation, you've got to stop this. There's just too much at stake.''

''Yes, Bill.''

''Understand. You're a good cop. That's not the issue. But I don't want to give *anyone* any excuses, legal or otherwise, that will let these bastards slip away. If we make a mistake, everyone'll be all over us. You know that as well as I do.''

He finished his lecture. Terry tried relaxing. Bill Reed was, after all, her friend. She had learned a lot from him over the last couple of years. In fact, she credited Reed with her ability to ''read'' people. Reed could sometimes judge a person's character quicker than she could. To any of his acquaintances, Bill Reed was as dapper and clean inside as he was outside. Only his close friends, like Terry, could occasionally see the frays in his pressed suits, his broken marriage, his workaholic mania.

''Bill?''

Reed waited.

"I'm sorry."

"So am I."

Terry wouldn't talk, and Gordon wondered how to shake her out of her silence. He had to speak with her, but she had become too withdrawn for normal conversation. He also wanted to know what had happened during Griffin's interrogation. He was as much a detective as she, and he didn't plan on spending the rest of the investigation waiting outside an interrogation room or acting as a glorified chauffeur.

He was reminded of this when Terry settled in the passenger's side of their car. Gordon just as naturally settled behind the steering wheel, turning the ignition and gunning the engine. The car roared. He pressed the pedal several times before shifting gears and turning on the heater. Warm air blew on their feet.

"What did he want?"

Terry shrugged.

"Well?"

"If there was anything you should know, Gordon, I'd tell you."

Gordon turned away, disgusted. Once again, she had succeeded in making him feel like a jerk. "Where to?" he asked.

"Uptown."

"Anywhere in particular, or just all of it?"

Terry looked at him coldly and he shut up, concentrating on the evening rush-hour traffic that had tied up the F.D.R. Drive. Between the stop-and-go traffic and the glare of headlights, he slid into a worse mood, swearing every time his foot tapped the brake pedal. Damn her! he thought. Damn this whole fucking city! It could blow itself up and he wouldn't give a shit.

Terry kept silent, her eyes on the cars while Gordon's anger turned into depression. He felt so inadequate with

Terry. "I just want to understand," he said. He sneaked another look at her as they passed the United Nations.

"You and Reed are like two peas from the same pod," he went on. "Both of you bottle everything up—except Reed doesn't have a partner, and you do. I can't trust someone who shuts me out."

The traffic clogged and Gordon stepped on the brakes. He used the brief stop to turn completely on Terry.

"I get scared wandering into dark buildings, Terry."

"You think I don't?"

"At least you know what to be scared of. You don't tell me everything you know. When you interrogate suspects, you throw things at them I've never heard."

"That's not true," she said. "I tell you everything I know."

"Bullshit!"

"Gordon, I tell you everything the moment I know it," she insisted.

The traffic moved and their car eased forward.

"I *do!*" she insisted. "That's why you're so upset with me. The way I pick up information doesn't make sense to you. But it doesn't make sense to me, either."

They drove past the Triborough Bridge, up the Harlem River Drive, exiting at Dyckman Street to avoid the Jersey-bound traffic. Terry gave Gordon the Clover Pub's address, and they moved along Broadway for the remainder of their trip. He parked near 207th Street underneath a subway trestle, and then they walked to the bar.

The Clover had a thick oak counter that curved into darkness. Some of the cushioned seats were occupied; others simply kept the crushed imprints of past customers. The regulars looked as if they'd come with the furniture, and well before the color television and the pinball machine.

All of this surprised Terry. She had expected the Clover to harbor a younger crowd—people who would make good cover for Griffin, Larry, and their friends. She sat at a table while Gordon bought two beers. "Know a guy named John Griffin?" he asked.

The bartender shook his head and shrugged.

"He's friends with someone named Larry."

"Larry?" The bartender pointed to a man watching television. "That guy's named Larry."

Gordon looked carefully at the man—in his late fifties, dressed in a baggy suit, a tie loosened and pulled to the side. Not even close to what they wanted.

Gordon carried the drinks back to Terry. "Nothing."

"Give it time."

She gave Gordon a photograph of Griffin and had him show it to the bartender. The bartender studied it. "Sorry," he said. He smiled wanly and walked to the other end of the counter. Gordon returned to Terry.

"Well, what do you want?" Gordon asked. "Should we hang out here?"

"For a drink or two."

"Maybe we should take a look in the other bars? I haven't cruised Irish bars since I was in Dublin," he said. "You ever been overseas?"

"A couple of times," Terry said. "Artie and I went to Venice for our honeymoon. We spent about a month there."

"A long time."

"Too long, too short," she said vaguely.

They sipped their drinks and watched a man swagger into the bar, metal tools poking out of his belt. Terry and Gordon looked once and then ignored him. Someone played a Doors song on the jukebox.

He waited.

"Look," Terry finally said, "you keep talking about my 'feelings' as if they're something special. But they're not. I know two or three good cops who have the same experience. Each has an instinct—a little voice inside that tells them when they're on the right track. It makes them seem to pull leads out of thin air. They have minds so quick that they seem to know everything about everyone they meet. But it's a trick, that's all.''

''Don't give me this Sherlock Holmes crap.''

''It's *not* strange,'' she insisted. ''I think it's just that, subconsciously, some people are quicker at picking up on the details. And when we do this too quick, it's almost like a magic trick.''

Gordon dropped fifty cents on the table and reached for his coat.

''Gordon, do you understand what I'm saying?''

''I hear you,'' he said coolly. They walked onto the street, and Gordon headed toward a second bar.

''But can you believe there's nothing strange going on?'' asked Terry. ''I'm not some witch out of Salem.''

''I never said you were.''

''You know what I mean.''

''Like I said, I understand what you're saying,'' he said. ''But I think it's bullshit.''

Terry sighed. ''You're not being fair.''

''And you're not telling me the truth.''

''Damm it, Gordon!''

He opened the bar door. ''Go ahead,'' he said. ''You ask the questions, I'll drink the beer.''

She left Gordon and walked to the bartender. For the next two hours, Gordon and Terry barely spoke to each other, preferring instead to shadow their own corners and tersely compare notes on the street. With Gordon's insecurities and her own temper, Terry realized it was probably the only way they could have spent the evening together. The respite, however, ended close to midnight, when, on a final check, they again returned to the Clover Pub.

It had changed. Earlier, Terry and Gordon had been the youngest there. Now they blended comfortably into a crowd that belonged to a singles bar, not an Irish pub. It hadn't occurred to Terry that a bar open until three in the morning would have different drinking crowds at different times of the day.

They sat near the pinball machine.

"Hell," she said, "it's almost midnight and I forgot to call Artie."

"I called him for you," said Gordon.

"When?"

"About eight, when I called Sharon," he said. "I told him you'd be home around one."

Gordon's brief moments of thoughtfulness always surprised Terry. At the same time, she knew she should have called Artie herself; but she wasn't quite ready for him. Artie would spend the entire call nagging her. As always, her responsibilities to her family ran smack into the responsibilities of her job.

She watched Gordon slide onto a stool and work his way toward a girl. For a detective, Gordon was incredibly obvious. He could have saved himself trouble by whistling and grabbing his crotch.

"Got any food left?" Terry asked the bartender, the same one Gordon had talked with earlier.

"Sandwiches." He pointed at a blackboard menu.

Terry ordered and enjoyed a brief flirt with a man standing near Gordon. There was an atmosphere in the small room that excited her—a wave of mystery and expectation. It was the sort of feeling that came from waiting impatiently for a lover; a feeling similar to the one she had felt earlier in the day, but not so unexpected. Before, when she had imagined herself in the body of a man, she was a victim of her strange feelings. Now those feelings were settling inside her and wouldn't leave. She savored them because they came from her future, not her past. They didn't belong to Artie or the kids; they belonged only to her.

114

"Still don't remember that face?" she asked the bartender.

He looked curiously at her. Terry felt foolish; the guy could care less about the photograph.

"John Griffin," she reminded him. "Had a couple of friends?"

"Yeah, I remember," he said. "You might want to talk with that guy." He pointed to a corner table and walked away.

The table was surrounded by a small, huddled crowd of people, hidden by a full coat rack and a table of drinks. Even after Terry had worked her way closer to them, the low lights made it impossible to see anything particularly well. The few full glances she had were obscured by layers of cigarette smoke and raised beer mugs.

Three people. Or was it four? No matter how she wriggled about, however, the poor light kept the details a secret. That was exactly why a terrorist group would hang out there, if they were going to hang out anywhere. The Clover Pub offered discretion and claustrophobic anonymity, just like the entire city. She concentrated on a young man with curly hair because he was the only person at the table she could really see. He was also the first to reach for his coat.

Terry looked for Gordon. Nowhere. She tried looking for his pickup, wondering if he had dared to walk out on her, overtime or not. The one moment all evening Terry needed his help, he had disappeared. Meanwhile, Terry could only watch as the small crowd pushed away from the table and squeezed its way to the front door. Terry shuffled behind the group, wondering if she should find a phone and call in for help.

Gordon stepped out of the restroom.

"Get the car," she told him.

Perplexed by her sharp tone, he nonetheless pushed his way outside. Terry followed, searching the street for her suspects. She saw no one, heard nothing—except for the sound of a car engine. Near the corner was a cab. Its engine was idling and its headlights had just flicked on. Uncertain what else to do, she waved her hand and stepped carefully off the curb. When the cab came toward her, she stepped in front of it, still waving, pointing uptown. The cabby beeped and waved her away. Terry didn't move. Finally, the cabby stopped. Terry slid up to the driver's window.

"Off duty," the cabby said.

Terry studied his young face; the cabby stared back.

"I want to go uptown," she said.

"I said I'm off duty." He rolled up his window. Terry grabbed the door handle.

"Police!" she said.

The taxi's engine roared, and Terry spun to the side, her bruised ribs hitting the car door. By the time Gordon pulled alongside, the taxi was disappearing to the south. Terry fell into their car, slammed the door, and fastened her safety belt.

Gordon pulled into the outside lane. He saw the cab swing left and out of sight. He raced through two sets of red lights, his fist hard on the car horn, now following the cab west. He crushed out a cigarette in the ashtray and asked, "Who is it?"

"Larry."

The Fairmont rose over a crest in the road and sped past a blinking yellow light. Terry reached under the dashboard and switched on the siren. A bread truck drifted out of a cross street. She braced herself for the crash, but Gordon jammed into low gear and powered them over the sidewalk. They made it around the corner in time to see the cab narrowly escape a collision with a station wagon.

"Jesus!" Gordon murmured.

They were gaining on the cab. Terry called in their position. Cars pulled to the side, ducking behind double-parked trucks as the chase now took them up toward Amsterdam Avenue. Gordon had the car straddling the center line, the siren screaming. The cab veered left. They followed, the Fairmont's tires catching a patch of ice and slamming them into a mailbox. Gordon wiped his face with a sleeve. All his concentration was focused on catching the cab—four blocks ahead, three blocks, then four again. Their car bounced over a rise, their rear dragging and sparking as the muffler grazed the street. Terry watched the speedometer—fifty m.p.h., fifty-seven, sixty-three . . .

Their wheels clipped and mounted the curb, a street pole barely missing Terry's side door. She slapped the dashboard.

"Go straight down," she said. "The street curves back toward Broadway."

The Fairmont slowed, squealed, and ended up heading west on Dyckman when the cab shot across Payson Avenue—closer, but still a block in front of them.

"We're gonna lose him," Gordon said, his knuckles bloodless from gripping the steering wheel. Terry pushed on the dashboard, trying to heave their car closer to the cab. Sixty-seven m.p.h., sixty-nine, seventy-three . . . She begged their car to go faster.

The taxi swung violently to the left, trying to make a turn into Staff Street.

It missed. Gordon slammed on the brakes as the skidding cab careened into a row of parked cars. Terry watched as the taxi lifted into the air and rolled over, wheels still spinning, settling on its roof.

Their own car jolted up the curb and stopped. Gordon jammed the Fairmont into reverse and drove a jagged route back to the taxi. They could see the cabby hanging upside down, his arms fighting to open his door. Gordon jumped out of the car with his gun drawn.

"Get out!" he shouted at the cabby. "But do it slowly."
He pointed his revolver at the cabby's head.

Terry glanced at a street sign, ready to radio their position to the 34th Precinct. It took her a moment to see the flashing blue lights. They were surrounded by patrol cars.

Nine

That night, Terry dreamed of Venice.

Touring Venice had been the most romantic part of her honeymoon. She liked to remember the hours Artie spent leading her aimlessly through the city, while pointing out crumbling churches and villas. He had spent a summer there as a teen-ager, promising himself that one day he would return to the Adriatic as an artist. He became an architect instead, but he kept his passion for Venice—a passion he had shared with Terry.

If she could spend all her nights dreaming of such days, she might have spent the rest of her life in bed. At least, Terry liked to think she maintained such dedication to her husband.

In this dream, however, the city was different. It was a brooding, lonely place—a gloomy maze where all routes bent in circles and brought her back to the same place.

Her steps echoed as she walked lightly to the crest of a

humpbacked stone bridge. She paused above a canal and stared down at the water, unable to see her reflection because of a low white mist. She looked to the stone banks, where streetlights glowed through a vague infinity. The lights were the only sign of life. In her dream, Terry was lifeless.

She turned and watched a new light bob gently in the distance. She waited as it slowly drifted forward, rocking from side to side, and becoming a gondola. She recognized her children sitting on its forward benches. They were alone and wore their best clothes, and Terry felt a sense of sadness as they passed underneath the bridge. Her sadness turned to horror. She realized too late that the gondola would not make it to the other side of the bridge. Instead, the tunnel led into a terrible darkness.

She jumped off the bridge and sank into the cold water. Somewhere in the darkness she heard her daughter laughing, but then the laughter faded, and all Terry could hear was the slapping of the water. The sound wrapped around her. Then it began to change. It was no longer the sound of breaking waves, but of her heart, growing louder.

It's just a dream, she told herself. Get *out* of this. She gripped the edges of the bed and groaned, terrified that she might die if she didn't wake up. But she couldn't pull herself out. She was no longer in control of her dream.

When she jumped off the bridge, she had jumped out of her mind.

The darkness gradually disappeared. The mist was no longer a fog, but dust blown by a hot, stinging wind. And her body was no longer soaked with the water from the canal, but with her own sweat, squeezed by a sun that blistered the skin. Only it wasn't her skin; it was the skin of a young man.

She passed down the tan-colored street of an African village. Black faces with bloodshot eyes watched her passage, their heads protected by dirty turbans and caked

119

mud. They relaxed outside peeling whitewashed huts made from cinder blocks and galvanized iron. The houses were little more than one-room, fetid squares that lined either side of the street like a set of irregular, unhealthy teeth. At most of the doors, men and women sat spread-legged on the front steps or in wooden chairs. One man lazily peeled vegetables; another spoke a few words to a companion; and a woman kicked a starving dog away from the potato shavings. The dog yelped and fell on its hind legs, stumbling into a shadow where its mate sat placidly curled against the sun, licking itself.

It was an assault of unfamiliar details—memories from a life that was not her own. The buzzing irritation of flies, the wrenching smell of a rotting carcass—these were not creations of *her* mind. They belonged to *him*. The man who was in the taxi. She could almost see his face, hear his name. . . .

There was an explosion, and the blast blew her to the ground. A nearby house disappeared in a pall of dirty smoke and debris, and the lazy afternoon was lost in a welter of shouting and wailing. When she kneeled, Terry saw a severed, bleeding hand, its forefinger twitching, as if to lead her forward. She shuddered and again tried to pull herself out of the dream. The smells and smoke became thicker, the screams of the villagers broken by the chatter of gunfire. Sporadic bursts from automatic weapons stitched the ground in front of her. She dropped back onto the dirt, bleeding, screaming for help. *Take me from here,* she prayed. *Let me wake up; let me go—*

She opened her eyes and stared up at Artie's face.

"You're having a nightmare," he said.

She was too withdrawn to answer. Artie lay down, his arm casually wrapping around her waist. Terry rolled away from him, stretching over the edge of the bed, vaguely recalling the dark passage beneath a bridge in some strange city. She finally fell asleep listening to the humming of the bedside clock.

"You want to tell me what happened yesterday?" Artie asked.

Terry stirred her coffee and ignored him. Both waited for the children to finish their breakfast and leave before the argument started. Terry had cleared the table and was at the sink when Artie finally said, "Are you trying to kill yourself? We don't count for anything, is that it?"

"Don't be a jerk, Artie."

She turned toward him, not knowing how to close the distance between them, a part of her wondering if she should. They were losing each other. She knew it last night, and Artie knew it today.

Terry carried her third cup of coffee into the living room and sat on the sofa. She felt she deserved a reprimand—a family rebuke. Her talent for investigation was becoming increasingly dangerous. It wasn't just the car chase; it was also the explosion in the tenement, the death of fellow officers, the explosives Gordon and she had found in the back of the cab. She had misbehaved last night. Gordon's reaction had been the right one—seal off the area, keep well back, and phone the bomb squad. Instead, Terry had ignored the cops from the 34th Precinct and opened the cab's trunk. The explosives enticed her. She had wanted to play with them. She was possessed by a fever that was putting everyone near her at risk.

"We've got to start talking to each other again."

Artie stood in the doorway and waited for an answer.

"Tonight," Terry said. She pushed past him into the kitchen and dropped her cup in the sink. Outside, a car horn beeped outside.

"Gordon's waiting," she said.

"Goddamm it! Give me a *break*!" he said. He stopped her in the hallway. She pulled free and sought refuge with

121

the children. He followed her, and she picked up a couple of toys, curtly telling Sean to get ready for school. She followed him out.

"Every time we don't talk it costs us, Terry," Artie warned her.

"I've got to go to work," she answered. "I told you, we'll talk about it tonight."

The car horn beeped again. Terry couldn't afford to waste any more time. She needed to interview their latest suspect—a man who could bring her closer to what she wanted. If only she knew what that was.

"What little surprises you got for us today?" Gordon asked. He looked more closely at her. "You look terrible."

"You're no oil painting yourself." It was cold in the car, and the glaring sunlight sparkled off the salted roads into Gordon's tired eyes. Even with sunglasses, he felt defenseless.

They drove down the West Side Highway to Fourteenth Street, then headed south. They went nine blocks and found a parking spot on Hudson. While Gordon locked the car, Terry crossed the street and entered the main headquarters of the New York Police Department's Intelligence Division.

The division was headquartered near Canal Street, a few blocks from the traffic barriers that led into the Holland Tunnel. It was a forgettable part of Manhattan with one advantage—the odd location gave the division anonymity. This was no small matter; over the years, the division had made many enemies.

The Intelligence Division began in 1912, after a surge of European immigration into the city. Seeing a connection between the immigrants and the rise in labor disputes, New York created an arm of the police called the Radical

Bureau, with the express purpose of investigating foreign-born anarchists.

In the years that followed, the division went through several name changes—from the Radical Bureau to the Neutrality Squad; then the Radical Squad; the Public Relations Squad; the Bureau of Special Services and Investigations; finally, the New York Police Intelligence Division. Only two things remained constant: its mandate to investigate dissidents, and a nickname created by the division's critics. That nickname was The Red Squad.

It stuck to the division during the early twenties, when the Radical Bureau spent much of its time inciting riots at Communist Party meetings, and stuck again in the fifties, when the Bureau of Special Services and Investigations opened its files to Senator Joe McCarthy. The derisive name made a third appearance in the late sixties, when the division put agents into deep cover in the student movements until they reemerged as confidants in such groups as Students for a Democratic Society and the Black Panther Party.

The division's agents watched college campuses the way baseball clubs sent scouts to check out opposing teams. When talented dissidents rose to power, the agents rose with them. The division was proud of the fact that an undercover detective had been Malcolm X's right-hand man. It was the detective who had administered first aid to the dying black leader on the stage floor of the Audubon Ballroom.

Still, critics argued, if the right to dissent was part of the Constitution, why keep files on the dissenters?

When it was revealed that detectives from the division had been covertly trained by the C.I.A., the entire department came under attack. The "plumbing" jobs, the wiretapping, the bribing, the "deep throats"—everything went public. The F.B.I. had suffered and survived similar attacks. The Feds even got a brand-new building for their troubles.

The Intelligence Division, however, was not so lucky. It suffered the disciplines of reform. By the mid-seventies, it had been cracked open and aired out. Years of files were discarded and agents taken out of cover. What remained was left forgotten on Hudson Street. Its new objectives became youth gangs, gambling houses, and occasionally terrorists. To its critics, this meant the division would have to forget "political extremists" and concentrate on less-glamorous criminals. Bill Reed didn't agree. Intelligence gathering meant stopping the criminals as they organized. Let the precincts play cops-and-robbers; the Intelligence Division was there to keep an eye on people intent on becoming criminals.

To Bill Reed the lesson of the seventies was simple: Keep a low profile. What was not seen did not need explaining. It was a lesson he expected his detectives to memorize. He wanted to keep the anonymity of the address on Hudson Street.

The D.L.P. was threatening to change all that.

Terry Cooke passed beneath the security cameras and entered the reception area, tapping on the bulletproof Plexiglas that protected the receptionist. The woman smiled and pressed a buzzer, freeing the door that led back to the offices and interrogation rooms. Terry slipped inside and chatted briefly with a shirt-sleeved detective, then made her way to the file clerk's office.

"Hey, Terry." The clerk smiled and he pointed to the wall. Terry saw the magazine cover photo of her and Griffin arm in arm, buddies forever.

"Pull the D.L.P. files, will you, Bennie?" she asked tiredly.

"Can't," he said. "Lieutenant took them."

"Terry?" Reed called to her.

124

She left the file clerk's office and followed Reed into an interrogation room. Terry closed the door.

"What's the matter?" she asked.

Reed sat on one of the hard wooden chairs and spread the files on the table.

"Your fiasco with Griffin. I've got to go to the prosecutor's office and deliver some papers. Then I'm off to see a judge to beg that the proceedings be closed."

"Why?"

Reed looked at her, exasperated.

"Think about it," he snapped. "I don't need my undercover cops getting their pictures on the front page of every city newspaper. Maybe once, but not twice or three times or however many times it may happen. And believe me, if there's an open trial, it's going to happen to you one helluva lot." He left his seat and began pacing the length of the small room. "I don't like my detectives taking the stand, Terry. I don't like them telling the goddamned world how we operate around here."

"You're being paranoid," she said. "Anyway, Griffin's pleading guilty."

"He *was*, so long as he was only charged with manslaughter. Now the city won't plea-bargain with a copkiller."

"What about our agreements?"

"This whole affair is a mess. And your antics last night didn't help."

Terry tried her "I can't stop being a cop" line. Reed ate it up.

"Oh, yes, you can," Reed retorted. "That's *exactly* what I expect. I don't care how good you are at it, you're *not* a street cop. Leave the car chasing and the bombs to the precincts. You've been here long enough. It's about time you understood what this division's all about."

"Bill?"

Reed settled back in his chair and tried to calm down.

"I'm really close. I can feel it."

Reed covered his eyes. "That's not what I want to hear, Terry."

"Seriously, Bill—"

"Have't you heard a word I've said? Do you understand the word *compliance*?"

"But I only want to look at the bio sketches," she said.

Reed stared at her, incredulous. He couldn't believe her arrogance. But when he looked into her face, he didn't see arrogance, only endless patience. It was an unhealthy look, and he felt uneasy at the sight.

Terry reached across the desk and gathered up the biographical material.

"Thanks, Bill," she said lightly. "I'll think about everything you've said. I promise."

Terry left the room, and Reed watched her pass the receptionist.

"Hope your kid feels better soon!" she shouted back at him.

Reed watched her go, wondering how the hell she knew his kid was sick.

His full name was Lawrence Kruger. He was a scrub-faced man of twenty-four, with curly ginger hair. He worked part-time as a hack for a Yellow Cab company in Brooklyn, and was also a supplier of explosives to the D.L.P.

Kruger was propped up in a bed, a month-old magazine on his lap. A bandage covered three stitches near his left eye, and his right leg was suspended several inches in the air. Kruger barely seemed aware of his injuries. He glanced up as Terry and Gordon entered, then returned to reading.

"I'm Detective Sergeant Cooke," said Terry. "This is Detective Weiss."

Gordon closed the door, while Terry walked over to the bed.

126

"Larry, we want to talk about the explosives found in your possession."

Kruger continued reading. Terry sat on the edge of the bed, her composure complete. Kruger looked up at her and grinned, shifting his attention to Gordon. Gordon took another magazine and settled in a chair.

"Just get me an attorney," Kruger told Terry.

"He'll be here soon," she said. She carefully examined Kruger's injured leg. A nine-inch wound was sutured along the length of his upper thigh. Terry had forgotten the jagged edge of glass that had cut Kruger. When they'd dragged him out of the cab, Kruger had been screaming from pain.

"That must hurt," she said.

Kruger shrugged.

"Does it?"

Terry rested a hand on his leg.

"It's fine," he said.

"Tell us about the explosives, Larry."

Kruger chuckled. She looked at him curiously.

"John already told us about you. John Griffin? Why do you think we were at the Clover?"

"A drink?" He smiled to Gordon. "She's weird." Gordon ignored him. Kruger turned back to Terry. "I drive a cab. People put all kinds of crap in my trunk. Phone the boss, he'll tell you—"

"Don't waste my time," she said. "Tell me about your other boss. Tell me about Meagan."

"Who?"

Terry ran her forefinger along the stitches crossing his thigh. She rested on one of them and delicately plucked it with her nail. Kruger's smile disappeared.

"Tell us about the explosives, Larry," she said. "Tell us about Meagan."

She hooked her nail and pulled. Kruger winced and swung down at her hand, but Gordon was quick to protect

Terry. One hand grabbed Kruger's wrist and the other held his throat.

"Say something intelligent," Gordon said to him. He looked down at Terry, playing her game, wishing he wasn't.

"This is illegal," Kruger managed to say. His eyes darted from one officer to the other.

Terry dug her nail into his skin. Gordon stifled Kruger's scream.

"Who's to say?" Terry answered. "What do you want? A cop? A *doctor*, maybe?"

Kruger tried saying something, but Gordon's hand muffled the words.

"I'm going to pull these stitches out of your leg one by one until you tell me what I want to know."

"Tell her," Gordon whispered. He relaxed his hand, letting Kruger breathe.

"I don't know anything." Kruger closed his eyes as Terry's finger brushed his skin, picking at a second stitch. When he screamed again, Gordon smothered Kruger's face with a pillow.

"I pulled out a stitch," Terry said.

Gordon leaned into the pillow, feeling nauseated.

"Don't worry, Larry, this is all off the record," she said. "No lawyers, no witnesses. Just a little secret between friends."

Kruger struggled. Gordon removed the pillow and clamped an arm about Kruger's throat. He held Kruger painfully tight, hoping Kruger would break, suddenly certain that Terry's sadism wasn't an act. Gordon worried how far Terry was going to go. She was enjoying this.

"You know where Meagan is, Larry," Terry said. "I can feel it. You don't want me to—you're trying to hide it—but it'll all come out." Her voice became soft. "Say it, Larry. Tell me where she is. Tell us about the explosives."

"No—" Gordon again choked off Kruger's scream.

"I can almost hear it. Her full name."

Kruger gagged for breath. Gordon was concentrating so hard on Terry that he had forgotten the strength of his grip. Terry let go of Kruger's leg and reached for his face. Kruger thought she was reaching for the stitches above his eye and rolled away.

"Louder," she said. "Think about Meagan."

She rested a hand on Kruger's cheek and pressed her fingers into his chin. Kruger's lips pursed open, a run of spit slipping down his day-old beard. With his eyes bulging out, and his nostrils flared, he looked like a corpse.

"Say it, Larry. Meagan Donahugue? Meagan Donnely?"

Kruger felt the inside of his head tingle. He imagined the teeth of a rake running through sand. He imagined a hand shuffling through papers, refiling memories. He felt a dozen sensations and formed them into a dozen images, but none of them made sense. When he tried to talk, a low, empty breath whistled out of his mouth. He felt reborn, released from body, time, and pain. Pain? What pain?

"Meagan Donnely?"

Yes. Meagan Donnely, he thought. *Meagan Donnely, 100 Sickles Street.*

"One Hundred Sickles Street?"

Meagan Donnely, 100 Sickles Street. Yes. Meagan Donnely, 100 Sickles Street. Yes . . .

"And the explosives? Where are the explosives?"

. . . 100 Sickles Street. Meagan Donnely . . .

"Some more names, Larry. What are some more names?"

Meagan Donnely. Yes.

"Names, Larry."

100 Sickles Street . . .

129

Terry dropped her hand, and Gordon relaxed his grip. Kruger collapsed on the bed.

"That's it," she said, looking up at Gordon. "Meagan Donnely, One Hundred Sickles. Call the office."

Gordon didn't move. He was too frightened.

Terry massaged her head. "We have to be careful, that's all," she said. "Bill said to leave the arrests to the precincts, so that's exactly what we'll do."

"Arrests?"

"Sure. We'll go there, but stay in the background."

"You mean to Sickles Street?"

"Yeah."

"And that's where we'll find this Meagan Donnely?"

His tone had been a bit too curious, and Terry looked at him. Her expression was one of annoyance. She was sick of Gordon's jealousy.

Gordon left the bed and leaned against the wall, his hands jammed in his pants. He didn't know what to say. His mind kept going over what had happened—the torture, the questions, the answers. Except there hadn't been any answers! There had been Gordon, and Terry, and this body. Kruger had been unconscious. Still was. Had Terry cracked up, or was something else happening? Gordon certainly didn't want Terry to be crazy; on the other hand, what if there *was* a Meagan Donnely at 100 Sickles Street?

"Terry?"

It was as difficult answering her as it was thinking. How had Terry got her information?

She looked hard at him.

"You're not coming with me, are you?" she asked.

Gordon remained silent.

Terry frowned. There was no memory of Gordon her partner. Now it was Gordon her enemy. That simple. Gordon saw the betrayal in her eyes. Within seconds their camaraderie had fallen victim to Terry's new passion—the same passion that she had unleashed on Kruger.

130

"I don't like this, Terry," Gordon said defensively. "We tortured him."

"He won't remember."

"I would."

"He won't remember," she repeated.

"This another one of your feelings? How do you know, Terry?"

"I just do," she replied.

"This the same feeling that told you about Meagan Donnely? And One Hundred Sickles Street?"

"Kruger told me. You heard him."

Kruger groaned and rolled on his side. Gordon watched him. Thank God she hadn't killed the guy. "He didn't say anything," Gordon said.

Terry's fury pushed inside Gordon's head and he stumbled backward.

"He's unconscious," Gordon said. "Look at him!"

"You're crazy."

"Terry—"

"I heard him!" she shouted. "If you're too deaf to hear—"

"I'm telling you, he didn't say a word. He *couldn't*."

"Just stop it, all right?" Her voice trembled. "I know what I heard. And I know you heard it, too." She grabbed her purse and headed for the door.

"Terry . . ."

She stopped. Gordon looked to the floor, uncertain what to say.

"I won't say anything about this," he finally said. "I'll stay here and straighten things out."

She didn't hear him. She heard her own voices—voices that told her she finally had the D.L.P. When she talked with Bill Reed on the phone, she spoke with such urgency that by noon, Terry and four patrol cars were at 100 Sickles Street with a warrant, ready to bring the D.L.P. to a decisive end.

What they found were the remnants of a bomb factory. Terry shouted a blur of orders at a sergeant. Then she returned to her car. She sat still, staring out the windshield.

Ten

Never in her life had Terry felt such despair. She was losing her family, failing friends, and being consumed by her responsibilities as an Intelligence officer. Beneath her self-confessed destruction was a vague awareness of something inside pushing to the surface. She was becoming aware of a second consciousness that threatened to strip her of the little trust she had left in herself. She was trying hard not to think about it, even when resistance was impossible, but sooner or later, she knew the "monster" inside would make itself known. She wondered if she'd lose her mind altogether when the time came for it to surface.

She wasn't crazy yet, though. She *had* heard Kruger tell her that address. It was only a whisper, but she'd *heard* it. Gordon should have heard it, too. If he said he didn't . . .

She stopped the car and closed her eyes. The information had been accurate. The address had been correct. They *did* find traces of a bomb factory. Why wasn't she vindicated? Why did she only feel worse?

For the first time, Terry doubted herself. Any insecurities had been kept in check for years. In hindsight, she knew it was a quality that had attracted Bill Reed's attention. He had not picked Terry for her expertise but for her persistence and character; she had the ability to achieve results with the thinnest of leads. Now she was ensnared by doubts and felt as though her career was based on fraud.

Terry left the car and went inside her house, waiting for the children to shout in her ears and make her forget the day; but it was eleven o'clock and they had been in bed for more than an hour. Only Artie greeted her, and she could tell by his expression that they had drifted further apart.

"Don't say a word," she warned him. She shook her dark hair and climbed the stairs. He sat on the sofa, watching her disappear into the bedroom.

Terry turned on the light and fell heavily on the edge of the mattress. *Our* bed, she reminded herself. She kicked off her shoes and let them lie on the carpet. *Our* carpet. Our house, our car, our children, our neighborhood.

Artie stood in the doorway. She looked up at him, then covered her face.

"What's happening, Terry?"

She listened out of habit. Artie stepped closer to the bed. He was uncertain whether to hold his ground or hold his wife. Whenever they were together, he felt weary and terribly resigned to letting their life together slip away. They needed to be rescued, but Artie felt unable to rescue anything.

"What can I do?" he asked softly.

"Nothing."

Artie kept silent.

Terry added, "You *could* leave me alone." The words were harsher than she had intended. "You could sleep downstairs."

"I intend to," he said.

It was a painful moment of understanding. Until now, they had kept their conflict beneath the surface. It was finally out in the open.

He turned off the bedroom light and closed the door, then walked to Jennifer's room to watch his daughter sleep. Jennifer had managed to curl up near the foot of the bed. He untangled her and made certain the blankets were tucked under her chin. He still couldn't understand how such a small child could be so restless. Terry and he had once found her curled up near the window. As a result, they had decided to keep the protective rail along the open side of her bed.

Preventive measures, he thought. The same sort of caution he should use to keep Terry and himself together.

Artie closed the door and went downstairs.

A long time passed before Terry could relax. Although the semidarkness of the room should have calmed her, a throbbing headache turned the bedroom into a mausoleum. If only she could stop thinking and give in to sleep. Sleep was similar to death—both, after all, meant an end to resistance. It would all become so simple once she stopped resisting.

But her mind kept drifting back to the day. There was something wrong, she thought. She wasn't losing control of herself—she was *giving it away*. To whom, or to what?

The idea disappeared. Succumbing to sleep was her only freedom. All these years, she thought, she had been so careful about how she behaved, fighting a world that taunted her with stupidity and jealousy. A world that demanded explanations when she had none to give; a world that she sometimes saw through as easily as glass.

There was no reason to fight, not when surrender promised rest, or something close it. A state between dreaming and being awake. A world that somehow freed the mind without abandoning the senses.

134

Even as these thoughts drifted, she felt the light breath of someone behind her—a man, pressing himself gently along the length of her body.

Fantasy, she thought. If she opened her eyes, she would find nothing there. But the touch was real. She could feel his hands slide across her stomach. They were coarser than Artie's.

She guided them to her breasts.

A breath of air warmed her back; then lips softly kissed a shoulder. She surrendered to her dream, wondering if this was what she had hoped to find in that bomb factory— something new and exciting, something that would possess her with a lover's passion.

What does it mean, she wondered, when you dream of an invisible lover?

The question rolled out of her mind as a hand slipped between her legs.

She turned onto her stomach, legs apart, feeling the weight press down upon her. She moved with his rhythm, losing her breath, catching it, slowly aware that something was not right. Betrayal to Artie? Partly. But this was a dream. She couldn't betray Artie in a dream.

The headache came back, nicking her like a knife point. With every quick stab, her lover disappeared and came back. She could feel him struggling to hold on, trying to revive her passion, grasping at her body. Terry wrestled with her apparition, but lost him with every painful throb. She felt him tug her hair as if he were slipping off a rope. He wanted so much to hold her, but Terry's dream was taking her somewhere else.

She was a child again, locked in a crib, struggling to catch a rainbow of lights that danced around her fingers. She leaned so forcefully against the crib that it toppled over. She crawled toward the window. She wanted to follow the light outside, and pulled at a curtain. Instead, the curtain came down upon her head. Breathless, suffocating . . . the light gone and the curtain taking away her breath . . . No, not her breath; Jennifer's. Jennifer's tears, Jennifer's screams . . .

"Jennifer."

Terry stumbled from the room, bumping into Artie on the landing. They turned on Jennifer's bedroom light and found her in a tangle of blankets.

"She's dead!" Terry cried.

Artie freed the child. A bedsheet was wrapped through her arms and knotted about her throat. He quickly untied the sheet.

"She's tangled up, that's all," he said. He pressed a hand on Jennifer's chest and felt her cheek. Jennifer began coughing, whimpering, and finally howling. Artie hugged her tightly, brushing Jennifer's hair and whispering to her.

Terry leaned against the doorway. She was afraid to touch her daughter. She didn't move until Artie put Jennifer back in bed. Then she kneeled beside her, holding her hand tightly.

Artie finally pulled Terry away and led her into the hallway.

"Leave the door open," she insisted.

Satisfied with Jennifer's safety, Terry followed Artie downstairs. She sat on the sofa while he stood in the shadows.

"God help us, Terry."

She looked at him. "Have you been talking with Gordon?" she asked.

Artie nodded.

Terry turned toward the stairs. Was Jennifer sleeping soundly? Could anyone in this house sleep soundly?

"Gordon's a liar," she said.

Artie laughed.

"He's a liar," she insisted.

"Doesn't sound like the Gordon I know."

"If Gordon had been in this house instead of me, Jenny would be dead."

Artie leaned closer. "You *heard* Jennifer scream?"

"Of course I heard her," said Terry.

"The child was *suffocating*, Terry. She couldn't have made a sound."

"Artie, she was screaming. I heard her!"

"She *wasn't*." He sat on the coffee table and faced her. "I was in the hallway, outside our room. I thought I heard someone in there. I thought you were . . ." He bowed his head. "Anyway, if Jenny had been screaming, I'd have heard it."

Terry looked at her husband, remembering the coarse hands of her imaginary lover, certain she had betrayed their marriage.

"What are you saying?" she murmured. For the moment, they needed each other badly.

"I don't know," he answered.

Early the next day, Artie phoned Bill Reed. He explained that Terry was sick and staying home. Reed listened carefully and realized Terry was having some sort of breakdown.

Shortly before Artie hung up, Reed suggested a psychiatrist—Samuel Becker. Artie jotted down the phone number, then slipped the piece of paper in his pocket before Sean and Jennifer ran downstairs for breakfast.

"Quiet," he said. "Your mother's still asleep."

The children plodded into the kitchen. Sean poured two bowls of cereal.

"Mom okay?" he asked.

"Sure," Artie replied. He bent down to examine Jennifer's throat. "How are you doing?"

She shrugged him off and reached for the milk. Just like her mother, Artie thought. But he was pleased the child was all right.

"Take care of your sister," he ordered Sean. Sean nodded and pushed Jennifer away from the milk. Jennifer started whining and Artie hushed her. Then he went to his office in the study.

Artie sat there a long time, trying to decide whether to call the psychiatrist. As it turned out, Becker phoned him.

"I hope you don't mind my calling," Becker said.

No, Artie said, he didn't mind. If Reed had been overworking Terry, perhaps this was a way to pay them back. Becker explained he was in Washington, but would be in the city by noon. "Can your wife come by this afternoon?"

"I'll ask her when she wakes up," Artie said.

He decided to bundle the children off to school before waking Terry. The last thing she'd want was a herd of little feet trampling on her nerves. "Come on, guys," he ordered, helping Jennifer dress and prodding Sean. He took Sean to school and Jennifer to the nursery, all the time wondering what would happen when Terry awoke. He remembered the previous night—standing outside her room, hearing the sounds of . . . of what? Of nothing. He knew there was nothing. There couldn't have been.

When he returned home, he found Terry in the kitchen boiling water.

"How are you?" he asked. He draped his coat over a chair and sat down.

"Better," she said, smiling weakly.

"Let me do that." Terry didn't fight. She was too exhausted.

Artie poured the coffee and sat opposite his wife, uncertain what to say. He certainly didn't feel like reaching out and holding her as he had during the night. In the daylight, he couldn't stand her rejection.

He reached in his pocket and showed Terry the phone number.

138

"Bill Reed gave it to me," he said.

Terry stared at the paper. Artie braced himself for the argument.

She looked at him with a compliance that was frightening.

"What time's the appointment?" she asked.

Becker's New York office was on Fifty-third Street, off Park Avenue, in a building guarded by two doormen and a wall of security monitors. Terry was walked to an elevator and went to the twelfth floor. When the elevator doors opened, she found herself at the entrance to Becker's anteroom.

It was a small room with clean, white walls that made a tight box around the secretary's desk. A large painting of bright, splashing colors hung over a corner filled with chairs.

"Detective Cooke, isn't it?" inquired the secretary. "If you'll please wait a moment."

Terry sat beneath the painting and flipped through the pages of a magazine, resisting the urge to pace, too aware of the secretary's attention. She wondered if the woman was also a nurse. Would a psychiatrist need a nurse? Not normally, but maybe Becker needed one. Maybe five minutes with Becker started his patients convulsing on the floor.

Terry turned another page. The secretary smiled benignly and listened to an intercom, then began scribbling notes on a pad. Terry hoped Becker was canceling their appointment. Maybe he'd send Terry off with a prescription for nasal spray. "Nothing wrong with you, dear, that a few drops of antihistamine can't cure," he might say.

"Doctor Becker can see you now," the secretary said.

Terry glanced at the door. She rose and nervously smoothed her dress. A moment later, Becker appeared.

"Terry Cooke," he said with a grin. They shook hands;

Becker added a little reassuring muscle to put Terry at ease. He was in his mid-forties, relaxed, and with a practiced manner that made him seem the perfect middle-aged man. Terry wondered if Becker and Bill Reed used the same tailor.

As Becker led her into his office, Terry said, "Bill Reed wanted me to see you."

"He told me the same thing."

"How do you know Bill?"

She waited for the answer, but Becker didn't provide one. Maybe Reed was seeing Becker on a professional basis?

Becker adjusted his glasses and looked over some notes.

"Is it Terry or Theresa?"

"Terry's fine."

"All right, Terry. What can I do for you?"

It was the sort of question she expected from an M.D. or a bank teller, not a psychiatrist.

She thought hard, as uncertain of her problems as she was of her marriage and everything else. "I'm not behaving normally," she said at last.

Becker waited.

"I'm not—" She tried to press her nightmares, her job, her visions into one word. Somewhere there had to be a word for it. "I'm not myself." She tried again. "It's as if my mind is running ten steps ahead of my body."

"You don't feel in control, is that it?"

She looked at the doctor, still struggling, letting her frustration show.

"What are you trying to say?" Becker asked.

Terry gave up. "I don't know."

"Are you fighting with your husband?"

"Not really."

"Are you having a fight with yourself?"

Terry nodded. He'd gotten that right, anyway.

"Fine," said Becker. "So what's the fight about?"

There was a long silence. "What I want to do."

"You mean, where you think your life's going?" Becker suggested. Terry looked down and twisted her ring.

"I'm scared of what I am—what I might become."

Becker leaned forward, trying not to look confused. "I know it doesn't make any sense," she said.

"It doesn't have to." Becker smiled. "Tell me about your work."

She told Becker about the Intelligence Division and her earlier job as a liaison officer. She spoke about her admiration for Bill Reed and her mothering of Gordon. She talked a long time about being a woman cop. She recalled the previous week as if she were reading from a diary. The explosion, Griffin, the car chase, even Kruger.

"You've been busy," Becker said.

"I suppose so."

"Maybe too much," said Becker. "Want me to ask Bill for a vacation for you?"

Terry looked hard at Becker, shocked, suddenly realizing she was talking herself off the job. She didn't want to stop working—not when she was so close to finding the D.L.P. and the man in her dreams.

"Tell me about your daughter's accident."

So Becker knew about Jennifer. "I was lying in bed when I heard Jenny screaming."

"Your husband says she didn't make a sound."

"Then maybe it was maternal instinct," Terry said tersely.

"Were you asleep?"

"How could I have been?"

Becker raised his eyebrows.

"All right, let's move on."

"Fine."

"You told me just now that your suspect,"—he glanced down at his notes—"Lawrence Kruger, gave an address. I understand that may not be the case."

"Who told you that, my husband?"

Becker didn't answer.

Terry was furious. The little bit of trust she had left in Gordon had flown out the window. Gordon told Artie everything.

"Look," said Becker, "it doesn't matter who talked with—"

"It's not true," Terry said. "Gordon's a liar."

Again Becker didn't reply.

"He's a drunk," Terry said. "It's what ruined his marriage. He's—" She stopped, as if a new idea had entered her head. Slowly, she said, "You didn't talk to Artie about this. You talked to Gordon."

Terry's anger trained on him. She spoke with dead certainty.

"Am I right?" she demanded.

Becker watched her, fascinated, perhaps too afraid to argue. "You're right," he admitted. He wiped his face, as if to wipe away his thoughts. "Tell me, do you know what I'm thinking right now?"

"Of course not."

"I'm thinking of a number. Try guessing it."

"No."

"Why not?"

Terry shrugged. "Nine."

"Wrong."

"So?"

"So, nothing," he said, again changing topics. "Relax. Tell me about your family."

Terry had given up understanding Becker. "You mean Artie and the kids?"

"Forget them," Becker said. "Tell me about your parents."

She thought about her mother and father, her memory drifting back to her fall out the window. "My father was a cop in San Diego."

"What grade?" asked Becker.

"Desk sergeant. He was a patrolman before that."

"Why San Diego?"

"He had been an M.P. at the naval base."

"Are your parents still alive?"

"Sure."

"Do you see them often?"

"Not often," she answered.

"Do you love your parents?"

"Of course."

"Why 'of course'?"

Terry turned away.

"Do you have a favorite?"

Terry became suspicious of his questions. "My father, I suppose."

"Artie told me you were frightened by your mother."

Terry hated this man.

"She scared me *once*," she said. "When I was a kid. It was a long time ago."

"Tell me about it," said Becker.

Terry paused, remembering the moment she had first acknowledged her "feelings." She had been six years old. "Help me, Terry," her mother had begged. "Your brother's in trouble. Can't you feel it?"

Terry wanted to help her brother, but she didn't know how. She barely knew him. He was a merchant marine who had been at sea for years. Her mother crouched beside her.

"He's drowning," her mother said in tears.

Terry struggled, but her mother held her hands tightly, forcing her to listen.

"We've got to help him! You and me together. I can't do it on my own."

Terry had stopped fighting and listened carefully to her mother, afraid, and uncertain what she should do.

"Deep inside, Terry," her mother pleaded. "It's there—look for it."

Terry felt her mother's guidance take hold of her. Her body had begun to tingle, and she forgot who she was. She tried to help her brother, feeling the cold rain, the wind, the waves. *Don't die!* they pleaded together. Terry felt her brother's head lift above the ocean, then just as quickly drop. A gulp of salty water filled her young throat, and she began choking. "Help him, Terry!" her mother cried.

A wave swept over her head, and Terry sank into a darkness that felt empty and eternal.

Her mother wailed.

Terry remembered crying and watching her mother, wondering what had happened, certain she had somehow killed her brother.

She looked up at Becker. "I don't want to talk about it."

Becker slapped a hand on the desk. "All right. I want to get together again tomorrow."

Terry didn't answer.

"I'm taking you to a place for some tests, that's all," he continued. He smiled. "Better paranoid than paranormal, right?"

"What the hell's that supposed to mean?"

"What it says."

Becker wrote an address on a sheet of paper and handed it to her. Terry read it, surprised.

"This is ridiculous," she said.

"Humor me," Becker said. "My secretary will phone you in the morning. Until then, keep your day open. I'll do the same."

"I don't—"

"*Tomorrow,*" Becker finished.

Terry didn't answer. Instead, she crushed the address into her purse and left the office.

144

Eleven

The building was a ten-story rectangle of dark glass and stainless steel—an ominous structure that reflected the street like a muddy pool of water. Inside, a wooden plaque was braced to the side of a reception area: THE NEW YORK INSTITUTE FOR PARAPSYCHOLOGICAL RESEARCH.

Terry passed through the revolving door, and Becker broke off a conversation with a guard. He greeted her, pinning a visitor's badge on her lapel. ''Glad you're here,'' he said. ''I want you to meet Emily Goldin.''

They took an elevator upstairs, passed a red-haired receptionist, and continued through a hall of medical offices. Becker was obviously familiar with the institute—a fact that didn't surprise Terry. The previous afternoon she had checked into Becker's background. Doctors Emily Goldin and Samuel Becker had been colleagues in Washington, and both were currently under contract with the Department of Defense. Although Terry could not collect details about the contract, she knew it had involved research into paranormal experiences.

They found Goldin in a storage closet, shuffling through a box of wires and tape. Her straight hair had been tied into a long, thick ponytail. Terry saw a flat-faced woman with hardly any makeup. Goldin turned and smiled warmly.

"Hold on a minute," she said. "I've got to finish just one thing. Then maybe we can get started. I'm sorry, Sam."

"No problem," Becker said.

Becker and Terry followed Goldin from the closet to the institute's laboratories. "This will just be a quick stop," she promised, ushering them into a small control booth. Through a long pane of glass, they saw a woman lying on an examination table. The woman was fully dressed, and electrodes had been attached to her face and arms. Next to the table was an abandoned wheelchair. Except for the woman, the table, and the wheelchair, the room was bare.

Terry watched Goldin enter the room and finish taping electrodes. When she returned to the cubicle, she spoke into a microphone. "Are you still comfortable, Ruth?" The woman nodded. "Breath deeply." A speaker amplified her long, deep breaths. "Everything's fine," Goldin told the woman. "Just wait a moment, and we'll get you going." She turned to a technician, whispered orders, then turned back to Terry and Becker. "I'm really sorry about this. It's tough getting people to volunteer their time," Goldin said. "This woman's been coming in twice a week, and I don't want to break the routine."

"Why is she here, if you don't mind my asking?" Terry said.

"Oh, a little unorthodox therapy," Goldin said. They left the room and walked back to the elevators. "Her husband was killed ten years ago in a car crash. Ruth survived the accident, but she experienced complete paralysis from her neck down. At first we were sure there must have been spinal damage. But there's nothing wrong with her physically. The problem's in her mind."

"Hysterical paralysis," Becker said. "Interesting, but hardly paranormal."

146

"When she enters a trance, Ruth is able to move her limbs after gaining the permission of her dead husband. A kind of one-woman séance, if you like."

"The woman's got problems," said Becker. "You've admitted that."

"Certainly she has problems," Goldin answered. "But that still doesn't explain one interesting thing." To Terry, Goldin said, "We attach a microphone to her chest to monitor her breathing."

"What about it?"

"When she enters her trance, we can distinctly hear the sound of two people breathing."

Becker coughed and covered a smile with his hand. Terry didn't know what to say. Goldin gave them both a playful look of horror.

"Which brings us to you, Mrs. Cooke," said Goldin. "Any voices from the dead—that is, besides Sam's?"

"Nothing like that," Terry said.

"Well, glad to have you here, anyway," said Goldin. "We can always use the volunteers." Goldin paused, then asked Terry, "Do you think you're telepathic?"

"No."

"Is that because you've never had a telepathic experience or because you don't believe in mental telepathy?"

Terry didn't answer, and Goldin stopped smiling. "I do take this seriously. From what Sam's told me, I wouldn't be surprised if you were sensitive to some of our experiments. Most of us are psychic to some degree."

"Which is not at all my conclusion," Becker said.

"Yes," said Goldin. "I presume you brought Mrs. Cooke here to prove me wrong."

Becker smiled. "I wouldn't be disappointed."

They went to the seventh floor and turned into a hallway. Goldin tucked a hand under Terry's arm and drew her aside. "Personally, I find it strange when anybody rejects the existence of the paranormal out of hand. Did you know Freud and Einstein believed in psychic phenomena?

"The interesting thing is that I find more and more people willing to give us our fair share of credibility. I like to think this has to do with the higher standards of research. It tends to diffuse some of the skepticism that's directed at our work. Telepathy, incidentally, is one field of psychic research in which we've made a certain amount of progress."

Despite herself, Terry asked, "What is it?"

"We've tentatively defined it as the ability to send or receive messages without oral, visual, or physical communication. It's one of the simpler psychic skills, and certainly the easiest to prove, even to skeptics like Sam. The navy's been experimenting with it for a long time."

"Nothing's conclusive," Becker said.

"For some psychics," Goldin explained, "performing in a lab is too inhibiting to be successful. Anyway, we've certainly got enough tests to thoroughly check you out. We have another volunteer here at the moment. I thought later on we might put the two of you together and see if anything comes of it."

As they walked past a waiting room, Terry noticed someone sitting in a chair. She saw only the person's legs. He or she wore denim jeans and was hidden by the partially closed door. Goldin closed it completely.

"That's our guest," she said. "It's better if the two of you don't meet for the moment."

"Fine," said Terry.

Goldin led her into a room with several computer terminals.

"Just bear with me a moment longer. The mind essentially works on two levels: the conscious and the subconscious. Now, our conscious mind is responsible for our actions. Our subconscious mind is at the root of this behavior."

148

"Okay," Terry said warily.

"Most scientists believe the subconscious mind is incapable of tangible, independent action—that is, without the support of the conscious mind. Here, however, we believe that telepathy, psychokinesis, and other psychic phenomena are moments when the subconscious mind overcomes this barrier and exerts a 'physical' influence on the world. Commonly, these moments occur during times of extreme stress—rage, terror, danger, whatever. But if we stop thinking of telepathy as an odd occurrence, and instead think of it as a skill—like being a musician—then it would seem the more one relies on a telepathic ability, the more developed it becomes. Once you've opened the 'door' in your head, so to speak, you can't close it."

The lecture was interrupted by a computer technician who changed the printer's ribbon and fussed over a terminal, accessing a program.

"So what are we going to do?" Terry asked.

"We're going to test your ability to tap your subconscious," said Goldin, "presuming, that is, you don't have any objections. A positive attitude does help with these experiments."

The technician motioned toward the computer and left.

"The first thing we'll do is give you some Zener tests," Goldin said. "The original ones used a deck of twenty-five cards with one of five designs on each card: a circle, a cross, a square, a star, or wavy lines. One test required the volunteer to predict the design of the card before it was turned over. A second test had a sender attempting to transmit the design of the card telepathically to the volunteer. In either case, the odds of getting it right are one in five, which means that out of a deck of twenty-five cards, the average person would guess about five right."

She directed Terry into a chair. As Terry made herself comfortable, Goldin leaned across her. PASSWORD??? asked the computer. Goldin tapped it in and pressed the

RETURN key. The computer hummed a moment, then flashed, PROBE #:XXXX-X. Goldin gave Terry a number and again pressed RETURN. TEST 4454-L COMCARD PLUS, the screen read.

"Everything's set," said Goldin. "The computer's going to act as your deck of Zener cards. It will ask you to predict one of five randomly chosen symbols. All you have to do is type the letter associated with the symbol." Goldin tapped the RETURN key, and the computer displayed the five symbols. Next to each was a letter. "Type 'A' for the star, 'B' for the waves, 'C' for the circle. . . ."

"Got it," said Terry.

"Fine. When you're done, I'll set up the next experiment. Meanwhile, Sam and I are going next door."

Terry thanked Goldin and turned to the screen. BEGIN? it asked her.

Terry hit the RETURN button and a sixty-second counter began flashing in a corner of the screen. SELECT CARD. Terry stared at the screen, wondering how on earth to predict the behavior of a computer. Was there a particular way she was supposed to think or feel? Should she close her eyes and ask the spirits to guide her through this stupid thing?

SELECT CARD, the screen insisted. The clock entered the final ten-second cycle. Ten, nine, eight, seven . . .

"Ridiculous." Terry sighed. She selected the star and pressed Return.

SHUFFLING. There was a brief hum, then: SELECT CARD.

Feeling foolish, Terry gave the five symbols passing interest, then made her selection. She wondered if the computer would ever let her know the score, but after each selection she was answered by SHUFFLING . . . , followed by SELECT CARD. With great efficiency, she hurried through the computer program.

END, said the computer. FORMULATING RESULTS.

150

Terry waited for further instructions. Nothing happened. STORING, it finally told her.

When the menu of programs appeared on the screen, Goldin came back.

"All right," she said. "Let's do the second experiment."

She leaned over Terry and punched in fresh commands.

"I'm going to open the line up to a machine in another room," she explained. "This time the computer will randomly select a symbol and then flash it on my machine. You'll be trying to read my mind in order to decide which symbol's been selected. You'll record your answers the same way as before. Understand?"

Terry agreed, and Goldin left the room. Soon a message flashed across her screen. READY WHEN YOU ARE. HIT [RETURN]. E.G. Terry followed the order, and the five symbols again appeared on the monitor. This time, at least, there was no annoying clock ticking away her final seconds. Terry concentrated on Goldin's thoughts.

After thirty minutes, a second message flashed on the screen. STOP. E.G. Terry settled back in her chair and waited for Goldin and Becker to return.

"What's the score?" Becker asked.

Goldin reached across Terry and typed, CALC: 4454-L. A board of numbers flashed onto the screen.

$$A=22, B=12, C=24, D=31, E=11.$$
$$4454\text{-}L: A=0, B=0, C=0, D=0, E=0.$$

$$T=0. \text{ MOE-4.5 PRE}=9.1$$

"All right," Goldin murmured. "Now the second test." The second set of calculations was identical to the first. Goldin ran a hand through her hair.

"What's it mean?" Terry asked.

Goldin sat beside her. "Well, the first subset of numbers tells us how many times a symbol was chosen by the computer. 'A-22,' for instance, means the star was selected twenty-two times. The numbers after your I.D. tag are the number of correct guesses you had for each symbol."

"You mean all the zeroes?"

"Yes," said Becker. "All the zeroes."

Goldin looked annoyed. "Undoubtedly Sam thinks your perfect rows of zeroes means you have no telepathic skills. I, on the hand, come to an entirely different conclusion." She tapped a finger against the computer screen. "See that last figure—nine-point-one? That's the computer's estimate of your telepathic abilities."

"Is that high?" asked Terry.

"Let's put it this way," said Goldin, "as far as the computer and I are concerned, it's almost as incredible to get two hundred answers wrong as it is to get every one right."

"That's where the machine and I differ," said Becker.

"The odds of anyone giving two hundred wrong answers for two hundred unbiased questions are long, Sam."

"So that makes me psychic?" asked Terry.

"I don't know," Goldin answered.

"That's hardly an answer," Becker said.

"We're not through yet," Goldin said. To Terry, she added, "I think we might get more positive results if you put up less resistance." She glanced at Becker. "Take her to an isolation booth, will you? I'll get our other volunteer ready."

Against her better judgment, Terry allowed Goldin and Becker to guide her into the hall. The whole experience was beginning to irritate Terry.

"What's going to happen now?" she asked.

"Now, we give Emily a chance to redeem herself," Becker said.

He swung open a door and turned on a fluorescent light.

It was a stark room, with soundproof walls and one padded, reclining chair. A loudspeaker was fitted in a far ceiling corner.

"You'll find a pad and pen on the chair," Becker said. "Just take a seat and wait until you hear Emily."

Terry obeyed, taking off her shoes and sitting down, while Becker left and closed the door. The moment the door closed, she felt she'd been sealed in a vault. She could see Becker through a thick glass window that framed the inside of the door, and then he wandered out of sight.

"Terry?" Goldin called.

Terry watched the loudspeaker.

"Can you hear me?"

"Yes."

"Good. We'll start in a few minutes. What we're going to do is fairly simple. You have the note pad?"

"In my lap."

"When I tell you to begin, I want you to think of a phrase no longer than five words. Write it down. Then concentrate hard on it until I tell you to stop."

"So I'm going to be the sender?" asked Terry.

"That's right," said Goldin. "Can you think of something?"

Terry thought briefly and jotted down, *The rain is heavy.*

"Ready," she told Goldin.

"All right. Now, without telling me the phrase, begin concentrating."

Terry concentrated as hard as she could. She directed her thoughts toward the loudspeaker, as if she could transmit the message through the electrical wiring. After four minutes, Goldin stopped her.

"That's enough," she said. "Number the phrase, set it aside, and think of a new one."

Terry leaned forward, again manufacturing a phrase. *I have two children,* she jotted down. Once more, she thought of nothing but her phrase, and again Goldin kept her concentrating for a long four minutes.

"That's fine," Goldin said. "Now a third time."

In the next hour, Terry "sent" a dozen short phrases. By the time Goldin told her to relax, Terry was exhausted.

"Is this going to last much longer?" she asked.

"Another hour," said Goldin. "I just want to turn the tables, that's all. Do you mind?"

Terry shook her head.

"What was that?" asked Goldin.

"I said 'no'. "

"Good. When you're ready, I'll have a message sent to you. I'll warn you when it's coming. This time, instead of concentrating on a phrase, I want you to open your mind. Make it accessible to whatever's being sent. When you think you've got something, jot it down on the note pad."

"Fine."

"I'm going to repeat the instructions to the other room. Then we'll start."

Terry leaned back against the chair, preparing herself. She didn't expect anything at all to happen. She wondered what to do if she didn't receive a "message." Would it be her fault if nothing happened? And what if something did happen? Did that mean she was psychic? Terry didn't want to be. Not at all.

"Everything's set, Terry," Goldin said. "Just try to relax."

Relaxing proved more difficult than Terry anticipated. She struggled to quiet her thinking, pretending she needed to nap. She forced her gathering dreams into one massive blur and waited for a message.

But it didn't come as a picture. It came as a voice. A man's voice that was so clear she thought someone had sneaked into the room and whispered in her ear.

Hello, Terry.

She opened her eyes.

154

"All right," said Goldin. "If you've heard anything, write it down on your pad before you forget it."

"Yes," Terry murmured.

"When you're done writing, relax and again clear your mind. Do you understand?"

"Dr. Goldin?" Terry wasn't certain what to ask. "Who's in the other room?"

"I can't tell you now," Goldin answered. "How about after the test, all right?"

Terry wondered if Goldin was being clever. There was something terribly wrong in what was happening. And the voice! It *felt* familiar. The voice of someone who was making himself at home in her thoughts. An invasion. No, more than that. Her mind was being raped.

Then he came again.

What happened at Sickles Street, then?

The voice was firm and mocking. Terry rolled off the chair and onto her knees, holding her ears. Why she held her ears, she didn't know. The voice didn't come from outside, it came from within.

"Write down anything you hear," Goldin said.

"No," Terry gasped.

"Excuse me?" asked Goldin.

Terry fought for her breath. "Who's in the other room?"

"I've already explained about that," said Goldin.

"What did you tell him about me?"

"Nothing."

"You *did*."

"This is just an experiment, Terry. Don't be so nervous. Anyway, what makes you so certain our guest is a man?"

Terry barely heard her. Another sardonic message came through.

You were great in bed.

Goldin sounded annoyed. "Terry? Are you ready for the next message?"

Terry rested her forehead on the cool floor, trying to recover her senses. She stood up like a drunk and fumbled toward the door, thinking if she could just escape the room, she would escape the voice. Her hand twisted the knob.

"Becker!" she called, falling into the hallway. She glanced either way, not knowing which direction was safe for escape.

"Becker!"

I love you, echoed the voice.

She fell against a wall, stunned by the surge of power. She looked up to see Becker and the technician running toward her. If she could struggle back on her feet, maybe they could get her away, out of the building and—

Don't fight me, Terry. I'll kill you if I have to. Don't make me do it. I don't want to. Don't make me. Don't . . .

The voice swept through her body. She was no longer in the institute—she was nowhere. His power smothered Terry, demanding obedience or oblivion. The longer Terry struggled, the darker it became. Her eyes rolled back and she screamed.

Chris Easton rose, wiped his forehead, and left the small, soundproof chamber. Shouts echoed through the hallways. For her, he thought. He had never meant to hurt her; he just wanted to warn Terry Cooke to get out of his way.

A hand touched his arm, and he looked to his side.

"What happened?" Goldin demanded. She held him firmly by the arm and stared up at his boyish face. "What did you do to her?"

"I just came to get myself tested, darlin'," he said. "It was very instructive."

"What are you talking about?"

Her fingernails cut into his wrist. He frowned and focused his attention on her.

156

Deaf, dumb, and blind, he thought. *Deaf, dumb, and definitely bleeding* blind.

Goldin froze.

Tricks, he thought. He didn't come here for this. He wanted more. That extra step, from the mind to matter. Psychokinesis—PK. It was there if he wanted it badly enough. On the brink. Mind to matter.

Then he understood—and stepped over the brink.

He almost had his finger on the elevator button when he pulled back. *Mind to matter,* he told himself; *mind to* matter.

He stared at the button, letting his subconscious project itself and wrap around the object, searching for a way to grasp it. Objects aren't people, he thought; they're made to be pushed, pulled, or destroyed.

Push! he thought.

Six feet away, the elevator button lit.

"PK," he whispered aloud. He said it almost tenderly.

Then the doors opened and he entered. He concentrated on the "L" button, and the elevator went down to the lobby.

Finally, he left the building. He walked outside and into the cold city, filled with a new power he had yet to comprehend.

PART THREE

PK

Twelve

After the downtown explosion, Chris's induction into the terrorist group proved quick and easy. Larry's mind, Chris realized, was easily invaded. Chris discovered this the moment he surprised Larry by climbing into his cab. By the time Chris and Larry reached the Clover Pub, Chris had complete control of the cabby's thoughts. As far as Larry was concerned, Chris and he had been friends since high school.

Larry bought two beers and looked for two men and a woman. The trio waited impatiently for Larry, not yet noticing his friend. Chris, however, saw them. He knew the woman through Griffin's memory, and the rest from Larry's—Meagan, Andrew, and Walter. The D.L.P.

Walter's nervous smile was partially hidden by his beard, and he edged closer to the wall. Meagan eyed Chris cautiously. When Larry tried making room at the table, Andrew grabbed his wrist. "Who's he?" he asked.

Larry looked confused. He struggled with Andrew, spilling the mug and soaking his shirt. Meagan caught Andrew's arm and told Larry to sit down. Chris slid alongside Larry and put a brotherly arm around him.

"Who are you?" Meagan asked.

"Chris."

She frowned. "Chris who?"

"Just Chris."

Meagan sat back, not at all pleased. Larry moved uncomfortably in the chair.

"Come on," he said. "Chris and me are old friends."

"Then *you* tell me his name."

"Sure." Larry opened his mouth, waiting for the answer. "Cooke," he said. "Chris Cooke."

Chris turned his attention to Walter, slipping gently into his head. Walter eyed him curiously.

"I know you, don't I?" Walter asked.

"Could be," Chris said.

"At the bookstore. You got rid of the police while Larry hid explosives."

"Something like that," Chris said. "Andrew took care of the cops. I delivered the explosives for Larry."

"That's right," said Larry. "I watched the car and Chris made the delivery."

Andrew glared with anger, still not part of the game. He pulled at his light brown goatee and studied Chris.

"You know him, too?" Meagan asked Walter.

"I've seen him," Walter said warily. "I'm pretty sure I know him."

"Of course you know me," said Chris. He looked at Meagan, and sank into her thoughts. "Mark Schneider introduced us."

Larry sat forward and said, "John got busted."

"Oh, Christ!" said Walter.

"We were both there. Chris helped me get out."

Andrew kept watching Chris, as if he knew what was happening. Chris again sank into Andrew's mind, not certain the job was done. Andrew's thoughts were a mess—the guy was a maniac.

"Let's get on with it," Andrew finally told Meagan.

"John's caught," Walter said with disbelief.

"He didn't know anything anyway," Meagan said.

162

"*I* never told him anything," Larry said. He sat back, holding his beer. "The only thing we got to worry about is the explosives."

"As if you got the balls to do anything with them," said Andrew. Larry lurched at Andrew.

"Stop it," Walter said. Chris held back Larry. Walter glanced at the bar, certain the bartender was watching, but the man was busy elsewhere. Meagan glared at Andrew and Larry.

"Make a scene," she whispered. "Tell everyone what we're doing!" Andrew reluctantly sat back. Meagan lit a cigarette. "How many cops were there?" she finally asked.

Larry sulked.

"It was a complete stakeout," Chris answered.

"Oh, Jesus!" Walter moaned.

"Shut up!" Meagan snapped. Andrew laughed nastily.

"Suppose John knows something?" Walter went on. "What if he talks?"

Andrew stretched his arms. "We waste him. No evidence. Good-bye." Again, he turned on Chris, staring hard. Chris felt certain Andrew was trying to sink into his head, but Chris felt nothing. It was only Andrew spilling out onto the world, with Chris in the way.

"John doesn't know anything," Meagan said.

"Why take chances? Waste him anyway," Andrew insisted.

"That's your answer to everything," said Walter.

"They'll be watching him every time he farts," Larry murmured.

"So we take out the precinct house," Andrew said.

"Make some sense," Meagan said angrily.

"I'm making perfect sense," Andrew continued. "Larry'll get the explosives, I'll wire it to Walter, and then we'll throw him and the bomb into the station. Simple." He smiled and watched the others over the rim of his glass.

"Very funny," said Walter.

"We could wire a car and park it outside," Larry suggested.

"No," Meagan said.

"What about a pipe bomb?"

"*No.*"

"This is bullshit," Andrew said.

"There's a world of difference between an empty bank lobby and a police station," Walter said.

"It'll focus too much attention on us before we're ready," Meagan said.

"It would be easy," Larry urged.

"It's stupid," Walter said.

Meagan stopped the argument. She turned to Chris. "What do you think?"

They all turned to him. Chris had slipped into each of their minds and left his suggestions. This was now his chance to ignite the action or smother it. He felt excited. A world of possibilities opened before him that he hadn't seen since Francine's death.

"Our trademark's lobbies, right?" he said. His voice was controlled and certain.

"You know it is," Meagan said.

"Well, there's bound to be a crowded one at La Guardia Airport."

Andrew smiled, tilting his head and studying Chris with renewed interest. "All right."

Walter groaned. "Meagan, what are you doing? We're not ready for this."

Meagan knew what she wanted. Chris's eyes held her, making her share his excitement. "I like it," she said. In a stronger voice, she added, "I like it very much."

"Good," said Andrew, finishing his beer.

Chris smiled at Meagan, and she was his.

"Let's go," he said.

* * *

164

Chris and Meagan left together, leaving the others in the bar. She took his arm, leading him to her car, never saying a word. There was no need to talk. He knew where they were going—Sickles Street.

She parked under the shadow of an oak tree. They approached the front door side by side, Chris certain of his steps, already knowing every detail of the house: the iron fence and gate, the rough granite steps leading down to the basement apartment.

She had "inherited" it from Mark Schneider. It was a little hideout where, at first, Mark and she had evaded the police, at least until he was invited to Nicaragua. Now it was all hers, just like the D.L.P. And it was all Chris's, if he wanted it.

The thought surprised her, but not enough to take hold. She unlocked the door and walked into the darkness, letting Chris turn on the light. He didn't.

He closed the door and became lost in the shadows. The cold winter moon frosted the window and outlined the apartment. One of the outlines was Meagan, leaning against the corner of a sofa, tugging at her T-shirt. Her arms crossed overhead and her breasts fell free. Chris put his arms around her. "Terry," he whispered. Meagan didn't hear. She pulled him down onto the sofa. Chris kissed her, excited her. Meagan held him tightly. They were naked on the sofa, their clothes carelessly discarded. Chris entered her. For an instant, he was also inside Terry Cooke. He was a child, reaching for a phantom that danced before his fingers, feeling a warm breeze blow on him as he climbed onto a windowsill.

"Mine," Chris whispered. Meagan kissed him. Chris and Terry fell together from the window as the phantom danced away. Far away they heard screams. Chris's mind flickered, fired. He struck the grass bank and looked up through Terry's eyes, seeing her mother's face at the window.

Meagan cried out as Chris possessed her. She was his. Meagan—Terry. They were both his.

When Andrew arrived, Chris and Meagan were finishing a light breakfast of toast and coffee. Now the apartment was grubby in the harsh morning light. The walls were covered by poorly balanced posters; forgotten furniture and a slightly burned rug filled the rest of the room. Sheets were carelessly piled on the sofa. Nearby was a small table with a full ashtray and a hash pipe. Andrew stretched out and lit the last of the marijuana.

"Thursday we'll hit the Chase Manhattan branch at La Guardia," he said, taking a deep breath. "Larry's getting some explosives this afternoon, and I'll make the bomb tomorrow. We'll let Walter deliver it."

Meagan searched the pockets of her coat for a new pack of cigarettes. "How much can he get?" she asked.

"Four pounds."

"What?"

Andrew shrugged. "Blame it on Griffin. Times are tough."

"You won't get the bleedin' door off with that," Chris said.

"Oh, really?" Andrew looked to Meagan. "Since when do your fucks start giving orders?"

Meagan lit her cigarette. "Chris is right," she said.

Andrew finally gave Chris his attention, and Chris returned it, tuning into Andrew's thoughts. Sooner or later, Andrew would try to kill him. Chris left an imprint in Andrew's mind, a feeling that if he followed through on the idea, it might bring him a great deal of grief.

Andrew sat forward on the sofa and said, "If the 'bleeding' doors won't come off, what does your twelve-inch prick have in mind?"

"I'll let you know this afternoon," Chris said.

"Real leadership," Andrew said sarcastically.

Chris rose and walked to the door. He turned back to face Andrew.

"This afternoon." He forced a smile. "Or would you like to share some more thoughts on the matter now?"

Andrew still didn't move. Chris left the door open and crossed to the sofa.

"You wanna play games with me, sunshine?"

Andrew rose, waiting for Chris to break. Chris didn't care.

"Come on, then," Chris taunted.

Andrew backed off. He glanced at Meagan and said, "He's a real motherfucker, isn't he?" She didn't answer. Andrew was on his own. "I'll tell Larry," Andrew said. He expected an answer, but no one spoke. The way Chris watched him, Andrew wasn't certain he'd make it out the door. He touched his pocket, rubbing his knife, waiting for Chris to attack.

Chris stepped aside.

"You and Larry come back here," he said.

"Don't worry. I'll be back," Andrew answered.

When the door closed, Meagan sat on the sofa. Chris leaned against the wall and closed his eyes.

"You don't want to do that," Meagan said. "Don't push Andrew."

He barely heard her. His head was filled with a new flurry of sensations—marvelously deadly. They came from Andrew, from Meagan. . . . It wouldn't surprise him to find that Mark Schneider had somehow sneaked in.

"I'll be back later," he said at last. "I've got to go to work."

"Work?" The thought surprised and amused her.

"I'll see you later."

He walked outside, slamming the door. Meagan went to the window and watched him climb the steps to the sidewalk. The sun bleached his face. She saw him squinting because of the harsh light, and imagined his relief when he was again hidden by the shade.

Murray's desk was a mess; it was not an unusual sight by any means, but this time it was hidden by galleys from the week's magazine. Along with the galleys was the published copy, complete with Chris's photograph of Terry Cooke and John Griffin, posing for the camera. A banner teased of more photos with a feature article.

"Hot off the presses," Murray said. Chris glanced at the copy. He looked and felt exhausted. Without an invitation, he settled on a sofa and threw back his head, opening his mouth. Murray settled back in his chair.

"You need some sleep."

"You always were quick, Murray."

"I can tell these things." Murray waved a copy of the magazine. "You know I didn't want you doing this kind of story."

"Here we go again," Chris said.

"Good stuff, though. *Usable* for a change. If you can get any more photos like this—"

Chris drooped forward, rubbing his eyes and finally giving Murray his full attention.

"I doubt it."

"Tom said you were on to a story."

"I've got a lot on my mind."

"What's that mean?" Murray felt annoyed. Chris always baffled him. "Anything you want to—"

"No. Thanks."

Murray looked down at his desk and pulled free some loose sheets of paper. "See this?" Chris took one of the sheets. It was an Associated Press wire:

A.P.—PESHAWAR, PAKISTAN. 4:15 A.M. A THREE-MAN B.B.C. CAMERA CREW AND FIVE TRIBESMEN WERE REPORTED KILLED TODAY IN HINDU KUSH,

AFGHANISTAN. THE BRITISH FOREIGN OFFICE THIS
MORNING LISTED THE NAMES AS EDWARD BOS-
WORTH, REPORTER, THIRTY-ONE, OF SURREY,
ENGLAND; ALISTAIR WATSON, CAMERAMAN, THIRTY-
SEVEN, OF DUNDEE, SCOTLAND . . .

Chris stopped reading.

"They were in the mountains with a rebel camp," explained Murray. "You remember Bosworth, don't you?
Worked with him once or twice in Lebanon."

Chris felt too tired to react.

"Thought you'd like to know, that's all."

"What were they working on?"

"Follow up on a Pentagon report. It's in the wire."

"I haven't read the bleeding wire."

"You're holding the fucking thing."

"Then I didn't read all of it."

"Agent Orange," said Murray. "Or some other goddamned chemical. The Russians are spraying the stuff all
over the mountains."

"Bloody typical." Chris rose wearily, giving Murray a
last smile. All Murray saw was a grimace. "Wonder if
Bosworth filed his story before they shot him."

"Probably," Murray said. "Get some sleep, all right?"

Chris left the building and walked east to the river. He
wandered to a forgotten dock that extended into the water.
He sat on a post and watched the water wash the edges of
the city, patiently picking at it; a piece of asphalt here, a
chunk of tar there. Hundreds of years. Thousands of years.
Made no difference. Sooner or later the river would win,
and the city would be worn down to nothing.

He climbed down to a concrete pile and slapped the
water with his heel. A bottle and a soggy cardboard box
floated past. Chris threw a stone, thinking of Bosworth,
wondering what it must have been like dying in the moun-

tains. Hell, Russians, Yanks, there was no difference. Bosworth had just learned the hard way.

Imagine, Bosworth—of all people. Some anonymous Soviet gunship swooshing down from the sun, the machine-gunner hanging out the open doorway spraying the campsite with tracers, rockets swishing in an arc, an orange trail of smoke behind them. The chaos below, the people diving for cover, some of them dead before they hit the ground. One of those bullets could cut a man in half.

Chris picked up a piece of brick and took aim at an aluminum can bobbing on the water. Then there was the D.L.P. What to do with them? How to use them? The bomb was incidental. An idea was slowly surfacing in his mind. If he gave it time, it would reveal itself, no doubt about that. He looked at a bottle twisting inland with the tide, its neck barely out of the water. It stirred a gentle circle. He concentrated on it. *Just keep it still,* he thought. *Hold the bottle motionless. Mind over matter—from the complex to the simple.*

Chris returned to Sickles Street at one A.M. Meagan was there. So were Andrew and Walter.

"We've lost the dynamite," Andrew said. Chris waited for an explanation. Meagan folded her arms and blew out a stream of cigarette smoke.

"Cops busted Larry," said Walter. "Grabbed him in his cab."

"And?"

"The dynamite was in the trunk," Andrew finished.

"There's nothing we can do," said Walter. "We can't do anything without Larry."

It was all so predictable, and it was all because of Terry Cooke. She was drawing closer. Soon Terry and Chris would again be close enough to touch. Chris sat down in front of Meagan. "Go and pack," he told her.

170

Meagan didn't seem to hear. Chris jerked her arm, pulling her toward him.

"What's the point?" she whispered.

"This place isn't safe anymore," Chris said.

"Larry won't tell."

"He won't *have* to."

"How else would they know?" asked Meagan. "John's never been here."

"I'm not thinking of him." He turned to Andrew. "You got a place where we can stay?"

"Sure," Andrew said, "but I'm not stupid." He glanced accusingly at Walter.

Chris reached for a pen and scribbled an address on the side of a grocery bag. He tore off his message and gave it to Meagan. She read it and passed it to Andrew. Andrew read the message.

"So much for secrets," Andrew said pointedly.

"Now, bugger off and find me some fresh explosives," Chris said to Andrew. "Walter, you get me a chemist. And you," he told Meagan, "come with me."

Andrew crumpled the message and threw it across the room. Chris picked up the paper, lit a match, and set the message on fire. He crumpled the ashes in a fist.

Andrew hid his anger behind a tired laugh. "He's not for real, is he?" he asked Meagan.

"Do as he says," she replied.

Walter touched Chris's arm. "Chemist?" he asked. "You mean for dope?"

"A biochemist," said Chris. "A good one."

"I don't know any biochemists."

"Try the universities."

Walter looked to Meagan for help. "I mean, once I find one, what do I do?"

"Just get me the name, all right, Walter?" Chris insisted. "That's all I need. Just the name. I'll take care of the rest."

"For what?" Andrew demanded.

Chris ignored him. Everything was fitting together. He felt contented, and it touched everyone in the room.

Then he thought of Bosworth, Francine, and the old Arab.

"It's time," Chris said.

Thirteen

The next day was when the police seized Meagan's Sickles Street apartment. While the local precinct sealed off the block, Terry Cooke and the bomb squad went systematically through the apartment, then the building. Nothing escaped their attention. Bomb-squad officers looked through the closets; Terry checked the sofa and tore open pillows. Together they pried up the floorboards. If there were no arms or explosives, she wanted clues. A fingerprint, a forgotten book of matches, a phone number scribbled on the wall. A forensics officer carefully took away a pile of ashes in an ashtray but in the end could do nothing with them.

Chris opened his eyes. He let the picture of police futility disappear and concentrated instead on the man in front of him. Stanley something with a biology degree from Columbia University. Associate professor, Walter had said. Chris had no reason to doubt the credentials; Stanley looked and talked the part. When pressed, he even had the patronizing temper of a teacher.

Stanley's disposition, however, was being kept in check. Chris needed information, not a lesson. Stanley frowned and scratched his chin, considering Chris's question.

"Well, I suppose if you could find a way to get the stuff active again, then you could make a soup of it. Of course, you'd still need a way to disperse it so the vapors were inhaled."

He paused, looking up, as if Chris had interrupted him. Chris had, but not with words. Andrew eyed them both with confused hostility. He did not like being left out.

"Yes," Stanley answered. "With some help, I could."

"Could what?" Andrew asked.

"Shut up!" Chris snapped. Stanley felt Andrew's distrust and wriggled uncomfortably. He was scared. He couldn't recall how he had come to be in this room with these people, and he knew he was completely at their mercy. Indeed, he felt his life depended upon keeping them happy. It was the most insidious fear Stanley had ever felt. And whenever the fear weakened, Chris bolstered it.

Stanley cleared his throat. "How many—?" He looked around the room for support. "How many bombs are we—?"

"Ten," said Chris.

"Which means, of course, we'll need at least a hundred pounds of explosives," said Andrew. "Which we don't have."

"Can you do it?" Chris asked the biochemist.

"Certainly," said Stanley. "I mean, I'll need a safe place, some equipment for a lab, a good culture."

"Don't worry about all that," said Chris.

"I'll take care of the place," Meagan offered. Hell, she thought. Why did I just volunteer to do that?

173

"It's Wednesday now," said Chris. "I want them ready by Monday."

"It all depends on the culture," Stanley said warily. Chris gazed at him. "It'll have to be healthy," Stanley dared to press.

"Don't worry."

"And we may need quite a bit."

"I said, don't worry. All right?"

Andrew laughed cynically. "Jesus Christ! Where are you hiding this stuff?"

Chris grinned. "I don't have to. It's lying in the ground in Scotland."

"That's right," Stanley said. "Gruinard Island. I should have thought of it myself."

"Never heard of it," Meagan said, lighting a cigarette.

"The place is completely contaminated," Chris said. "It's exactly what we need." He looked at Meagan. "Goes back to some tests during the war, when England developed an anthrax bomb to beat Hitler. Your lot built the thing, and our scientists at Porton Down designed what went inside and then tested it."

"Why didn't they build more of the bombs?" asked Andrew.

"Churchill wanted to, but the Cabinet stopped him. Fuck your atom bombs. We made one that could *really* do the job. Terrified everybody."

Chris sat back on the sofa.

"They *never* used it?" Meagan asked.

"It was too bleedin' dangerous, darlin'. Problem with it was you killed the land as well as the people. Would have made Europe a desert. They lost their bottle."

"Huh?" Andrew asked, irritated.

"Like I said, they got scared. Gawd-and-Bennett, they reckon anthrax was the fifth plague of Egypt. What do you think would have happened if they'd set off a few dozen plague bombs all over Germany?"

174

"Or New York, for that matter," Stanley commented. Chris eyed Stanley, amused with his biochemist.

"So what does this have to do with some shitty little Scottish island?" asked Andrew.

Stanley cleared his throat. "See, they didn't use the bomb, but they did test it—at Gruinard. Gruinard's in the Hebrides, about six hundred yards off the Scottish mainland."

"How big is it?" Meagan asked.

"What? The island?" Stanley asked. "Not very. Quarter mile, half mile—something like that. Big enough for a field and a dozen or so sheep. That's what the English did, you see. They put sheep on the island, waited for the wind to blow out to sea, then sent a plane over to drop the bomb."

"What's wind got to do with it?" asked Andrew.

"Think about it," said Chris.

"That's how anthrax kills," explained Stanley. "You inhale it. Doesn't take long before you get a high fever, and your skin breaks out. Then your lungs collapse. It's very unpleasant. Once the symptoms begin, it all happens so fast that by the time anyone's isolated the bacteria, the patient's dead."

"Highly contagious," Chris said.

"So they sprayed the island with anthrax?" asked Meagan.

"Not exactly," Stanley corrected. "The point of the test was to see if the bacteria could survive the high temperatures of an explosion."

"It did," Chris commented.

"Absolutely," Stanley went on blithely. "Unfortunately, they didn't foresee the bacteria settling in the ground, where it's still alive, forty years later. Be alive for God knows how long. The whole thing's kind of an open secret over there. One big, poisonous embarrassment." Stanley stopped talking, suddenly listening to himself. He

175

was being so cavalier, as if nothing would be more interesting than to explode one of these bombs in New York City. "My God!" he murmured.

"Must be tough to get at," said Andrew.

"That's the point," said Chris. "A few signs up, that's all. Skulls and crossbones."

"Come on," Meagan said. "There must be more to it than that."

"There isn't. Not one bloody soldier. They don't even patrol by sea. Who'd be stupid enough to go and get himself infected? There ain't no cure."

"You can see their point of view," Stanley interrupted.

"From their island to this one," said Chris. "Every fucking war in this world's been caused by profit and pig bloody ignorance. Enough is enough. It's time they realized their little game can't go on."

"What are you talking about?" Andrew asked.

"Nothing you'd understand."

Andrew calmed himself. There was a silent understanding between Chris and himself; Andrew would follow orders until Chris made a mistake. Then he would make his move. All of life should be so straightforward.

Stanley coughed into a fist, breaking the mood. "I'll need at least two days—"

"You'll get your culture," Chris promised. "I got just the man for the job." He entered Stanley's mind one last time. "When we're done with this, I don't ever want to see you again. Understand?"

"Sure," Stanley stammered.

"Make sure of it," Chris said.

As Andrew led Stanley to the door, Chris grabbed Andrew's arm and pulled him aside. "Don't fuck up, will you?" he told him quietly.

When the others had left, Chris took Meagan to bed. Only when they had finished making love did her doubts begin to surface—the sort of doubts usually whispered to

176

a lover. Doubts she had buried deeply since meeting Chris. He sensed the turmoil of her thoughts. She was his, but as she softly called his name, Chris also sensed her fear. Chris kept his eyes closed. He felt so tired.

"Chris, what are we demanding?"

His eyes opened and he looked at her. Her face was a pale, distant thing, almost forgotten.

"We've never done anything like this before, that's all."

Terry, he thought. Meagan, Andrew, Gruinard—an end to all the madness.

"What do we want, Chris? What did Mark tell you?"

Chris rolled on his side and faced her. "There's nothing we want from them," he told her. He could feel her confusion, filling and distracting his mind with useless thoughts. He wished she would stop so that he could think straight.

"What's the point, then?" she asked.

"Listen, darlin'. You Yanks in Vietnam, Central America, the Russians in Afghanistan, Poland. Everyone uses force to get rid of governments they don't like. That's all we're doing. That's all they understand."

"But why this?"

Chris turned to her for a moment. "Because I asked you to." Meagan had no ready answer. He rolled away from her. At times his head seemed full of other people's craziness.

Terry, he thought. He closed his eyes, drifting off to sleep. He imagined a bedroom window and felt himself rising from the bed. He walked to the window and looked down. He saw a little girl, curled motionless on the grass beneath, a bloody gash across her forehead. Her eyes stared blankly up at him.

Terry, he called to the child. He reached toward her and found himself on a bridge in Venice, a fine mist obscuring everything in view. He leaned against the parapet, watching the light of a gondola grow brighter. Two children

177

were sitting near the front and heading toward the tunnel. Chris saw the little girl look up and laugh, mocking him. He turned quickly and crossed to the other side of the bridge, waiting for the gondola to reappear. It didn't.

Time past, time present.

He was back in Mozambique, at the beginning of the road that had led him around the world to New York and the D.L.P. He was walking down a dusty street, surrounded by passive faces. He studied them one by one—the wrinkles, the etched-in dirt, the cracked lips and distended bellies. There was an explosion as a land mine detonated less than twenty meters away. Then came gunshots and screams. It was the first time he had ever witnessed anything quite like this. With all his other memories, there was still a freshness to this one. A continuing sense of shock and excitement.

Time past, time present.

Chris curled against the woman lying beside him. He could feel her attraction to him. His hands began caressing her bare skin. How could she resist? He felt the woman respond sluggishly to his touch, at first surrendering, then fighting the feelings he aroused. Together, they saw a hand beckon to them.

Time past, time present.

Chris was a child again. But it was different. The sights and sounds were nothing he had experienced before. They were *her* sights and sounds. Terry's. No, not Terry. Someone else—

Jennifer!

Time present.

Chris rolled onto his back. Something in Terry made him feel weak, but he needed her. He wished Terry was with him now.

Meagan snored softly. Chris rubbed his temples. In an act of casual tenderness, he formed a calming dream for Meagan and rolled away. She wasn't Terry, but so what?

178

Tomorrow, who knew where they all might be? Or, for that matter, who would be living?

Chris spent Thursday afternoon making preparations.

He took a seat in the corner of the British Airways office on Fifth Avenue and browsed through a *Visit Great Britain* magazine. Three operators in starched blue-and-red uniforms were busy. He waited for an opportunity, glancing at an article about a military tattoo held in Aldershot during the summer.

Chris noticed a young blond woman sitting by a computer terminal. He entered her thoughts and felt the keyboard beneath his fingers. He closed his eyes and in his mind saw the screen. He gave the woman his instructions, and twenty minutes later left the office. All he had to do now was contact his courier and the anthrax would be in Manhattan within forty-eight hours—provided, of course, the police didn't interfere.

To be certain he wasn't caught off guard, he returned once more to Terry Cooke. Such a difficult life she led— frazzled and deadly, comforted at the end of the day by a numbing suburban security. She was a long way from catching on to what he was doing. Chris did, however, take an interest in a trauma she now faced. She was on the verge of discovery—something Chris had gone through on his own many years before. Tomorrow was her day to be tested for psychic skills.

This would be no small discovery for Terry Cooke; Chris knew from experience. The moment of realization was one of awe and delight. In an instant, it gave the world a new dimension, new colors, new tastes, new smells. A place for tinkering, repairing, and creating in a way more fundamental than most people could imagine. Would Terry appreciate the pleasures awaiting her?

* * *

The next day, Friday, shortly before Terry arrived, Chris entered the institute, knowing exactly who to contact.

"I think I'm psychic," he told Dr. Emily Goldin. She looked up at him, taking a mild interest, busy with preparations.

Chris looked through the long glass window and saw two assistants wheel a woman into a laboratory. Goldin tried directing Chris to someone else.

"I'm really busy," Goldin said.

Chris pointed across the room. "What's it called when you can move things around just by thinking about it?"

"Psychokinesis."

"Yeah."

"Affecting an object without any physical contact."

"Yeah," said Chris. "Show me how you do that."

Goldin smiled, despite herself. "You sound as if you're in a toy store. That's one of the more elusive psychic abilities."

"But I'm already psychic. I just can't make things move."

"Already psychic," Goldin repeated, still amused. "Look, being a telepath doesn't guarantee you'll also be a psychokinetic." She stopped talking long enough to answer a telephone. It was Terry Cooke, on her way upstairs. "Anyway, we can test psychic skills, but we haven't had much luck training anyone."

"I'm different."

'What makes you so certain you're telepathic?"

Now it was Chris's turn to smile. "Why don't you test me?"

Goldin studied him a moment. Chris pointed toward the elevator as the floor lights flashed.

"Put me with *her*."

Goldin looked puzzled, but Chris pressed a finger to his lips and disappeared into a waiting room. She shrugged him off, glanced at her watch, and rushed to find some more equipment before Terry Cooke arrived with Becker.

Chris sat on the sofa, his senses growing stronger as Terry approached. He heard her steps, her voice. He felt her nervous energy pressing against the hallway walls.

"Name?" asked a secretary. Chris looked up. He tried thinking of a name. Something that would give Terry a clue.

"Murray Hunt," he said.

"Age?"

Chris lied. With each of the secretary's questions, he invented an answer. It was a short interview, over in a matter of minutes. By the time they finished, the secretary's profile sheet was nothing but fabrication.

The secretary glanced at the information. "All right, Mr. Hunt. Follow me, please."

"This is gonna be fun," Chris said brightly.

The secretary murmured agreement, not particularly interested. Chris was shown into a computer room and seated before a terminal.

"This is very simple," an assistant said tiredly. "The computer is going to randomly choose one of five different shapes stored in its memory. You've got to predict the shapes the computer chooses. Do you understand?"

Chris played with the keyboard.

"I said, do you understand?"

"How much time do I get?"

"An hour," the assistant said. "Up to a minute per question. Is that a problem?"

"No."

Chris finished the test in four minutes. No one had ever before tried to gauge his abilities. At best, he'd attempted to find his own limitations. He enjoyed being the center of all this scientific attention.

"These are amazing," Goldin told Chris when she saw his scores.

"I'm really interested in parakin-what's-it," he said airily.

"Psychokinesis," Goldin corrected him. "PK, for short." She looked to her assistant, waving a tear sheet of Chris's test results. "These can't be right."

The assistant pretended he hadn't heard.

"I want to do them again," Goldin said to Chris. "Would you mind?"

"PK," he said.

Goldin sighed. She looked to her assistant. "Let's just keep going, all right?"

Chris was growing impatient. Where was Terry now? What were they doing to her?

"You gonna put me and that bird together?" he asked Goldin. She looked surprised.

"As a matter of fact, I am thinking about putting you with *somebody*." She paused. "We'll put you in one room and our other volunteer in another."

Chris considered the plan. Terry and PK. Those were his goals.

"We'll have you take turns sending messages to each other. One of you sends; the other receives. Then we'll turn it around."

"Sounds fine," Chris said. "She'll be in one room; I'll be in the other."

"A *volunteer* will be in the other room," Goldin emphasized, carefully leaving out the gender.

"Whatever you say," Chris answered, delighted. "Let's get on with it."

Goldin had the assistant lead Chris into an isolation room. There were a few more rules to the game, but he barely listened. Instead, he concentrated on the small details of his padded room, particularly the door. He tried turning the handle without touching it. What a useful power that would be.

The rain is heavy.

182

It was a whisper, but it was clear. Terry was sending him a message. Chris listened attentively, and her psychic voice grew stronger.

The rain is heavy.

Terry was reaching for him, taking the first step. Chris congratulated her. There were so many things about this woman he admired. If only he could make her appreciate his feelings. If he could only make clear to her how dangerous it was to stand against him.

I have two children.

The words tickled him. They were shy kisses of introduction, welcoming him into her life. Terry and he were revealing more of themselves than any pair of lovers. He waited impatiently to become the sender.

When it came he whispered, *Hello, Terry.*

A pause. He sensed her startled reaction and smiled.

See, I know who you are. If you try hard, you'll know my name, too.

He felt her panic rising. He decided to taunt her.

What happened at Sickles Street, then?

He could see her struggling with the doorknob, trying to escape his voice.

I know all your secrets, Terry. There's nothing about you I don't know.

You were great in bed.

He could feel her fighting him, trying to get away.

Don't fight me, Terry. I'll kill you if I have to. Don't make me do it Terry. I don't want to. Don't make me.

Chris rose from the chair and left the room. He could feel the power flickering. When Goldin stopped him, he fanned it into a blaze, unleashing it on her. Then he rested against a wall, staring at the distant elevator. He folded his hands and gauged the distance. A few feet of air separated him from the button.

Chris concentrated, forming an image of the button in his mind.

183

Push!

The elevator button lit.

PK.

Suddenly there was so much more for him to see and to learn. He owed it all to Terry Cooke.

Now there was one final piece of the puzzle to set in place.

Chris knocked on the office door and looked inside. "Murray?"

Murray raised a finger, his head tilted against a telephone, scribbling notes with a free hand. Chris entered the office and closed the door, taking his place on Murray's sofa. Bright sunshine poured through the window and stung his eyes. Chris didn't block it. A little pain made the task easier.

Murray hung up the phone and smiled. "About time you came by." Chris smiled back, but his expression was bleary, his red eyes wet from fatigue. Murray felt more depressed every time Chris came to see him. Drugs, Murray thought. Chris was slowly killing himself.

"You keeping yourself entertained? Christ knows, you haven't been showing up here."

Chris looked past Murray to the window. His eyes turned directly into the sun. "I was walking down Fifth Avenue yesterday. I've been thinking about a few things."

The telephone rang, and Murray again raised his finger. Chris stopped talking, letting Murray take his call. After a minute, Murray shouted a string of curses and slammed down the phone. "Fucking thing never stops ringing. You want to go out for a drink? We won't get any peace here."

"No, mate. There's not enough time."

"What?"

"You're the last link, me old son."

Murray leaned forward, eyeing Chris curiously. Definitely drugs. "What the hell are you talking about?"

Chris said, "I've had enough, mate. I'm going to do something."

Murray wiped his face, helpless before such nonsense. "I don't understand a word you're saying."

"It's time for change," Chris said. "Time that the bubble was burst."

"It's time you saw a doctor," Murray answered.

Chris glared at him. "It's a farce, Murray. We're propping up a system that's been doomed for decades. We've always told ourselves that what we do is important, right? Informed people are educated people, ain't that what you told me once?"

"Well, I . . ." Murray thought hard, trying to remember if he had ever said any such thing. Maybe in a bar, while on the trail of some story in Nicaragua. Maybe not. Somehow most of what Chris said sounded as if it belonged to someone else. "I don't remember."

"Of course you don't. You're like all the rest. You don't care. But you're wrong. I'm sick of hearing about 'special considerations' to be made by the politicians and the bankers and all the other bastards. No one wants to take any responsibility. No one important ever says, 'Let's help.' They're too eager to drop a bomb on someone instead and steal what's left. Who needs it? Nobody gives a shit. The only time human beings ever do anything is when it hurts."

Murray began rising from his chair.

"Sit down!" Chris shouted.

Murray's legs collapsed. It was as if someone had severed his spine.

"Jesus Christ!" he muttered.

Chris left the sofa and paced in front of the desk. "No more and that's it, you know? It's time to stop the bastards."

"Chris, my legs—"

"That's why I'm here, Murray. You're my friend. But I ain't got no more friends. There's no other way. No friends means freedom, see? I'll be able to breathe again." He rubbed his aching head, out of patience.

Murray stared at Chris, terrified. Chris *was* crazy. Worse, he was trying to make Murray crazy, too. He pushed up at his seat, leaning on the desk, shouting for his secretary.

Chris took away his voice.

"We don't need them anyway," Chris told him.

Or at least Murray *thought* Chris was talking. He waited for Chris's lips to move, but they didn't. So how the hell could he hear Chris?

Oh, my God, Murray thought.

You're my way out, Chris thought, his voice echoing inside Murray's head. *See, you're perfect for what I need. You travel to Europe all the time. Five or six hours to Scotland. Back by dawn. Common sort of trip for you.*

Oh, Jesus!

And getting you to fetch it makes you part of it all, makes me more committed. A friend to the fire, so to speak. We finish tonight, you and me, and there's no turning back for either of us. I'm sorry.

The telephone rang and Murray flinched, his hand instinctively reaching for it. Chris looked at the phone. Before Murray's hand touched the receiver, the phone slid across the desk and flung itself against the wall.

Chris felt pleased. "I had to tell you all this," he said aloud. "Call it a final gesture, if you want. We was friends when I came in here, but I ain't got room for such things no more."

Murray opened his mouth, gagging on his thoughts, trying desperately to speak. His face darkened and distorted as he struggled for a sound. The agony ended the moment Chris took complete control of Murray's mind.

At three o'clock, Chris brought Murray to Kennedy Airport. Murray paid for the first of the tickets Chris had reserved. Then he boarded the three-thirty P.M. flight to London's Heathrow Airport. Chris went to the parking lot and watched the hooknosed Concorde take off.

When Murray arrived in London, everything happened quickly. Once Chris had planted the details in Murray's head, Murray himself made the final arrangements. A helicopter ferried him to Gatwick Airport, where a charter flight flew him to a small airfield in the Hebrides. A hired car was waiting. Murray tipped the driver, dismissed him, and took the keys. He would drive himself. He had some speed limits to break.

The ten-foot fishing boat bounced through the waves, its propellers rising out of the choppy water and frothing the surface. Murray sat at the stern, the tiller held tightly under his arm as he steered toward the dim outline of Gruinard Island. He felt a strange elation as the hill of An Eilid rose out of the moonlit, early-morning mist.

He ran the boat up a stony beach and dragged it out of the water. Then he leaned against the timbers to catch his breath. Out of shape, he thought.

He looked at his watch, clumsily holding his flashlight as he pulled back the cuffs of his coat. Two-fifteen. A chilling southeast wind blew in from the Hebrides. Murray reached back in the boat, leaned over the gunwale; and retrieved a large, round metal canister. The wind snatched his breath as he walked along the beach, the flashlight catching the shingle just before his shoes crunched down. A strong, fresh smell of heather stung his nose, and he tucked his coat collar about his throat. He blew on his gloved hands, trying to warm them, his flashlight momentarily blinding him.

Gradually, his eyes became reaccustomed to the moonlight. The beam of the flashlight caught a large warning sign, its writing faded after forty years of exposure. The beam went beyond the sign, sweeping the island. Murray

187

trudged toward the hill, his legs now deep in rhyme-encrusted heather and gorse. The beam picked out wild new growth to his left, perhaps the legacy of a brush fire. He moved away from it, heading up the slope of the three-hundred-fifty-foot hill. He passed the abandoned remains of an old crofter's cottage. The moon was slowly descending and the top of the hill cut a sharp curve against it.

Here was a spot. Murray dropped on his knees, tossing the container to his side. It hit a stone hidden by a clump of frozen heather. The sound died quickly in the wind. Murray lifted the canister, checking its sides and unscrewing the top. Satisfied, he settled both near the flashlight. He grasped a heather bush by its roots and heaved back. A plug of dirt came out of the ground. Murray threw away the heather and dug into the small pit. One inch. Two. Fresh, lethal dirt from Gruinard Island piled around the hole. Some worked its way inside the sheepskin lining of his gloves. Murray brushed out the dirt, grimaced, and dug deeper, bending low over the hole to see what he was doing. He had to dig deeper. The soil sample was better the farther down he went. More alive. More deadly.

He paused and straightened the flashlight a last time. Then he grasped the canister, plunging it deep into the pit. Damn the gloves. He took them off and scraped at the dirt, shoveling handfuls into his canister.

The dirt moved easily beneath his fingers and the wind caught it. Murray coughed as the fresh earth sprayed into his face.

Fourteen

"Terry?" Artie whispered, leaning over the bed. He pulled the blanket up to her neck and tucked it in.

Terry didn't move. She heard his voice but couldn't answer. For hours she had been listening to another voice—one inside her head. A voice that forced her into the past.

"Terry?" Artie repeated. He laid a hand on her shoulder. Artie could whisper all he liked, but Terry was gone from him. She was fourteen years old again, in the rear of a classroom, waiting impatiently for the sister to end Bible class.

"The Ninety-second Psalm, Theresa?"

Terry had hated her school. Her parents sent her there less for the religious instruction than the discipline.

Terry stood up and recited: " ' O Lord, how great are Thy works! And Thy thoughts are very deep. A brutish man knoweth not; neither doth a fool understand this. When the wicked spring as the grass, and when all the workers of iniquity do flourish; it is that they shall be destroyed forever.' "

"Catherine," said the teacher, "continue."

Terry sat down. The other girl rose and recited: " 'Mine eye also shall see my desire on mine enemies, and mine ears shall hear my desire of the wicked that rise up against me. The righteous shall flourish like a palm: He shall grow like a cedar in Lebanon. . . .' '' The endless drone of verse continued. The words went in and out of Terry's ears.

"Theresa," said the sister. Terry stood up.

" 'To shew that the Lord is upright: He is my rock, and there is no unrighteousness in Him,' " she said.

"And what does that mean, Theresa?"

Terry looked blankly at the sister. What did *what* mean? When she recited a passage, she didn't *listen*. It was too boring. "That the Lord is the source of all goodness; that our strength comes from the Lord, and no one else," she said.

"Yes," replied the nun. "Exactly my thoughts." She gave a quick, thin smile. Terry sat down. The class repeated the phrase together, with Terry as lifeless as the others. She was always being teased for saying just the right thing in a pinch.

Artie. Tell me about him, a man's voice commanded.

In her dream, Terry found herself wandering in a hazy gallery of her life. Artie. They had married when she was nineteen. In hindsight, she was really too young, but at the time it was all she had wanted.

They had met through a mutual friend. Artie was Terry's second boyfriend. While not particularly shy, she had rarely taken an interest in dating. Before Artie, she had preferred staying at home, where her father and his cop friends traded stories over a poker table littered with beer cans.

Terry had always presumed she would lose her virginity to one of her father's buddies. She felt their eyes whenever they visited the house. But during one particularly long autumn weekend, it was shy and intense Artie who became her lover.

Why him? the voice asked.

190

Terry had no answer. Artie was neither handsome nor especially clever. He was someone she had met by chance while attending classes, another set of eyes that watched her as she walked in the hallways. Yet, for a while, he had been a kindred spirit. Someone to talk to and with whom to have fun.

Once she encouraged him, though, there had been no refuge from his affection. Her mother said Artie was obsessive. Terry, lacking any experience, couldn't tell the difference between love and obsession. If it was obsession that drove Artie, then it was obsession Terry wanted. They married, and within a few months Terry felt Artie and she were devouring each other. At the same time, Terry's classes gave her a way out.

She was saved by an obscure pre-law U.C.L.A. teacher—a man who would never know his profound influence on her. Still, without his lessons in law, Terry would never have discovered her own passion. Law. People needed laws more than doctors, perhaps even more than they needed each other.

They moved east, and Terry discovered she wanted to administer the laws, not write them. What better place to enforce rules than the unruly streets of New York City?

A wonderful place, the voice agreed.

A place of darkness, Terry thought.

Yes.

A city in need of rescue. Purge the tenements of their demons and ghosts.

Purge them, or join them?

Purge them. For Sean and Jennifer. For Artie and herself. She wanted to keep the world sane.

Another memory stirred into life.

"I was in the top five of my class," she heard herself say. Terry saw fat Harry Caruso reach across his desk, his pudgy fingers patting her hand.

Oh, yes. The Intelligence Division interview. Harry Caruso, an instructor at the New York Police Academy. Also an I.D. recruiter. Terry had worked hard to win this man's attention, first as a student, then as a liaison officer. If Caruso liked her, and if she didn't screw up, she'd make I.D. despite the hiring freeze. I.D. could do that.

"I'm not a kid," Terry said.

"Oh, I know that," said Caruso. "You've got two of your own, though, don't you?"

Terry didn't answer. Caruso studied her. "Mrs. Cooke?"

"So, I've got two kids," Terry said defensively.

"Be difficult to manage a couple of kids and a job like this, won't it?"

"No."

He leaned back in his chair and smiled. "Every twenty-five-year-old thinks he's—excuse me, she's—got the world by the balls. When you get older, you realize it's the other way around."

"Women don't have that problem."

Caruso grinned. "That's right." He closed her file. "Incidentally, there's no need to be modest. You were head of your class, not just in the first five."

Terry waited. The job was hers; it had to be.

"I'll think about it," Caruso said.

"I want this job," Terry told him.

"Maybe." He smiled and extended a hand. They shook. She'd earned this job. Terry was ready for investigations. Damm it—what more did they want?

You got the job, the voice asked.

Yes.

But not from Caruso. He didn't like you, did he? He chose someone else.

Caruso's a shit, she thought.

Who cares? You got the assignment. *You got rid of Caruso. Put him in a rehab clinic with a little push of the old psi.*

192

No, she thought. *Caruso was near retirement. He got upset, and started drinking, and—*

He laughed at her.

Caruso fell apart because you went into his head and grabbed him by the balls, the voice said. *You made him lose. You don't give up easily, do you?*

I didn't, she insisted.

It's your strength. Look at the way you trapped Artie. The way you get every bloody thing you want.

No!

Peas in a pod, Terry. You and me, peas in a pod.

"No," she murmured aloud. "God, no."

The door's open, Terry. Can't be closed. You'll find out. I can help you. Trust me.

Fifteen

Three hours later, Terry was in the kitchen making coffee. She wore no makeup and had on jeans and a black, shapeless polo-neck sweater. She waited until the black liquid was slapping the glass dome, then switched off the percolator and poured herself a full cup. She drank it without milk or sugar, and, more important, *alone.* The other chairs were pulled tightly against the table.

Terry was relieved by her temporary isolation; no children drained her energy, and no husband demanded her time and attention. She assumed Artie was in his study working. There was no other reason for this rare moment; he was always hovering over her these days. Terry could see that now—her dream man had helped her see it.

What was his name?

Terry rubbed her eyes, still tired. Fifteen hours of sleep didn't seem enough. If only he could leave her head and sit at the table for five minutes. What would he look like? Would he be an enemy or a lover?

A door opened somewhere in the house, and Terry heard the shuffle of Artie's steps.

Go away, she pleaded silently.

"I didn't know you were up," Artie said. He pulled out a chair and sat across from her. "How are you feeling?" There was a faint resignation to his tone. Terry bowed her head, her hands pushing away her fallen hair.

She finally looked up. Artie was pouring himself a cup of coffee. He peered into it, rubbing his beard stubble.

"Terry—"

He touched her arm and she flinched.

"Anyone would think you'd been given a month to live," he said.

"I'm fine."

"No, you're not."

"The doctor said I was perfectly healthy."

"*Screw* the doctor." His hand snaked out and grabbed her wrist. He was convinced his grip was the last hold he had on her. His fingers pressed deep into her skin.

"For Christ's sake, Artie!"

Terry's thoughts were clear. She knew all he wanted was a sign of encouragement from her, something that showed she still wanted him in her world.

"Let go," she said calmly. Artie's grip tightened and he leaned toward her.

"What's wrong with you?" he insisted.

194

"Nothing," she said. "There's *nothing* wrong with me."

She spoke his name softly. Artie barely noticed.

"I wish you could see yourself," he said.

He let go of her. There was a long pause, while Terry rubbed her wrist, holding it close to her chest. Terry shivered. Her mother had once said that whenever a person shivered, someone had just walked on their grave.

"I'm frightened," she admitted quietly. "Everything's out of control."

He let out a deep breath. "Whose fault is that? Mine?"

Terry was quiet a moment. "Until a week ago everything was fine," she said.

"No, everything wasn't fine. Not here." There was no reply. "There's always this wall with you, Terry. There's a part of you nobody can reach. I used to think it was just some annoying trick you picked up at work to make you seem more mysterious. Then I realized half the time you don't even know you're doing it."

She hesitated, wanting to be honest, but certain her honesty would complete the disintegration of her life.

"What?" Artie prompted.

"I feel numb. To everything." She looked into his eyes, but he avoided her gaze. "I did love you, Artie. I just don't know anymore."

He felt sick. "Nice to hear," he murmured.

"I'm sorry."

"Sorry?" He turned back to her, feeling drained, wondering why he was in the kitchen instead of working. Certainly not to lose his wife. The habit of loving someone was hard to break. "When are you going back to work?"

"I've got a couple of things to do this afternoon. Monday, for sure."

"*Christ*, Terry."

"What's that supposed to mean?"

"You know damned well what it means." His eyes glistened. "Anything rather than deal with the real problems in your life."

"Stop being a bloody idiot!" She caught herself. Shit! "He" was in her *voice* now.

How could this be happening? Artie wondered. Was it all his fault? He recalled the helplessness he had felt outside their bedroom a few days earlier, listening to what he thought was his wife making love. That was ridiculous, Artie knew, and he felt ashamed. His lack of trust was a symptom of their marriage's disintegration. Still, perhaps if he'd had the courage to open the door and look inside . . .

Artie felt weak and foolish. He had always drawn his strength from Terry; now it was gone.

"Ironic, isn't it?" he finally said. "You're pulling away from me, and I keep thinking it's my fault. I mean, deep down I know it's not, but I can't stop thinking it is."

"It's not you."

He watched her, feeling helpless.

"There's something else," Terry said. "I can't describe it." She poured more coffee, using the moment to think. "It's some elusive 'thing' I've been chasing for years. And now it's dangling in front of me, and I still don't know what it is. But I have to catch it." She stopped, again feeling frustrated. "I just can't deal with anything else right now."

"Something you've seen?"

"No."

"Something *I've* seen?"

"It's something you can't see," she said. "Something inside me."

Artie tried smiling. He reached for her again, but she turned away.

Goldin was undergoing treatment at St. Luke's—a Manhattan hospital close to the institute and ready for patients needing police protection. Until Bill Reed had an explanation for what had happened to Terry Cooke and Goldin, he wanted Goldin under wraps. If there was a conspiracy, and if Terry was now known to the D.L.P. . . .

Damn. All his problems had begun with that screwed-up stakeout. Terry never should have let her picture be taken. Another detective would have to take her place.

Reed played carelessly with a pencil, turning it over between his fingers.

But who else knew the case as well as Terry? Gordon Weiss, maybe; but Weiss couldn't command an operation like this.

Who else, then? No names sprang to mind. Besides, it wasn't as if Terry had been shot or anything. Something strange had happened to Goldin, and by coincidence, *maybe* something had also happened to Terry.

Reed tapped the pencil on the desk.

Half the time the doctors were guessing anyway. Terry was under a lot of pressure at home. Reed recognized the signs; he'd been there himself not so long ago. Work would be the best thing for her. Give her something to focus on. It would certainly be best for Reed. This investigation was requiring all the ingenuity he could muster.

Terry Cooke, still in charge.

The thought made Reed uncomfortable, and he threw the pencil.

Why wasn't there someone—*anyone*—else he could trust with this job? Depending on random intangibles was not how Bill Reed liked to work an investigation. And Terry Cooke was definitely an unpredictable force at the moment.

He hunched over the D.L.P. files on his desk. It would have to be Terry Cooke. She was the only one who could slam the door shut on the D.L.P. Reed would just have to make sure she didn't close it on him as well.

* * *

"This way, please."

Terry was ushered into a white hospital room. On a bed, near a battery of machines, rested Goldin. A bright neon light washed Goldin's face, yet she was oblivious to it. The doctor explained to Terry that the patient was in a state of severe shock.

Terry tried to remember precisely what had happened that afternoon at the institute. All she could recall was a sense of mounting panic and a man's voice echoing inside her head. Her dream man, promising, cajoling, threatening.

She slid a chair close to the bed, sat down, and squeezed Goldin's hand. There was only a slow response; Goldin had been sedated to stop a spastic twitching in her arms and legs. Terry squeezed harder and placed her other hand on Goldin's forehead. Terry closed her eyes, trying to imagine the woman as she had been—concentrating on yesterday's Emily Goldin, not the patient lying in bed.

"Emily," Terry murmured.

Terry found herself back in the institute. There was Goldin working in a laboratory, Goldin programming the computers, Goldin talking to an assistant and preparing Terry for the final test. The images ran through Terry's head like a movie.

"Help me!" Terry saw herself shout. She watched Becker lift her, then Goldin turning to someone by the elevators. Terry and Goldin ran toward the man, shouting. They tugged at his arm. The man turned, smiling, pouring into her head.

Monster! Goldin cried. *He's going to do terrible things. You must understand me. He's crazy. He's shown me things—*

A second surge of power struck Goldin with a terrific force—a bore of energy that closed her off from the world, her senses clipped at the nerve. Terry and Goldin were left alone in a cloying darkness.

198

Terry opened her eyes and returned to the hospital room.

Goldin stared sightlessly up at the hospital ceiling, her face soft and without expression. Terry had only visited Goldin's isolation, not found a way to help Goldin out of it. To do that, she would first have to find the proper way in.

For that, she needed a teacher.

"Terrible thing, wasn't it?" the young receptionist said. It was more a statement than a question. Terry slipped her police I.D. back into her shoulder bag, behind the pistol. The hall where Terry had once collapsed on the floor was again a quiet thoroughfare of sterile efficiency. But Terry sensed a hint of "something" still in the air, a residue of energy in the building. "It was so sudden, you know? Shook everyone up."

"I'm sure it did."

"Wouldn't be so bad if any of it made sense."

Terry gave the secretary her attention. "You were going to show me the records?"

The receptionist turned to her computer console and quickly typed a few keys. Terry waited patiently. There was a beep, then CODE? flashed on the screen.

"I'll send it to the machine in Dr. Goldin's office," the receptionist said. She led the way down the hallway, guiding Terry into a cramped office. There was a lingering odor of cigarettes. "There's more files in the bookcase," the receptionist explained. "I hope this will be useful."

"It can't hurt."

The receptionist adjusted the monitor's brightness and punched a few more keys, bringing to life a jumble of names and numbers. Terry turned to the bookcase, fingering a box of cassettes, examining the titles. Telepathy, Clairvoyance, Precognition, Retrocognition, Psychokinesis, Psychobiology, Apparitions, Poltergeists . . .

"What exactly do you want?" the receptionist asked.

199

"Do you keep a list of visitors?" Terry asked.

"Oh, sure."

"I'd like to see yesterday's."

Terry watched the list crawl up the screen. It was a scroll of about a hundred names.

"This is everyone who came into the building while we were open," the receptionist explained.

"Is there any way of separating Goldin's people?"

The receptionist typed another command. "That's Friday morning, right?" Four names became highlighted on the screen. Ruth, Goldin's first patient; Becker, Terry . . .

"This one," said Terry. She pressed her finger on the glass. "Do you remember if he had an accent?"

"I think so," said the secretary.

"English?"

"Maybe."

"Remember anything else?"

The receptionist shook her head.

"Was he tall? Short?" asked Terry. "Thin? Fat? What?"

"Yeah. Tall. And sort of skinny." She grinned. "Nice smile."

"Was he—"

"And he was carrying a black bag over his shoulder."

"Could you see what was in it?"

"It was leather, I remember that. Expensive, by the look of it."

"Anything else? It's important." Terry restrained herself, waiting for more details.

The receptionist shrugged helplessly. "Sorry," she said. She tapped the monitor. "I'd like a hard copy, please."

"Sure," said the receptionist, relieved. She pressed a button, and the list began to print out.

Terry slipped a cassette into the car stereo and sat back. She had borrowed it from the secretary just before leaving.

"August 15, New York University," said Goldin. "Parapsychology conference. Lecture number six: Psychokinesis."

The overdubbed lead ended, and the sounds of a full student classroom echoed through the car's speakers.

Goldin tapped the microphone. "Psychokinesis, or PK, is probably the ultimate psychic exercise. It's the ability to move objects using psi, or the power of the mind. In this manner, subjects can affect the physical environment by a change in psychic mood or a shift in thought.

"It is also a skill that's rarely been established, and, when demonstrated, usually disbelieved. . . ."

Terry ran the tape forward, listening selectively.

". . . . You'll read about one particular subject who showed strong indications of psi during early testing. He demonstrated a remarkable ability in the Zener tests, and a higher-than-average success rate, generally, in telepathy. When we created an isolated environment conducive to concentration, we recorded him bending a thin laser beam.

"Yet the question remains: What is the maximum influence a psychokinetic can inflict on the physical world? In a modern laboratory—with the necessary precautions to guard against fraud—not a great deal has been proven. There's something about the scientific environment that intimidates many volunteers. It's as if they're afraid we scientists will steal their power through analysis and rationalizations. In some cases, psychics are scared of having their abilities confirmed, often because they can't control them. It is not always a pleasant revelation."

The tape ran forward.

". . . skilled psychic I personally ever met was a man from Chicago. He was a private detective who managed impressive telepathic demonstrations under strict conditions. But he couldn't perform in a laboratory. His psi ability would freeze up. In the field, though—in his every-

201

day life—he did things that are impossible to explain, except by psi.

"A typical episode involved locating a divorced husband who had defaulted in his child custody payments. By concentrating on a photograph of the man, this detective formed an aerial picture of where the husband was living. The detective described seeing a coastal town with a rugged shoreline, a nearby lighthouse, and lobster trawlers. Once he had a clear picture, he then heard sounds. Sea gulls, passing traffic, a fog horn. As it turned out, the horn belonged to a ferry boat that loaded in Portland, Maine. The missing husband was a deckhand on board.

"PK was another practice of this detective. Just as I saw him track a divorced husband, I saw him use his mental powers to balance a chair on two legs. He claimed to link his telepathic skills with PK. As his abilities increased, he succeeded in balancing a chair on one leg. We introduced him to a clairvoyant, and discovered the more power in his presence, the more he could accomplish. He could, for example, use psychokinetics to balance two chairs at once.

"You may wonder what finally happened to this man. He died last year, and his wife is now writing a book on his experiences. Here's a final footnote, however: About six months prior to his death, this detective swore off all psychic experiments. Because of his psi experiences, his mind had become a patchwork of memories. His thoughts, he said, were simply not his own. They were shared by all the people he had ever psychically encountered. Hours from his death, his identity, according to his wife, was continually changing.

"I should also add that the detective died of a heart attack, though neither he nor anyone else in his family had a history of heart disease. His last investigation, however, involved tracking a suspect who did have chronic heart trouble. Indeed, *the suspect* died of a heart attack the same afternoon as our detective.''

Terry stopped the cassette player and turned her attention to the receptionist's printout. It was a list of all the people Dr. Goldin had seen the day of the incident. Four names. All of them known to Terry except one.

Ten-thirty-five A.M. *Murray Hunt, 100 Sickles Street, Manhattan, N.Y.C.*

The address was the clincher—Sickles Street. The investigation and the incident at the institute *had* to be connected. All of it was linked to the D.L.P., and there could be no doubt that whatever Murray Hunt's plan of action, it was deadly. Was that really his name? Could the guy be that arrogant?

She used a corner phone to call Bill Reed. "I've found something," she said, telling him what she knew.

"Hunt," Reed repeated when she'd finished.

"We know the address, but not the name."

"Some asshole's playing with us," Reed said.

"It has to be the D.L.P."

"So one of these punks goes to the psychic institute the same day you do. What's he want?"

"I don't know."

"Was he following you?"

"I don't think so."

Terry heard him sigh. The Cubans, the Puerto Ricans, the Croatians, and now this. His streets were being overrun by Marxist maniacs.

"As long as you're checking on Hunt, have someone check out a few recent visas, will you, Bill? I need a list of all the Englishmen who entered the city in the last two months."

"Agreed," Reed said. "Call me later."

"Fine."

"And be careful."

Terry hung up.

Be careful? Her dream man was never far away these days. Some moments, his presence was so tangible she glanced about, certain he was beside or behind her, almost seeing him out of the corner of an eye.

He loved her; he had told her so during their encounter at the institute. He might also kill her. There were times when she was eager for both. During these moments, Terry felt she was a woman hurtling blindly forward, out of control.

The moments were becoming more frequent.

Sixteen

While Reed's department tracked down Terry's leads, she parked her car on Fortieth Street and ran into the main branch of the New York Public Library.

It was a vast building with sixty-foot pillars and gray granite stairs that stretched for a block. With the exception of the federal courthouse downtown, the main branch of the library was the closest thing the city had to the Parthenon.

A guard inside directed Terry to an information desk, from which a librarian sent her to the second floor. The soft hum of a thousand whispers echoed through the chamber, greeting her like ghosts in a tomb.

"I'm looking for the travel section," she told another

librarian. Terry was given a room number and pointed toward another hallway. She followed the directions and became lost in a gallery of ancient Egyptian glassware. With more help, she was directed through a doorway that led into an apparently endless stack of law journals. After a short search, Terry found the card-index room. She walked to a file cabinet, pulled out a drawer, and carried it to a nearby desk.

England—Historic

Terry flipped through more cards.

England-Tourism

Her eyes moved slowly across the list of book titles.

A Traveller's Guide to Great Britain and Ireland.
England on $20 a Day
England: A Pictorial Guide

She reached in her bag and took out a pencil and paper.

England: A Pictorial Guide

Terry noted the catalogue number and quickly searched the stacks for the book. Then she sat at a small side desk, hidden from the lobby, in an isolated part of the library. She fingered the photograph on the front cover. Big Ben's face showed noon, while a knot of London traffic was frozen around Parliament Square and on Westminster Bridge.

She paused. How did she know the names? She'd never been to England.

Terry grinned. *Just beyond the picture is Victoria Street,* she thought.

Terry opened the book: *Welcome to London* read the first chapter. *Home of Prince Charles and Lady Di, Fleet Street and Bond Street, the Tower and Nelson's Column.*

Beneath the paragraph was a map of London, several streets carefully highlighted for tourists.

London: a sprawling, cosmopolitan city that, to the casual observer, seems to make no sense. Yet to a Londoner, there is nothing to equal it. It is an English town multiplied perhaps a hundred times in little communities throughout the Greater London area.

Terry ran her finger through the introductory chapter, reading the names of English towns and villages, scanning pictures. There were familiar fragments of memories surfacing in her mind—pieces of someone else's memory—and she wanted to make sense of them. Dorchester? Windsor? Vaguely familiar. Odd-sounding names. Middle Wallop, Upper Wallop, Piddle-on-Trent, Aldershot . . .

Aldershot. She stared at a photograph of a narrow street. According to the book's author, this was a typical example of a village ruined by modernization. In the picture, greasy oil slicks stained a river. Terry turned the page and saw a couple of youths standing on a street corner. Behind them, at an intersection, was a Whimpie's burger shop. Terry pressed her finger on the photograph, tapping Whimpie's, as if by touching the image she could melt inside it. She focused on the sidewalk. Vivid images flashed in her mind. *He* had been here. The tip of her finger traced the outlines of the burger bar.

There had been an explosion there, prior to Whimpie's. He had come from London to Aldershot and seen a pub explode. Yes. Definitely. Terry could smell the smoke now. She saw the flames puffing through the windows and billowing into the street. And where had he gone from there?

She tapped the page again, breathing deeply, struggling with the image, when her head began tingling. Terry kept absolutely still. The tingling grew worse, settling behind her eyes.

Damm it! she thought.

He was in her.

Terry deliberately thought of nothing—of a blank page, a white library wall. Library? No; she needed him off guard, uncertain of her discoveries. How to do this, she didn't know. Maybe he was reading her thoughts right now. Maybe he already knew them; after all, he loved her. He had told her so. Otherwise, he would have destroyed her. He'd done it to others. He could wipe her mind clean this very moment, leaving Terry empty.

Shit! Are these my thoughts, or his? Terry wondered.

She refused to open her eyes. This time she would beat him. She *had* to.

He waited.

Terry listened. Someone was nearby, searching through the stacks. She heard a book slide out of place. Terry guarded her eyes and approached the shelves.

"Excuse me."

An elderly gentleman turned to her. Terry pulled away his book. "That's mine," she said.

The tingling spread through her body. Terry held the book up to her face.

" 'Chapter Three,' " she read aloud. " 'The Opossum.' "

Opossum?

" 'The opossum is a land mammal common in the eastern United States, seen as far north as New England and as far south as the tip of Florida. It is also common in northeast Mexico—"

Fuck the bleeding opossum!

Terry spoke louder. " 'It usually sleeps by day and hunts by night, living on such diverse foods as frogs, insects, and mice—' "

Stop wasting my bloody time.

" 'The opossum is low on the food chain, providing a tasty meal to any number of animals, including man. Roasted opossum is a special meal for many Georgia hunters, and —''

Screw the opossum. I want you. Where are you?

Terry broke into a sweat, gripping the book, tearing a corner of the page. Her vision blurred. She felt her eyeballs stretch and start to tear. She dropped the book and clapped her hands over her eyes, blocking her eyesight.

"The opossum," she recited from memory, seeing the page in her head, "survives by playing dead. Thus the term, 'playing possum.' ''

Her eyes distended painfully, as if they were about to explode.

"Playing possum!" she cried. "Hiding—dead.''

Gone.

Terry waited for something else to happen. Her eyes relaxed, sore but free, and she searched her mind, looking for damage, wondering if she'd escaped. Why didn't he just kill her? What did he want?

"Are you done with the book?''

Terry glanced up.

"Mammals of North America," the gentleman said politely. "You took it from me.''

She looked down at the book, confused by the picture of an opossum, remembering at last that she had stolen it from someone. "Thank you," she said. She bent down, retrieved the book, and handed it back to him.

"You read very well," he added.

"Excuse me?''

" 'The opossum is a land mammal common in the eastern United States, seen as far north as New England and—' ''

Terry stopped him.

"I love listening to an English accent.''

"What?'' She stared at him. What was he talking about?

The man looked over Terry's shoulder. He pointed at the book on the table.

"That's England, isn't it?"

Terry turned and followed his gaze.

"You planning a trip there?"

"No."

"You ought to. Beautiful countryside." He pointed at one of the pages. "That's Aldershot, isn't it?"

She looked into his eyes.

"Lovely town," the man said. "I have a friend who lived there."

She wiped her face and stared back at the man. *He* was there. The bastard had jumped out of her head and into his.

The old man grinned.

"Damn you," she said.

He didn't reply. Terry grabbed the man's collar and shoved him against the stacks. "You son-of-a-bitch," she began.

"Oh, God!" the man gasped in terror.

"Keep out of my head! Goddammit! Keep the hell away from me!"

"I—" He looked helplessly to his sides. "Please, what do you want?"

Terry released him and backed away, brushing back her hair with a shaking hand. "Damn him," she said to no one.

"Please, please don't hurt me. Here. My money . . ." He reached into his pockets.

Terry turned and left the library before she caused any more trouble. She walked to a street corner, stopped at a pay phone, and dialed Bill Reed's number. When he answered, she could barely talk.

"Hello?" Reed said. "Who is this?"

Terry spoke louder. "It's me, Bill. I've got some more information on our suspect."

"Go ahead."

Terry closed her eyes, recalling details that were now etched in *her* memory.

"He's from London originally, but he's something of a traveler. Spent some time in a place called Aldershot. It's connected with the British military. He was involved in a pub explosion there, though I don't know the details. Pretty long ago, I think, because the building's gone now. After Aldershot, he went abroad."

The traffic moved noisily about her, and it was difficult to hear Reed properly. She stuck a finger in her other ear.

". . . where?"

Terry closed her eyes and thought harder. "Central America, I think. Or the Middle East. Maybe both."

"Where was he before he came here?"

"I don't know," she replied. A cold wind brushed her, and Terry pulled her coat tighter. "One of them, but I'm not sure which."

Reed scribbled down the information. "All right, I'll see what we can find out. In the meantime, I've got another address for you. You got a pencil? Room PHO eight-four-five Columbia-Presbyterian Medical Center."

"What do you have?"

"Murray Hunt," said Reed. "Get there as soon as you can. The doctor says he's dying."

The Intelligence Division had found Murray by first going through criminal records, then running checks with the F.B.I., their own Intelligence Unit, Motor Vehicles, and the phone company. Within three hours, they knew Murray Hunt's Social Security number and place of employment, and after six hours they had the receipts from his flight to and from London. If they'd found Murray the same time they found his receipts, the Intelligence Division might well have pulled some information out of him. But they didn't trace Murray to Columbia-Presbyterian for

210

another ten hours, despite, or perhaps because of, a confidential report to the police commissioner's office, notifying him of a virulent case of anthrax infection.

"He showed up at E.R. late Saturday," said the doctor. "No explanation, no nothing." The elevator doors opened and Terry followed him. "At first we thought it was the D.T.'s or an O.D. Toxicology finally took a look."

"How deadly is it?"

"On a scale of one to ten?" The doctor looked through a plate-glass wall, his hands behind his back. On the other side was Murray Hunt. Murray was a deflated, pale sight, locked from the world in an isolation room. His mind had long ago been closed by fever, and the hospital had completed the isolation, securing him inside an oxygen tent. Outside the room was a guard, making certain that no one strayed inside. "I'd give it a nine. I keep ten for a bullet in the heart."

Terry looked at him. "Treatable?"

The doctor gave a short laugh. "If I could cure him, would I be here with you?"

Terry turned back to Murray, her reflection in the glass obscuring the view. "I'd like to see him."

The doctor agreed. He told a nurse, "She's going into eight-four-five." The nurse took Terry to a dressing room, where she was asked to remove her clothes and put on green disposable pants and a shirt. A cap was slipped over her hair and a mask drawn over her mouth. The nurse finished Terry's outfitting with a pair of rubber gloves.

"Draw them tight up the outside of your sleeves."

Terry did as she was told until the latex wedged into the webs of her fingers.

"You know he can't talk," the nurse said.

"Doesn't matter."

"What is he? A strangler or something?"

"A journalist," Terry answered. It was more than the nurse needed to know. The doctor met Terry in the hallway. He signaled to the guard and led Terry inside the room.

"In this particular form," he warned, "anthrax is extremely contagious." Terry lifted a chair and carried it to the side of the bed. She leaned closer, staring at Murray Hunt.

"I don't know what you expect to get from him," said the doctor. "We've tried five or six times. He doesn't hear a word and can't speak. Can't do much of anything."

Terry ignored the doctor. She concentrated on the patient. Her eyes took in the length of tubing that traveled to the I.V. needle in his arm. Wires connected him to an electrocardiogram. His pulse gave weak, irregular beats.

A soft rasping came from the still figure. Terry wanted to touch him, but they were separated by the plastic walls of the oxygen tent.

"Has he spoken at all?" she asked.

"No," said the doctor.

He excused himself and left the room, certain it would be only a moment before Terry followed.

What was Murray Hunt doing in London? she wondered. How did he get infected? How was he connected to the D.L.P?

Murray drew another rasping breath, and the E.K.G. machine answered. Terry edged closer. Somehow, she had to extract information from this man. That had been the *point* of using Murray's name at the Institute.

It's a game, Terry thought.

"Why you?" she asked aloud. Murray was oblivious to her question. A magazine editor, a solid, middle-class office drone. Nothing new on him since his days in the Middle East. His life was overweight conformity. So what was the connection? Terry was missing something important, she knew it. Bill Reed was going crazy waiting for an answer. Anthrax? London? The whole thing smacked of a major conspiracy. What the hell was the D.L.P. up to?

Reed was still talking with Scotland Yard's Special Branch and MI-6, and he had left word that Terry was to page him wherever he was, and at any time. They had to know how the D.L.P. connected London and New York, and why Murray Hunt had been the courier. There could only be three reasons why he'd take a trip like that: to meet someone, to carry something out of the States, or to bring something back in.

Her eyes flicked from the E.K.G. machine to the man on the bed.

Murray's breathing grew weaker. Terry closed her eyes. The moment they closed, she felt a freezing gust of air. It was followed by the smell of brine.

Terry became part of Murray's dreams. Her arms felt leaden and tired, her fingers long, raw, and cracked, stinging from salt. One of the hands guarded her face from the wind and the cold sharp spray of the sea. A name began to surface.

Craig?

The images came quicker than she could comprehend. The sea disappeared with the rise of a wave, and she found herself on her knees, still buffeted by the wind, scrambling in a pile of dirt. Murray and Terry were digging, coughing. Their fingers, numbed by raw cold, bled as they scraped deeper into the frozen earth. When Murray and Terry had finished filling a container, they rubbed the sore fingers against a pants leg.

Chris?

Terry and Murray looked up as a door opened. Her dream man was there to greet them. Chris—she knew his name now. He smiled at Murray. Murray walked wearily inside, collapsing on a sofa. Chris kept smiling. Terry felt he was smiling at her. Perhaps he was. This was Murray's memory, but the smile was meant for her.

"Put the canister down, Murray," Chris said.

Murray and Terry obeyed. A strange, balding man approached, lifting the canister with the help of large tongs. Chris and the stranger talked while Murray waited, the infection already gnawing at his body.

Easton, Terry thought suddenly. *Chris Easton.*

Then the walls of the room collapsed—not like plaster structures, but like walls of color that were melting and blending. Terry watched as the swirls of color gathered and drew her into a whirlpool. Everything about her was slowly draining into a familiar, frightening blackness she had seen under a bridge in Venice, and before that as a child. It was the same empty hole that had swallowed her brother.

She understood immediately. Murray Hunt was dying.

The doctor had told her, but now Terry could see it for herself, and she did not want him to die. She wanted him to fight for his life and tell her about Chris Easton. If he couldn't fight for himself, Terry would do it for him.

Where's Chris Easton? she thought.

The whirlpool turned her in a slow, circular movement of memories. A kaleidoscope of dreams, corkscrewing into the darkness. The gray, faded images of childhood slowly disappeared. A mysterious woman's face slipped past Terry. Beneath her, Terry watched the smiling face of Chris Easton stretch like an oil slick.

Murray's death was quicker now, and no matter how Terry tried, she couldn't keep the memories from disappearing. They poured into the maelstrom, twisting tighter, pulling Terry. She struggled to keep her head above the "water," but the colors swirled about her, turning her around, confusing her sense of direction. She was still swimming toward the vortex. It had grown, and still the memories rushed in. She looked into the hole. The emptiness terrified her.

She stretched out, desperate for something to hold. The darkness became her earth and sky. The colors collided, striking with incredible force. For a moment she was in a

214

strange suspension—a plug keeping Murray Hunt from finding his rest. The flood pushed against her, and Terry resisted. The darkness simply waited. There was no doubt who would win.

"No!" Terry gasped.

There was a terrible smell.

"Just sit up," said a voice.

A pair of hands pulled her back on the chair. She opened her eyes. The doctor and nurse were by her side, their faces hidden by masks. The doctor again waved the smelling salts under Terry's nose. She tried speaking, but felt too weak. And the light was too bright. It made her eyes water. She wanted to rub them, but the doctor stopped her. Instead, Terry stretched, then began to feel queasy. She watched a second nurse talk on a telephone. A moment later the nurse was back by the bed, disassembling the wires and tubes, turning off the E.K.G. machine. For a moment, the only sound was the crisp rustling of clothing. The rasping breathing had stopped.

"What happened?" she asked.

"You fainted," the doctor said. "Let's get you out of here."

Two interns pushed past her, eager to move Murray off their floor. They unfolded a plastic sack marked CONTAMINATED. In another minute, they had permanently sealed the body.

"Come on," the doctor insisted. He put more smelling salts under her nose. Terry turned her head and pushed his hand away.

"I'm all right."

She stood by herself. The nurse stuffed the bedsheets inside a plastic bag, then sealed and threw them into a cardboard box also marked CONTAMINATED. Terry walked unsteadily outside.

"Let's get those togs off," the nurse said. "Everything gets burned."

Terry shook her head. "Save the body."

"You'd better discuss that with the doctor."

"Don't burn him," Terry insisted, concentrating. She knew the nurse would obey.

Terry removed the disposable clothing and took a shower. Alone in the women's room, she was overwhelmed by sadness. She began crying quietly, mourning the death she had shared with Murray Hunt. She mourned, too, the knowledge that her dream lover had been responsible for what had happened. It clearly marked them as enemies. Yet he had brought her to the verge; he had something to give her that was unique.

Terry looked into the mirror, frightened of herself, her hands cupping her face. Her eyes were red and wide.

She remembered being a part of Murray's thoughts. That much she would admit. She recalled the brink of a terrifying blackness. But she had saved herself. Perhaps she had even helped Murray Hunt live a moment or two longer.

She also remembered her indecision. A part of her had been willing to risk death, because hiding somewhere in that darkness had been Chris Easton.

Terry gazed at her reflection, shocked. She had been willing to embrace death to find him.

She no longer knew whether this was what *he* wanted her to do or whether it had been her own idea.

She could no longer tell if she was in control of her own mind. What happened when she no longer wanted to resist him?

Seventeen

"I've got some names for you," Bill Reed told Terry over the telephone. "English guys given immigration or visitors' visas in the last two months. That's right, isn't it?"

"Yes."

"Fine," Reed replied. "So we've got a list of three or four hundred names. Now, some of them are businessmen. About thirty are diplomats—"

"Forget them."

"Okay," Reed went on. "I figured as much. So, chopping the list down, we're left with about a hundred names. How do you want to do this?"

"It's Chris Easton," Terry told him.

"Excuse me?"

"The guy we're after. His name's Chris Easton."

"Easton," Reed murmured. In a louder voice he said, "He's on the list, all right. Photojournalist. Flew in from Paris on—"

"Hunt brought him here."

"Hunt—"

"Hunt told me before he died."

"And you let me keep talking?" he sighed.

"Of course I was going to tell you," she said.

They were both silent. Terry could feel Reed's frustration and understood it.

"Look," he said at last, "I'll call Hunt's magazine and get someone over to Easton's apartment. Go home, all right? The only address I've got for Easton is the one he gave Immigration. I bet he isn't even visiting there anymore."

"I'll go," Terry told him.

"I'm sending O'Hallan," Reed told her.

"It's on Riverside Drive in the Nineties," Terry said. "Hunt gave me the address. You want two people to do one person's work, that's up to you. But this is *my* case, Bill. I'm going there now."

It took her twenty minutes to reach Chris's building. She parked and looked up at the building's red canvas awning. It was not what she had expected.

It was a twelve-story cooperative, built on a corner that overlooked Riverside Park and the Hudson River. An iron fence wrapped around the building and protected a set of picture windows on the ground floor. Similar windows balanced both sides of the broad entrance, multiplying up the building and ending at a penthouse. Looking straight up, Terry could see the bare branches of a tree in a rooftop garden.

"You can't park there."

A doorman stepped out of the lobby and approached her car. He was dressed in a dark brown uniform and braided cap. He waved a clipboard.

Terry showed him her I.D. "Does Chris Easton live here?"

"Suite six-fifty."

"Do you see much of him?" she asked.

The doorman took a closer look at her badge. "Not for a couple of weeks," he finally said.

"I'd like to go up."

"Sorry. I can't let you in without a search warrant."

"He might be up there," said Terry.

"Want me to ring his apartment?" asked the doorman.

"I don't think you understand," she said. "He might be *dead* up there."

The doorman eyed Terry curiously, buzzing 650. There was no answer.

"When was the last time you saw him?" Terry pressed.

"About a week ago last Monday."

"You actually saw him leave the building?"

The doorman frowned. "I don't remember."

"So he *could* still be up there, couldn't he?"

The doorman hung up the security phone.

"Anyone notice any strange smells in the hallway?" she asked.

The doorman glanced at the phone, then at Terry. Reluctantly, he dug into his coat. He took the master key off a chain and handed it to her. "Don't touch anything," he warned.

She took the elevator to the sixth floor and found suite 650, corner apartment. She turned the key and pushed in the door. She was greeted by a showroom for modern singles living: shag carpet, track lighting above a couch and matching chairs, a dusty glass dining table surrounded by stained-oak chairs.

Terry walked over to a mahogany coffee table and looked through a spread of magazines. *The New Yorker, Newsweek, Life, Illustrated London News, Paris Match, Der Stern.* She tossed them aside. They were all month-old copies and had obviously not been read. Behind the couch stood a floor lamp. She switched it on, then glanced at the small bar in the corner. The liquor bottles were still sealed, and the glasses were coated with a fine film of dust.

He's never lived here, Terry thought. She wandered around the apartment, finding her way to the refrigerator in the kitchen. It was empty.

219

She searched the bedroom, going carefully through the drawers. Empty. So were the closets. Terry moved back into the main room, again looking around. "This is a waste of time," she said aloud. Still, she searched under the bed, looked behind paintings, opened hall closets. Frustrated, she rubbed the walls, as if touching them could create some mystic vibration that would give her a clue to Chris's whereabouts. She gave a final look around the apartment, then locked it and went downstairs. Chris's real home was obviously elsewhere—someplace better suited to a Bohemian.

Terry drove downtown, listening to the car radio, caught for ten minutes in a snarl-up of traffic. The only person who might have had Chris Easton's address was Murray Hunt.

When Terry told her about Murray Hunt's death, Shirley, Murray's secretary, dropped back in her seat.

"Heavens!" she gasped.

Terry walked to the door of Murray's office and pushed it open. The room was an absolute mess. Books were piled up, and paper was crumpled and scattered around. Terry stood by Murray's desk, moving things about, trying to find his private phone directory.

Shirley stood at the doorway, weeping.

"Is this normal?" Terry asked, dismayed. She moved a sheaf of page proofs.

Shirley supposed so. Between tears, she could barely talk. Terry again swept her hand across the desk. "Has he got a personal phone book or Rolodex?"

"Try the left-hand drawer, at the top."

Terry opened the drawer and found the phone book. She tried "E" for Easton, "C" for Chris, "P" for photographer, "F" for friend. She went through all the combinations she could think of, but all she found was the address on Riverside Drive.

"You know an Englishman called Chris Easton?"

"He was the photo editor here," Shirley said. "Sort of still is, but no one's seen him in a while."

"What about him and Murray Hunt? Did they get along?"

"As far as I know. They worked abroad together a few years ago."

Terry closed the drawer. "Mr. Hunt must have kept a work diary."

"I don't think so."

"Do you know of any phone numbers anywhere else?"

"No."

Terry looked around the room. "When was the last time you saw Easton?"

"A couple of days ago. You should talk to his deputy, Mr. Johnson. He's handling everything."

Terry took the advice, going downstairs and standing before a network of office carrels. A photo technician pointed her toward a wall of offices that lined a far hallway, and Terry squeezed past the carrels, stopping at a room where Lyle Johnson was hanging a fresh batch of prints.

Johnson studied her, not particularly thrilled with human contact, even less so after seeing Terry's badge. He was a short, unshaven, scruffy man.

"What can I do you for?" he asked.

"I'd like to see some negatives, please."

"Negatives, photos—makes no difference," Johnson said. "We don't show pictures outside the office. Policy."

"I'd very much like to see Chris Easton's negatives," Terry continued. Johnson squinted at her and patted his shirt pockets. He found a crushed pack of cigarettes and lit one, blowing the smoke into his week-old beard.

"Easton?" he asked.

"Your boss," Terry said patiently.

"What's he been up to?"

Terry was silent. Johnson thought for a moment, then had Terry follow him. They entered an office that was in worse shape than Murray's.

"I haven't seen him for a couple of weeks," Johnson said. He rummaged in a pile of papers. "He's a crazy motherfucker." Hearing that from Johnson made Terry realize just how crazy Easton must be.

Johnson pulled out a photograph. "You want a picture of him? Here."

Terry took it and studied Chris Easton's gaunt face. "Do you know where he's living at the moment?" she asked.

"Riverside, somewhere."

"I mean his *real* address."

"That *is* his real address."

"I think he's living somewhere else."

Johnson considered this. "Ask Murray when he's back on his feet."

"Murray Hunt's dead."

Once again, Terry shocked someone with the news. Johnson's cigarette dipped. Then he took a deep drag on it. He closed his eyes and vanished behind a nicotine mist. "Shit!" he muttered.

"I'd like to see the last few rolls of film Easton shot," Terry said. "I'm particularly interested in any waste shots."

Johnson removed a piece of tobacco flake from his bottom lip. "Murray was okay," he said. Terry waited, looking sympathetic. Johnson pulled the cigarette from his mouth and crushed it into an ashtray. A stray wisp of smoke curled up.

"Easton have something to do with Murray's death?"

"I just want to talk to him," said Terry.

"Yeah," Johnson replied, certain Chris had everything to do with it. He cleared off a chair and asked Terry to sit while he ducked out the office door. "Myrna?"

A woman stuck her head over a carrel.

"Get Easton's last box of film from the darkroom, will you?"

Johnson touched Terry's arm and walked her to the darkroom. "I shouldn't be doing this," he said. Myrna stood over a filing cabinet. She pulled out a drawer and gave it to Johnson, who grabbed it without a word. He took Terry into the darkroom. The rolls of negatives covered the last two months of shooting. Johnson unrolled one and scanned it.

"They worked together in Beirut, you know. Then Murray got the editor's job here. He brought Easton over from Paris."

Johnson took a second roll of film and held it up to the light. "This box has most of the stuff he shot in New York."

Terry took one of the small canisters and examined the negatives. Johnson glanced at her, fighting his paranoia.

"How much time you got?" he asked.

"None," she replied.

Johnson opened the darkroom door. "Wait outside and I'll get this done in thirty minutes. All right?"

She studied Johnson, reluctant to move.

"Look, I don't have to do shit for you."

Terry slipped the roll of film back into its canister, handed it to Johnson, and left.

"Fucking cops," he muttered as he closed the door.

Terry sat on a chair and waited. It was forty minutes before Johnson emerged. When he did, he handed her a large manila envelope and walked away. Terry returned to her car with the prints.

She eliminated all but five black-and-white photographs. Two were inside an apartment, and three were of the New York skyline.

Of the two inside an apartment, Terry could make out the edge of a bed, a sink, and flowered wallpaper. Both

223

shots were overexposed. The wallpaper looked bleached and faded, and a strip of it had been peeled back, revealing a white plaster wall marked with deep scratches. In the corner of one photo there appeared to be the end of a suitcase, but she couldn't be certain.

Anywhere, U.S.A., she thought. She tossed the photos aside and picked up the ones of the New York skyline. All three had been taken from a window about four flights up—Terry was certain of this, judging the height from the view. They were also taken from the same window.

Terry spread the five pictures on the passenger's seat of her car. A thought occurred to her, and she rummaged through the toy cars and candy wrappers in the glove box until she found one of her son's magnifying glasses. She picked up the two daytime skyline pictures—both long shots of the street. She examined them through the glass.

The shadows were longer in the first shot. It was probably taken early in the morning because the street was narrow and there were only a couple of parked cars, but no traffic. Almost all the narrow streets in New York ran east–west, and if it had been early evening, the streets would have been busy.

Terry looked carefully at the image and spotted a street cleaner parked on a corner. She glanced quickly at the second photo, hoping to see a sign in one of the shots, but even without the cleaning truck there was no clue to the street or a building number. Well, at least she could call the Sanitation Department. That would put a time to one of the photos.

Terry looked at the third photo: a night picture, taken of a building across the street. A massive old structure, with a bare flagpole projecting from the bricks. Assorted lights reflected off the windows, but that was about the only difference in the three shots.

She returned to the first picture. If this was morning, and the shadows were stretching toward her, then the camera was facing east. In the second photo, traffic was driving toward her, which meant the street was probably one way, heading west. Most streets going west were odd-numbered: Fifteenth, Twenty-fifth, Sixty-first. . . . The architecture looked like downtown or maybe midtown—but she couldn't be certain.

Terry cursed. Now all she had to do was drive up and down all the odd-numbered streets in Manhattan looking for an old building with a flagpole. Presuming, of course, Chris Easton's secret apartment was even in Manhattan. Hell! Suppose the damned pictures had been taken on a Sunday? Lots of streets like this emptied for the day. Then the photo could have been taken in the morning or early evening, which meant the street could be going either east or west, which meant she had no clues at all.

Terry picked up the night photo and studied it again. Something in the reflections off the windows caught her eye. She could see the mirrored images of a small crowd of people hanging outside a doorway. Between the building entrance and the top of the photo, Terry distinguished part of neon sign.

"J-E-F-F-E-R," she read aloud. She took out her note pad and wrote down the letters. "Jeffer." She dropped the photo and went quickly to a corner telephone booth, dialing information. "I'd like the number for the Jefferson," she said.

The operator tapped in the request. "Hotel Thomas Jefferson, Hotel Jefferson, or Jefferson Hotel?"

"Give me all three."

The operator read her the numbers and the addresses: one on Fifth Avenue, one on Lexington, another on Thirty-first Street—a side street.

Terry hung up and drove crosstown to the Jefferson Hotel—less than two blocks from the magazine's offices. It was an S.R.O. boardinghouse for potential suicides and drug addicts who lived on welfare checks. And crazy photographers, Terry thought.

She went up to the front desk and asked for Chris Easton's room number. The woman behind the counter turned from a small portable TV to thumb through a register. Lunch crumbs covered the counter and her blouse. She ran a finger down a list of names.

"No Easton," she said.

"You certain?"

The woman's eyes were bloodshot, and her teeth—what was left of them—were stained dark yellow. "Cop?" she asked. Terry showed her badge, and the woman bent forward, peering at it a long time. She smiled. "Got your brother upstairs." The woman turned the register around and tapped it. "There you go. Terence Cooke—with an 'e.' Room four-oh-one."

Terry stared down at the register. "Does that room face the street?"

The woman took the key from a shelf. "All the 'ones' face out," she said. "One-oh-one, two-oh-one, three-oh-one, four-oh-one." She gave Terry the key. "If that don't work, just give the door a good shove."

"Is he upstairs now?"

"Ain't seen him in days."

Terry walked up the stairs to room 401. She opened the door carefully, then turned on the overhead light.

"Dear God!" she gasped.

She was surrounded by pictures of herself. They were on the walls and scattered on the bed. A hundred copies of Terry Cooke taking John Griffin out of the squad car, standing alongside him. A picture on the door had been slashed several times with a knife, a long cut slicing across her body. In another, Griffin had been sliced away and Terry had been blown up to poster size. Beneath it, a blood-red carnation lay on a pillow.

She sat on the edge of the bed. It was clear to her now. There was no need for her to pursue Chris Easton.

Sooner or later, he would come for her.

Eighteen

Once the other detectives arrived at the S.R.O., Bill Reed ordered Terry home. She spent the rest of the day vigorously putting her house in order. Artie watched, wondering if Terry's frenzy was a therapeutic release of energy. He asked her once, but Terry was too busy to answer him.

She wiped counters, vacuumed carpets, washed clothes, sponged windows. The children watched her apprehensively. There was too much force behind her mopping, too dangerous a swing to her sweeping.

Artie came out to give the children their supper. While they ate, he tried once more to talk with his wife. She ignored him.

Artie smeared a finger across the top of a shiny bookcase. "How much cleaner can it get?" he asked.

The children stared at them from the kitchen table.

"The place is spotless," Artie said. "Terry—"

She polished harder.

After supper, Artie sent the children to their rooms and waited upstairs for Terry. Surely, it would only be another half hour before she relaxed. Then he could take her into the kitchen for something to eat and reason with her.

At midnight, Terry was scrubbing walls that she had cleaned four hours earlier. Artie came back downstairs. "If this is just to avoid me, I'll sleep in my study," he said.

"*I'll* sleep down here," she told him. "Go back to bed." She wiped her brow with her forearm and pushed back her scarf.

"Fine. Sleep downstairs. But for God's sake, do it. You're acting crazy!"

"Because I want a clean house?"

"You're impossible, Terry."

"I'll go to bed when I'm tired."

Artie shook his head. "I don't understand you."

Terry turned aside from her work. Her face was soaked with sweat, her red and wrinkled hands gripped the scrubbing brush. Her knuckles were white.

Artie moved to the foot of the stairs. "Tomorrow I'm calling Bill Reed. Maybe he'll explain."

"Don't you dare!"

"I've had *enough*, Terry." Artie cursed her and went upstairs. Terry looked back at her wall. "Not tired," she whispered.

When she was, her day would be a success. She wanted to be exhausted. If her sleep was deep enough, she was guaranteed a visit from Chris Easton.

Terry ran a scalding-hot bath, then attempted to soak her tension away. Billowing steam clouded the mirrors and hung like a fog in the room.

There was no doubting Terry's earlier experiences in the hospital. She had first gone into Goldin's thoughts, then into Murray's. There was a strange power inside her, and Chris Easton was pulling it out. Or maybe she was pulling it out of herself. No matter. Chris Easton was the expert, and their secret meeting place was Terry's mind.

When her bath was finished, Terry wrapped herself in a towel and went to the living room. She took blankets and sheets from a closet and made a bed on the couch.

She lay restlessly, victim to her own anticipation. If Artie had his way, she would be chained to him forever. His love was as possessive as ever. But Artie would lose her because Terry needed to find Chris; nothing else was important. Her exhaustion finally took hold, and Terry drifted into sleep.

Dreams whispered at her, and she found herself walking along a wide, desolate street somewhere in Manhattan. Judging from the look of the neighborhood, she was in a *barrio*, a Latin ghetto where the streets tilted, echoing with the rhythmic jerking of salsa.

Terry stopped before the stoop of a building that had seen better days. A number was poorly brushed in black paint and ran in tears down the wall.

Here, Chris told Terry.

She entered, dreading the shadows; the dark hallways were infinite tunnels. She crossed to the elevator.

The peeling elevator doors opened. Terry noticed graffiti carved into the metal. She entered and the doors closed behind her. When they again dragged open, she entered a dark hallway: 3C, 3E. Half the apartments were unnumbered, others only vaguely marked. A "G" hung upside down on a screw. Terry moved to the end of the hall and stopped. The door she wanted was hidden in the darkness. Her nightmare waited patiently on the other side.

The door opened by itself, and Terry floated into the room.

"Well done," Chris said to her. "I knew you could do it if you tried."

Terry glanced around the room, its details strangely blurred. "Chris Easton," she said.

He didn't answer her. His eyes were wide, and a dreamy

haze brought him closer. The door slammed shut behind her.

Terry asked, "How did you do that?"

Chris grinned. "Don't be daft. This is a dream. Anything can happen in a dream."

Terry followed his gaze and, looking down, found herself standing in a bed of flowers.

"Try it," Chris said.

Terry concentrated on the window. She felt his help. The window stretched until it became opaque and changed into a door.

She looked around and saw Chris had moved near a bureau. He was a ghost, disappearing and reappearing at will.

This is only a dream, she thought. She felt cornered and glanced around the room. Terry turned back to the door. In its place was a wall.

Chris settled in a chair. The walls began to contract, and his chair stretched into a sofa. "Sit here," he told her.

Terry had no choice. She was already by his side.

"We're getting closer," Chris said. Terry didn't trust herself to answer. She tried stretching the walls, looking for the door. The walls only blurred and changed color. "When should we meet?" he asked her.

"That's up to you."

Chris held two thin champagne glasses and they filled themselves. He offered one of the glasses. Terry focused on them and they disintegrated. Chris looked surprised. Then he laughed. "Very good," he said.

"What do you want of me?" Terry demanded.

"You know already," he said. He walked to a wall and sank a hand through it. He jerked it back and the wall tore, revealing the city. It was ravaged by a holocaust limited only by his imagination—her dream, but his imagi-

230

nation. Flames enveloped the buildings. Terry felt their heat.

"Ever meet your brother?" Chris asked. "The one who drowned at sea? He's behind you, right now."

Terry listened to the footsteps. A soft, painful shuffling—the impossible steps of a man who died twenty years ago.

"The revolution's come," said Chris. "It's the rise of Mao and Che and Islam and Palestine. . . ."

She could smell him now—the scent of seawater, the growing odor of open, raw flesh.

"Violence is the only course of change. Death is inescapable. To die for change is to die for glory."

Water dripped on her shoulder. A hand pressed her cheek. Bloated fingers, sinking into her skin, the nails torn away, the knuckles blue and pussed. Terry screamed and spun to face him.

She faced Chris.

"I can do this in the real world," he whispered. "So can you."

They fell backward. She was lying naked on a bed, kissing Chris, enjoying it.

Just a dream, she forced herself to remember.

"Be with me," he said. His hands touched her body. Terry shuddered as she felt his mouth on her arms, her neck, her nipples. She resisted him.

"I'm going to stop you," she whispered. "I'll kill you if I have to."

Chris continued touching her. She pressed him closer. "I love you," Chris told her. "You were made for me. You're mine."

"Get off," Terry begged. She fought him. Chris trapped her arms, pressing down on her body, forcing her knees apart. The walls became bright with flames. The fire reached toward them, consuming their bed. Everything Chris embraced fed the fire.

231

Terry stopped fighting. The flames changed color to a pale blue. "Get off," she said calmly. The bed and the flames disappeared, and she was standing fully clothed. The room looked the same as when she had first seen it.

"This is my dream," Terry said angrily. "I don't want this."

Chris sat by the window. The throbbing salsa floated up from outside. "Maybe not yet," he told her.

Chris faded into the wall. Her body floated out of the building.

"Very soon," she heard him call.

When Gordon arrived in his Dodge at nine-fifteen A.M., Terry was waiting on the stoop. A thin layer of overnight snow blanketed the ground and the tops of bare branches. She walked briskly to the car, opened the door, and climbed inside.

" 'Morning," Gordon said.

"Let's go."

Gordon took a deep breath and started the car. Terry sat stiffly until they were lost in traffic. She relaxed and touched Gordon's arm lightly. "Thanks."

"For what?" The rush-hour traffic crawled toward Manhattan.

Terry smiled uncomfortably. "For coming here." She could feel his suspicion of her. Terry watched the cars press together, closing in on her like the walls of her nightmare. The world around Terry seemed no more real than the objects in her dream. Chris was shrinking the gap between dreams and reality.

PK.

"I'm glad you did," Terry said.

Gordon glanced at her, then back to the traffic. "Don't get carried away," he said. "Reed told me to come here and hold your hand."

"Oh."

Terry and Gordon were together, then, only temporarily. "I don't trust you and I'm not even sure I like you," he added. "The sooner this day ends, the better for me."

Terry settled back in her seat and looked out the window. "It won't be much longer," she murmured.

Gordon patiently played chauffeur, and twenty minutes later Terry told him to take a right turn. She had him park at One Hundred Sixty-third Street and St. Nicholas Avenue.

She climbed out of the car and looked to either side of the street. Gordon thought she was searching for a street sign, but Terry walked away from the corner, following a line of double-parked cars. Gordon watched her from the Dodge.

Terry carefully paced her steps, counting aloud, her breath white, stopping in the middle of the street. She seemed to be daydreaming. Gordon yelled at her, and she looked up in time to evade a speeding gypsy cab.

"What the hell are you doing?" Gordon shouted. He ran to her side and grabbed her arm. Terry's eyes were gleaming. "Terry?"

"I'm okay," she said. "I couldn't see the street corner last night, but it doesn't matter. I saw that store." She pointed to a *bodega*. "After that, all I had to do was count my steps."

"You're out of your fucking mind."

"I'm *okay*." She looked around, then added, "In there, third floor."

"You actually expect me to go inside that building?"

Terry didn't answer. She crossed the street, leaving Gordon. Cursing, he followed.

The building was much as she had imagined it, except for the people. A young mother sat spread-legged on a radiator, two children screeching by her feet. The door to an apartment was wedged open, and from inside came the blaring beat of salsa. The music echoed through the lobby and hallways, stirring the smoke of an incinerator.

Terry pushed the elevator button. Gordon caught up with her.

"What are we doing here?" he asked.

"Chris Easton," she said.

"Who?" It took Gordon a moment to recognize the name. When he did, he unbuttoned his jacket and checked his revolver.

The elevator arrived, and they stepped in. "Is he alone?"

"Yes."

"What kind of weapons?"

"He doesn't need any."

The elevator stopped, and the doors dragged open. They walked into the gloomy hallway.

"This is a D.L.P. safe house," she whispered.

"So where's our goddamned backup?" Gordon asked.

"That's why you're here. Wait by the stairs."

Gordon obeyed and crouched at the foot of the steps. Terry dried her hands on the back of her jeans, then took out her gun, trying to draw comfort from its weight. She released the safety catch.

"If anyone jumps out that door, don't stop to think, all right?" She softly pounded her chest.

She walked the last few steps to the doorway. What if Chris was really in there? Would she be able to stop him? That was why she'd brought Gordon along. Certainly, one of them would have to do it.

Terry stood to one side and rapped on the door with the muzzle of her gun. No answer.

"Police!" she called. She glanced back at Gordon, who trained his weapon on the doorway. The formalities were over. Terry tested the knob, taking a breath and pushing inward.

The worst would have been coming face to face with

her nightmare: Chris Easton, waiting for her, the walls of the room changing color, dissolving about her, watching herself in bed with him as his sacrificial fire devoured her.

Gordon watched Terry hesitate, then disappear inside. After a moment he left his position and joined her, stepping cautiously into the room and away from the open doorway.

It was the remains of an apartment. Gordon found a switch and flicked on a light. An earthquake seemed to have hit the place, overturning and breaking the few pieces of furniture that had decorated the room. Books were shredded, the window broken. A desk, table, and couch were lying torn or cracked on their sides, piled in the center of the room. At first, Gordon thought it was a barricade, but there was no one on the other side of the mess, only broken chips of plaster and more shattered glass.

He relaxed.

"Look's like someone had a good time," he said.

Terry held a finger to her lips and pointed to a door. Gordon opened it, with Terry close behind. A woman screamed. She was huddled on the floor, a blanket wrapped about her head and shoulders. Terry switched on the bedroom light. The woman flinched and hid deeper in the blanket.

"Meagan," Terry said.

Gordon bent beside Meagan and tried to lift the woman. Meagan beat him back, grunting in anger. When Gordon touched her again, she squealed like a pig and looked up.

Gordon screamed.

Meagan's face was a grotesque distortion—her nose squashed and flattened; her cheeks puffed and stretched. Her head fell to one side, unable to support its own weight. Scars like thumbprints scored the sides of her balding skull. She tried to hold a hand over her face, but the fingers had melted away into raw stubs. Gordon turned away quickly and threw up.

235

Terry gingerly helped the woman onto the bed. A note was pinned to Meagan's T-shirt. Terry unfastened it, and the woman again curled into a ball.

Gordon came back into the bedroom and wiped his mouth with a handkerchief. He peered over Terry's shoulder and read the note:

THE WOMAN BETRAYED US.
THIS GOVERNMENT HAS POISONED
DEMOCRACY. IT MUST BE PURGED.
D.L.P.

"For once in your life, Terry, tell me what the hell's going on." His voice was shaking, but Terry didn't notice.

She left him and went downstairs to call the precinct and Bill Reed. Paramedics soon took control of the place. One of them took a look at Meagan and passed out. Two others cradled her onto a stretcher. The blanket was thrown over her head.

Terry paced the room, mesmerized by what she had seen. She circled the pile of broken furniture and touched it carefully. It felt warm. "He did all this," she murmured. "Just by thinking about it."

Gordon tried to understand. "Easton?"

Terry didn't reply. She was listening to other voices, feeling a power gradually building inside her. She reached on top of the pile and pulled down a chair. She tossed it aside, then pulled uselessly at a bureau.

"Terry?"

She kept heaving away at an overturned table.

"Come on," Gordon said softly. "Let's get you out of here."

Terry pulled a last time at the pile and, failing to dislodge anything else, fell to her knees. She stared across the room at a shattered clock. Its frame had been twisted and its guts scattered. Gordon watched her, feeling helpless, looking at the clock. Christ! Was the second hand starting to turn?

Gordon suddenly didn't want to understand. He waited for Terry by the car.

Chris, Terry thought. *What do you want with me? Where are you? What do I do to stop you?*

Leave me alone, she pleaded. *Go away. Go back to Lebanon, or South America, or wherever you came from.*

She had to get away.

Terry went downstairs. "I'm heading downtown," she told Gordon. "I've got to meet Artie for lunch, and I'm late already."

"What about the freak? When do we talk to her?"

Terry walked over to the stoop and looked up at the gray sky. A storm might be brewing. "When I get back," she answered Gordon.

I can *beat you, Chris Easton,* Terry decided.

His voice swept through her.

Today, it told her.

Terry nodded. Today.

Nineteen

Chris locked the apartment door after Walter and Andrew left with the bombs. Then he made love to Meagan one last time.

The D.L.P. had been a means to an end for Chris. Now, its usefulness was almost at an end. The terrorist closest to Chris—Meagan—had been guilty of duplicity. She had shown him the facade of loyalty, but whenever he entered her thoughts, he felt fear and distrust. It grew worse each day.

Deep down, Chris knew he was partly to blame. After all, he had changed her memories and tampered with her emotions. He had tried making her like Terry. At times, he had almost succeeded.

Chris stopped thinking and listened as Meagan rolled restlessly in bed.

There was no doubting it; she was a threat he could not ignore.

Meagan simply wasn't strong enough for Chris. She was feeling panic, fearing that something was killing her and stealing her mind. Rather than hear Chris's voice, she was starting to hear the voice of survival, warning that unless she escaped, she would be completely destroyed. Run, it warned her. Find Mark; he'll save you. Go to the police, or the F.B.I., or the C.I.A. Do something. *Anything.*

In the morning, Meagan sat up in bed and put on her T-shirt. Chris propped himself against the arm of the sofa bed. He read her thoughts. Then he wasted no more time and unleashed his power. Chairs and tables smashed together in the center of the room. The windows imploded, showering the floor with glass. Chunks from the ceiling bellied out, cracked, and collapsed onto the pile. Chris ripped apart Andrew's apartment, disposing of the D.L.P.'s last safe house.

Meagan hugged her knees, terrified. Chris's eyes glowed when he looked at her.

Meagan screamed. Her cheeks began stretching, as if somebody had put a fist in her mouth and punched outward. She felt her jaw crack, her teeth splinter, her lips bloat. Then the fist punched again, crushing her nose. She fell backward, holding the bedpost for balance, losing sight of everything as she collapsed on the floor. Her eyes were expanding. They grew until they bulged out of their sockets, the eyelids drawing back and tearing at the edges.

She screamed and her tongue flapped out of her mouth—a long, swollen tongue, fresh and pink. She screamed again—a horrible sound. An animal's sound. The bed slipped out of her hands. When she tried to catch herself, her fingers disappeared. Almost in unison, they retracted, as if her fingers were claws on a cat.

Meagan waved her arms in the air, begging. Her skull expanded until her head lolled on one shoulder, unable to bear its own weight.

Chris leaned over her and pinned a piece of paper to her T-shirt. Meagan was no longer a threat.

Chris yawned. He stood on the street corner, waiting by a phone booth, wondering if there *were* any limits to his power. When Terry Cooke was finally his, everything would happen.

He smiled and watched the passing traffic. He thought about Terry with the nervousness of a groom. Theirs would be the ultimate union. Total joining of body and mind. They would discover powers Chris had not yet imagined, and they would be able to change the world. But first, people had to be made to listen. That was why he arranged to poison eight million of them. No one would ignore him after that.

The pay phone rang and Chris lifted the receiver.

"Yes?"

Walter breathed heavily. Nervous, Chris suspected. He was simply not made for this business. Walter was not only frightened of Chris; he feared the police, the F.B.I., the token clerk . . .

"Walter?"

"I'm here."

"All done?"

"Yeah. Like you said. Grand Central, Penn Station, Times Square—"

"The Times Square one," Chris said. "Where did you put it?"

"Eighth Avenue, near the I.N.D. Right across from the Port Authority."

"Perfect," Chris said. "You've got one more job to do. I want you to find the nearest cop and tell him what you've done. Show him one of the bombs—just one, mind you—and then tell him the others will be detonated in twenty-four hours. We'll be in touch."

Walter listened, but couldn't believe it. "You mean give myself up?"

Chris entered Walter's thoughts.

"Tell them anything you want, except where to find the other bombs."

"Don't say anything about the bombs," Walter repeated.

They hung up. A faithful soldier, that boy. Predictable. The same could not be said for Andrew.

The pay phone rang again. Chris lifted the receiver. "Andrew?"

There was a long pause.

"Shouldn't use names on the phone," Andrew said finally.

Chris grinned. "Everything all right?"

"Of course. Let me talk to Meagan."

"She's not here."

"Where is she?"

"Back at the flat."

Andrew was quiet.

For a moment, Chris thought he had left the phone. "Andrew?"

"I'm here," Andrew answered. "Walter's gone, too, huh?"

240

"He's doing a job for me," Chris answered.

Andrew controlled his laughter. "I bet," he said. "Look, meet me at One Thirty-three Bleecker in two hours. After that I'm old news, man." He hung up.

Terry arrived at the Fortieth Street precinct at two o'clock.

"Detective Cooke," the desk sergeant said by way of making an introduction, "meet Mr. Walter Beal."

Walter looked up at her, his mouth hanging open, waiting patiently for something to happen.

"He came in here about an hour ago babbling about a D.L.P. and some kind of poison bombs," the sergeant said. "Says he planted them all over the city."

"Find any of them?"

"One," said the sergeant. "In Penn Station, right where he told us."

"Did they take it apart?"

"Not yet. Didn't want to risk exploding it with people around."

"What sort of poison?" Terry asked.

"Anthrax." The sergeant looked at Walter. "At least, that's what Beal says. The lab's still checking it out."

She listened carefully, beginning to understand. "So what does he want?"

The sergeant shrugged. "Don't know. He hasn't made up his mind."

Terry drew up a chair alongside Walter. He looked blankly at her. "Walter?" He did not respond. "Why are you here?" she asked.

He tilted his head to one side. "I represent the Democratic Liberation Party."

"Who sent you? Was it Chris Easton?"

Walter looked to the sergeant. "Ten bombs are hidden throughout the city. Inside each bomb is a deadly virus known as anthrax. Inform the mayor that he has twenty-four hours to satisfy our demands. After that, the bombs will be detonated.''

''Where are they?'' Terry asked.

''You can find one bomb in locker number B-two-six-three, Pennsylvania Station.''

''What about the others?''

Walter sat silently.

Terry glanced at the sergeant. He stood over Walter, frowning, as if that would be enough to make Walter talk. Terry grabbed hold of Walter's jacket and pulled him closer. ''What do you want?''

Walter didn't answer. She pushed him back into his chair.

''When will you tell us your demands?'' she asked quietly.

Walter coughed, then spoke so quietly Terry had to lean forward to catch his words. ''A billion dollars.''

''You said one *million* an hour ago,'' the sergeant said.

Terry started again. ''Tell me about the bombs, Walter,'' she said.

''Ten bombs are hidden throughout the city,'' Walter repeated. ''Inside each bomb is a deadly virus known as anthrax. Inform the mayor that he has twenty-four hours—''

''Where are they?''

''You can find one in locker number B-two-six-three—''

''Where are the *others*?''

Walter looked at his feet. Terry began pacing. She stopped behind Walter's chair and slipped her fingers in his hair. Chris would have done something to Walter's memory, of course, but perhaps she could find a crack. She concentrated, searching Walter's mind for a weakness in Chris's programming. A woman's face began to appear. Somehow, Walter had found the strength to squeeze this memory under the barrier.

''Where are the other bombs?'' Terry whispered.

Walter said nothing, his mouth open, his eyes closed. The image of the woman became clearer. It took Terry a moment to recognize her.

"Tell me for Meagan's sake, Walter," Terry said to him. "She wants you to tell me."

"No," he murmured.

"Meagan's in the hospital," Terry went on. "Chris put her there."

"No."

"She's dying, Walter."

"You're a liar," he said hoarsely.

"Excuse me," said the sergeant, "but what the hell's—"

"Don't ask," Terry said quickly. The sergeant shrugged and walked away. Terry again immersed herself in Walter's thoughts. There was a wall, and there was Meagan. Walter would do anything for Meagan.

Terry began to change his memories.

This is how he works, she thought. He not only reads minds, but he also changes them. It was so easy! All she had to do was touch Meagan's face. The features began to coalesce and then blur. Another shift, and Terry could begin to see her own face in their place. Soon, all Terry saw was her own face reflecting back to her.

Walter's confusion disappeared as Terry and Meagan merged into one picture.

"I missed you, Walter," Meagan seemed to say.

Walter's eyes grew wet. "I'm sorry," he said, collapsing against her shoulder. Tears streaked his cheeks.

"We've got to stop Chris," she said. "He's going to ruin everything."

"Stop Chris," Walter agreed. "But he didn't tell me where he hid the rest of the bombs."

Terry looked for the sergeant and saw him behind the front desk, too far to hear them. Walter and she were alone in their own world. "Where?" Terry whispered. She

243

kneeled in front of Walter and held his hand. "Tell me. Where are the other bombs?"

Andrew slid his knife into a front pocket of his jacket and ordered another beer. The bartender topped his mug, placed it on the counter, and quickly collected five other glasses.

The Bleecker Café was a classy restaurant and pub that lulled its customers with light jazz. Its clientele was part of the youthful affluence that made up Greenwich Village—none of that "T-shit" crowd from nearby New York University.

Andrew wiped his mouth with a coat sleeve. He looked around the room, feeling envious. These people—eating their Coquilles St. Jacques and crêpes Suzettes—were secure in money. Safe, hip, and protected by a wall of co-operative town houses. Might as well have a security monitor pointing north of Eighth Street.

Still, in this bar, Andrew believed he had the advantage. He didn't give a crap if anyone saw him cut Chris. He was looking forward to the theatrics. Sticking it to Chris in front of a crowd of assholes! Chris, however, wouldn't do anything here. Andrew was betting on it, even though he had no idea what Chris might do. Andrew fingered his knife, drained his mug, and called to the barman. "Fresh one!" he shouted.

"Make it two."

Andrew turned. Chris was at his left side, cramping his hand. Andrew again tried reaching for the bartender, but Chris pulled his hand down.

"I'll get them."

Andrew relaxed. He didn't want to make his move yet, not until Chris was off guard.

The bartender brought two beers and Chris picked one up, throwing a five-dollar bill on the counter and ignoring the change.

244

"Cheers," he said. He raised the glass and smiled.

Andrew muttered something and slowly sipped his drink. All the time, his eyes flicked to Chris's hands, looking for a weapon, ready to jump if Chris made the slightest move toward him.

Chris leaned against the counter. *"Vive la révolution* and all that, eh?" A faint smile spread on his lips.

"Sure," Andrew agreed. He twisted about and raised his mug to the rear dining room. *"Vive la révolution!"*

The diners quieted, regarding him cautiously. Andrew was embarrassed. He turned back to the bar and smiled nervously at Chris.

"You sure everything's set?" Chris asked.

"Told you already, didn't I?"

"Fraunces Tavern, Citicorp, the U.N.—"

"It's done." Andrew added, "And I don't like the way you talk to me."

"I'll talk to you any way I bleedin' like."

"That's where you're wrong, 'mate.' I'm not Walter or Meagan." Andrew again looked at the diners and shouted, "Fuck all you assholes!"

He turned back to Chris, but Chris was no longer beside him. The bartender grabbed Andrew's arm.

"What's the trouble?"

Andrew shrugged the hand away, leaning forward and grabbing the bartender by his cardigan. He pulled the man across the counter. "There's too many faggots in this place. The smell makes me want to puke."

The bartender glanced at the cash register, then back to Andrew. Andrew's eyes began to glaze, and he dropped his voice to a whisper. "We got packages all over the city. All over. Maybe next to your house. Who knows?"

He looked over his shoulder and spotted Chris in a corner. Chris nodded, and Andrew shoved the bartender back into a shelf of bottles and glasses. Then he pulled out his knife. The bartender grabbed Andrew's arm, struggling for the knife, managing to wrench it free.

"Gimme that!" Andrew demanded. He dived over the bar at the bartender. "Gimme that *now*!"

The bartender straightened, holding a small gun. He had every intention of shooting Andrew, but the gun pulled itself from his hand and flipped through the air. Andrew caught it and glanced at Chris.

Do it, Chris told him.

Andrew shot the barman in the face. The man collapsed backward in a shower of blood and glass. Someone screamed.

Andrew moved from the bar and reached over a table, pulling a young woman to her feet. She was dressed for an expensive evening, her throat decorated by a string of pearls. Light jazz continued whispering through the dining room.

Andrew stepped back to the bar with the frightened woman. He shifted until his arm was around the woman's throat. Then he shouted, "Everyone, on the floor!"

The woman's companion came forward, pleading for her. Andrew pressed the muzzle against her temple. "Sit down with the others," Andrew demanded.

The man backed into a table as the door behind him opened and a patrolman wandered in. He took one look at the room and stopped. "Holy shit!"

"*Freeze!*" Andrew screamed.

"Okay, okay," the cop said nervously. He raised his hands. "Anything you say. Just keep cool, all right?"

"Hey, Eddie," a voice called from outside, "you all right?"

"Wonderful," Eddie called to his partner, his voice tight. He watched Andrew, wondering what would happen next. Eddie inched backward, his arms raised, the smile on his face beginning to ache. No one would shoot a guy with a nice smile, right? "See, I'm leaving. Okay?" Eddie jammed his heel on the door. Andrew watched him, the hysterical woman still gathered tightly in his arms, the revolver aimed at the cop. He didn't know what to do.

"I want safe passage!" Andrew shouted. He tightened his grip on the woman's throat. "I'm warning you!"

Eddie stood with his hands in the air. There were voices coming from the kitchen. Where's Chris? Andrew thought. Where the hell is—

Andrew couldn't remember Chris's name. He searched nervously around the crowded room for a familiar face. They all stared back, each masked by a look of fear.

What am I doing here? Andrew thought.

The woman stumbled. Andrew jerked her up and pressed the gun into her temple.

"I'll have to call," Eddie said. He motioned to his radio. Andrew nodded, his eyes wide. "Take it easy," the cop muttered. The woman was sobbing and trembling in Andrew's arms.

Eddie wiped his hands.

Andrew's nerves were alive, and a sheen of sweat dripped off his face. *What the fuck am I doing?* he thought.

"*Slowly!*" he shouted at Eddie. The cop froze.

"Hey, man, calm down. We can work it out, okay? What's your name. Everyone calls me Eddie."

Andrew tried massaging the pain in his head.

"Stop talking!" he shouted at the customers. "I have to think! I need safe passage out of here!"

"Sure," Eddie said. "Anything you say. But first you got to let some of these people out. Think about it. How you gonna keep an eye on all these people? Let the women out. What do you say?"

Andrew swayed, unable to make a decision. His hostage kept crying and curling away from him. Andrew pulled her back, using her as a shield.

Chris took a sip of beer.

Let them go, he told Andrew.

"Okay," Andrew nervously agreed. "The women go. The guys stay."

"Fine," said Eddie. He carefully edged away from the group of customers. The women shuffled hesitantly, then moved quickly for the doorway.

"Everyone else, in the corner, on your knees," Andrew said.

The men obeyed and collected against a wall far away from the front door. Andrew dragged his hostage across the room and stood alongside the men. The cops wouldn't dare fire at him now for fear of hitting someone else.

"Hey, you," Andrew said to Eddie. "Where's the car?"

"Give me a break. These things take time, you know?" Eddie went back to smiling. "What's your name, anyway?"

Andrew glanced around. His wandering attention finally fixed on the cop again.

"John Griffin."

"Okay, John. Here's the thing. I'm gonna do what I can, you know, but it's gonna take a little time. You've got to keep your head."

"There's no time left!"

"Sure, there is."

Eddie glanced around. Across the restaurant was the bathroom, partially hidden from Andrew's view. Two cops in bulletproof vests had silently worked their way through a bathroom window and were now behind a room divider. The lead cop crouched and raised his automatic with both hands.

"Everything's gonna be fine," Eddie continued calmly. "No one's gonna get hurt because we're all calm, right?"

Moment of truth, thought Chris. He watched the patrolman move forward. Chris could feel Eddie's heart pounding, sensed the fear.

"I want you to move away from those people, John. We

248

don't want any accidents. We don't want anyone shot because of an eager trigger finger. What do you say, pal?''

Chris looked at Andrew.

There's one behind the room divider, his mind whispered.

Andrews's expression changed, and he swung his arm toward the hidden cop.

''No!'' Eddie shouted.

Andrew fired, the explosion deafening in the confined space. The hostage pulled away and stumbled for the door. She pushed past Eddie, who was reaching for his service revolver. Andrew fired again, and the force of the bullet took Eddie off his feet, throwing him against the table. He slumped to the floor, looking stunned, bleeding heavily from the chest.

Then everything seemed to happen slowly.

The third cop swung around the divider. Andrew stared at the injured patrolman, then at his weapon, as if seeing them for the first time. He saw the cop standing spread-legged, aiming an automatic, a slowly widening pool of blood spreading between his legs. The cop fired and hit Andrew with three shots in quick succession. Andrew fell on top of Eddie. The cop moved quickly forward, his weapon trained on Andrew's body. He drew level and kicked Andrew's gun away as other cops burst in through the front door.

Before the place was completely controlled by the police, Chris slipped out the back door, through the kitchen.

No more loose ends, he thought. Now there was only Terry.

He walked down the street, keeping to the shadows, escaping the lights and sirens of the nearby police cars. He concentrated on sending a message to Terry Cooke.

It's time, Terry. Come to me.

Twenty

Soon, he had said. But what was Terry to do? How could she hope to stop someone with that much power?

The hideous image of Meagan would not leave Terry. The shock of what she had witnessed and alone understood overwhelmed her. What he could do with his mind!

"Sorry," she said. She had bumped into a crowd of teen-agers. One of the boys stumbled back and cursed. Terry again apologized. She had been walking at a breakneck pace, as if running from her own thoughts. Now she stopped long enough to catch her breath.

Noise came from a nearby schoolyard, just beyond a mesh-wire fence. Terry leaned against the fence and watched a stream of first graders race across the yard to waiting parents. A convoy of yellow schoolbuses was double-parked along the street.

Terry hooked her fingers into the wire mesh and watched the children play. They were oblivious to the cold, screaming as they scattered in different directions. "You're it! You're it!" Their breath shot out in small white clouds as they twisted and turned. A little girl with pink earmuffs gave chase.

Her children would be coming out of school now, too,

Terry thought. She closed her eyes to imagine Jennifer's face. Instead, she saw Meagan's.

My God! she thought. *How could anyone do such a thing? How can you stop someone like Chris Easton?*

The noise in the playground had subsided, and most of the children were off in a distant corner. There remained a little boy, a year or so younger than Jennifer, sitting on the wooden seat of a swing. He gripped the chains and feebly kicked his legs in the air in an effort to gain a little momentum.

Just what I need, Terry thought. A little momentum.

Remember when Sean was that young? Remember Sean at all? Damn it! She *loved* her children, but this *thing*—this *man*—was trying to make her give them up. Keep her from ever seeing her children grow. She wanted to cry. The worst part was that he had already succeeded. He had changed her life irrevocably, no matter what happened. Damn him! How dare he!

She pressed against the fence and concentrated on the little boy. He was watching a group of older boys playing football, hoping one of them would come over and give him a push. That's all he wanted, Terry thought. Was that so much to ask?

She stared harder at him, brushed past his hair, touched his cold cheeks, ran her mind against the knitted canvas of his down jacket.

"Push," she whispered.

The breeze caught the boy, swinging him slightly. He kicked and jerked his body back against the chains.

Push.

The boy looked to his sides, then kicked again, his woolly red hat falling to the ground.

Push! Push!

She let out her breath and turned away from the playground. PK—damned if she could do it.

The cold wind pushed her toward the darkening street.

He was near, right now, looking for her. She heard his voice, carried on the wind.

Tonight, he promised, ruffling her hair. *Born anew from the water. When the time comes, I'll take you there. Wait for me, Terry.*

Artie walked into the kitchen in time to see his daughter balanced precariously on a chair, trying to reach a high shelf.

"What on earth are you doing?" he shouted.

Jennifer was wearing a yellow nightgown. She stretched upward, standing on tiptoes, wobbling. When she turned to answer her father, she lost her balance.

Artie caught her and swung the child playfully into his arms. She looked at him seriously and said, "I was making you some coffee so you could wait up for Mommy."

"That's very nice, but you know you're not supposed to stand on chairs. We put things up there so you can't get at them. What would happen if you'd hurt yourself? We'd have to rush you off to the hospital and cover you in sheets and stitch up your fingers and feet and ears."

Jennifer giggled and Artie held her tighter. "So why aren't you sleeping?"

The child hid her face in his shoulder. Quietly she asked, "When Mommy finds this man, will she come home?"

"What man, sweetheart?"

"Mommy told me she'd come home after she found him."

"When did she tell you this?"

"A little while ago."

"Mommy hasn't been home since this morning. You've been dreaming."

"No, I wasn't," Jennifer said. "Mommy came upstairs and kissed me good-night and told me about this man."

Artie thought it best for both of them to drop the subject. Jennifer was always talking to invisible friends. He

252

flipped her on his back and gave her a ride to the bedroom. She slumped tiredly over his shoulder. When Artie dropped her across the bedsheets, it was hard to believe that minutes earlier she had been daring to make him coffee.

"Jenny," Artie whispered, "where did Mommy say she was going?"

Jennifer rubbed her eyes. "What?"

"Your mother. You said she was going to see some man?"

"It was on a boat or something." She curled up, already drifting off to sleep. Artie sat beside her and stroked her hair. When the phone rang, he glanced at his watch.

Ten o'clock.

Jesus! Where the hell was Terry? She should be home looking after her kids, not stuck in some phone booth in Harlem or Inwood, or wherever the hell she went.

He went downstairs and answered the phone.

"Artie?" asked a voice.

Artie put a hold on his temper. "Yes, Gordon. What do you want?"

"Sorry, but there's a few things I wanted to check with Terry."

"She's not here."

"Any idea when she'll be in?"

"None at all."

"I wanted to talk with her about something we're working on."

"Well, she's not here," Artie said. "She's *never* here."

"We didn't exactly part the best of friends this afternoon. Sometimes your wife can be a very difficult person to get along with. Frankly, she can be fucking weird."

"Tell me about it." Despite himself, Artie relaxed. "I haven't seen her since this morning. Why don't you call Reed? She works for him. I'm just her husband."

Gordon didn't answer. Artie realized Gordon wouldn't be calling if Bill Reed knew where to find Terry.

Damn her for doing this to me, Artie thought.

Gordon stayed on the line, talking, listening. Artie answered, speaking without thinking. Gordon pumped him for clues to Terry's whereabouts. Artie finally repeated what Jennifer had told him, more to shut Gordon up than anything else. It worked.

"You there? Did I say something?" Artie asked.

"No, no," Gordon muttered.

"Do you know what Jenny was talking about?"

Again, Gordon was quiet.

"Gordon?"

Gordon hedged. "Did she say where Terry was going?"

"I told you. Jenny said something about a man and a boat. But the kid's five years old. Half the time she's living in her own little world." Another pause. "What's the matter?

"Nothing," Gordon replied finally.

Artie was sick of all this discretion. Just once he'd like to be given a straight answer to a straight question.

"Have Terry call me the minute she gets in, will you? Tell her the freak died this evening. Whatever the time, Artie. It doesn't matter."

Artie hung up. He slowly made his way back upstairs, looking in on Sean, then finding himself drawn to Jennifer's room.

As usual, she was sleeping restlessly. Artie sat on the edge of her bed for an hour, watching her. Strange mother, strange daughter, he thought.

He finally leaned forward to kiss her forehead and leave.

As he did, she woke up screaming.

Twenty-one

Gordon was not an intuitive cop like Terry. Cops who worked off hunches had always made him nervous. Gordon was a plodder, putting pieces together until he had enough of the picture to see it clearly.

He prided himself on deduction. He was, after all, a *detective* with the New York Police Intelligence Division. So he was particularly pleased with how he had connected a number of facts concerning the D.L.P. case.

First, Terry was acting totally fucking strange. *Obsessed* was the best word. Today, she'd been impossible. Irritable, disconnected, flaky; and it was more than just her problems with Artie, Gordon was certain.

Second, Bill Reed had sent her to a psychiatrist, and the psychiatrist had sent her to a center for weirdos. On top of that, Terry used the place to lock on to a lead—Murray Hunt, a wealthy magazine editor dying of anthrax, of all things.

Third, Terry had lied. She'd told Gordon she was meeting Artie for lunch, but, in fact, she'd disappeared. And all the really strange stuff had started after she and Gordon had crossed paths with the D.L.P.

Fourth, Artie's kid said Terry was going off on some boat trip. Was the kid imagining things, or had she really talked with her mother? Artie reckoned the kid had made it up, but maybe Jennifer and Terry *had* talked on the phone.

All these facts pointed to three possibilities for Gordon: Terry had dumped her job and her family—which he thought highly unlikely; she was in some kind of danger—very possible; or, far more likely, she was following the trail of whatever it was that threatened her—hence, all the secrecy.

Gordon returned to a note pad and reread what he had jotted down:

> D.L.P.—Goldin—boat (?)—Murray Hunt—
> Anthrax—Meagan—Easton.

Those were the clues. Scratch Goldin; she couldn't say a word. Then again, Hunt had also been comatose before he'd died, but Terry got information out of him.

Gordon cursed, feeling his familiar frustration with Terry Cooke. He switched off the desk lamp and leaned back in his chair. It was here—somewhere. If Terry Cooke could find it, then goddamn it, so could he.

What were the combinations? Gordon leaned forward again, switching the light back on. He circled "boat" and put another question mark beside it.

D.L.P. and Meagan. D.L.P. and Goldin. Terry and Goldin. D.L.P. and Institute. D.L.P. and Murray Hunt. Murray Hunt and anthrax. Murray Hunt and Terry. Terry and D.L.P.

Gordon rubbed his eyes, tiring of his game.

Terry and boat. Hunt and boat. Easton and Hunt. Anthrax and D.L.P. Anthrax and boat. D.L.P. and boat.

In large black letters, Gordon wrote:

EASTON

256

He stopped making his list. Some of these could be easily checked out with a few phone calls.

He once more ran through the notes on his desk. In one pile he had collected his information on Meagan; in another was a computerized profile of the late Murray Hunt and the copy of Hunt's magazine with Terry on the front cover. It was an expensive glossy, and Gordon bet whoever owned it wallowed in big bucks. Enough bucks to own a boat, maybe?

Gordon flipped through the magazine, scanned the masthead, then dialed the number of Murray's office.

A half hour later, he was parking beneath the F.D.R. Drive overpass near Twenty-fifth Street.

He turned off his car headlights and gazed into the dark sky. It was going to snow tonight.

He checked his revolver one last time before locking his car, then put the gun in his overcoat pocket. He walked across the cobblestone street, his shoes slipping on frosted oil slicks. The east-side traffic rumbled above his head.

Gordon escaped the protection of the overpass and was immediately buffeted by an icy wind. It swept up the New York Bay and along the Manhattan shoreline, chopping the water into white waves, freezing everything in its path. Gordon set his back against the wind and pushed his way toward the river. The cold sliced through his overcoat. He turned up his collar and folded his gloved hands under his armpits.

Fifty yards away was the boat basin—a shadowy mass of masts, booms, and cabins.

A gust blew down his collar and up his pants.

I'm freezing my ass off, he thought. He jogged onto one of the docks. He was looking for the magazine's boat— the *Ambrosia*—hoping to find the yacht before the wind made him permanently impotent.

"Terry?" he shouted.

The first few flakes of snow drifted down, settling in his hair. The wind snatched his breath away. Calling out was useless. A light shone from across the water. Aside from the headlights from the F.D.R. Drive, it was the only light in the neighborhood. Gordon slid on a patch of ice, cursing as he almost tumbled over a pier post and into the water. He regained his balance and ungloved one hand, sticking it in his overcoat pocket for the reassuring feel of his revolver. Gordon looked at the transom of a yacht. A small deck light shined over the word "Ambrosia."

"Jesus!" he moaned. He walked up the exposed gangplank, and the wind stung his eyes. He wiped away his tears. The ratlines were humming, and flurries of snow were settling on the curved deck and cabin roof.

The boat was a sixty-footer. Its two masts were covered with glistening sheets of ice and towered into the scudding winter clouds. Gordon walked toward the bow. He slid his feet along the bulwark and grabbed the cleats to keep his balance. When he reached the bow, he climbed on top of the foredeck and looked into the bridge. It was empty.

Well, at least we're not going anywhere, Gordon thought. He took a step and slid off the foredeck, landing heavily on the deck below. "Motherfucker!" he yelled. He kept sliding until the only thing keeping him out of the water was a coat sleeve hooked on a cleat. Gordon clambered back on board. He leaned against the cabin wall, catching his breath.

Had to be fucking Terry doing this to him, didn't it?

He worked his way carefully back toward the stern and found the cabin door. He'd had enough. Just let it be locked, he prayed. That would be the end of Gordon's evening and he could go home with a clear conscience. But it wasn't. He swung the door inward and stumbled into the darkness, slamming the door shut.

A light flicked on.

Gordon spun around, his numb fingers fumbling for his

gun. He relaxed when he recognized Terry. Gordon leaned against a bar stool and said, "It's goddamned freezing out there!"

Terry glared at him. "Get out of here, Gordon."

He looked around for a heater. "Christ, Terry, it's as cold here as it is out there."

"Go *away*," Terry said. She leaned out of the light. Gordon rubbed his jaw, trying to work some life into it.

"What's going on?" he asked.

Terry didn't answer.

"I said, what's—"

"None of your bloody business," she said.

Gordon continued to look for a heater. He finally said, "Easton, right?"

Terry glanced at her watch. Gordon went to the door and rubbed the ice off the glass, pressing his face to the window, trying to see into the night.

"Want to get him on your own. Is that it?"

He moved toward her. For the first time he realized just how awful Terry looked. She rocked back and forth in a steady, hypnotic movement. He stopped in the center of the cabin. The place was luxurious, with a bar and a row of observation seats along the cockpit. His feet had tracked wet snow onto the carpet.

"I'm getting you out of here," he said. "You need help." He started forward, then suddenly stopped, putting a finger to his mouth and listening.

He stepped quickly through a hatchway and slipped his revolver out of his pocket. Terry looked at him, then back to the cabin door. Now the footsteps were distinct. Gordon cautioned Terry, then ducked out of sight.

Chris came through the doorway.

Terry could feel him running through her. He was drawing her power to the surface, just by being near. She clutched her shoulder bag and stood up.

"You gonna arrest me, then?" Chris asked. His grin

became broader. "What have I done, darlin'? What can you prove, eh?" He paused, lifting his hands in mock surrender. "You want a drink before we go, 'ocifer'?"

He glanced over to the bar. A moment later, he was sipping a whiskey sour.

Terry brought up her gun and pointed it at Chris's chest.

"I know where the other bombs are," Terry said.

Chris smiled. "Do you, now? You willing to gamble your kids on that?"

"Penn Station, Times Square."

Chris waited.

"Empire State, U.N., City Hall, World Trade Center . . ." She hesitated. "Fraunces Tavern, Police Plaza, Port Authority—"

"You read my mind well," he said.

"Walter's," Terry said.

"Walter's?"

"He told me everything."

"I'm impressed. You're better than I thought." Chris sipped his drink. " 'Course," he added, "that assumes Walter knew everything that was going on." He sat back on a bar stool.

Terry slowly understood. "There's more," she whispered.

"Ain't you clever, then." He smiled. Terry focused on his thoughts, searching. *Another bomb. In a Christmas box* . . .

"Like I said, you willing to gamble your kids on it?"

Terry's gun was still aimed at Chris, but her hand was frozen. Why couldn't she shoot him? All it needed was a slight squeeze.

Chris watched her struggling with the revolver. "Fingers a bit stiff, are they?"

He moved toward her, his mind caressing her before his hands. He reached inside and tried to calm her.

Join me, he told her.

260

"No," Terry said aloud.

Become one, his mind whispered.

Gordon stood up.

"Police!" he shouted.

Chris turned to the hatchway, and Gordon fired. He shot at an unarmed man, trying to kill the son-of-a-bitch, wanting nothing less than to see Chris Easton dead at Terry's feet. He pumped the trigger, waiting for Chris Easton to drop, ready to follow him to the floor.

The bullets never touched Chris. They simply disappeared with little flashes of light.

Terry watched, shocked. Gordon looked helplessly at his partner. "Terry?" he pleaded.

She turned away.

Chris eased his neck, and Gordon was flung against the bar. He struck hard and slid to the deck.

"Terry?" Gordon begged.

He rubbed his cheek, suddenly feeling very warm. It felt as if his skin was melting.

He looked down at his hand. It was covered with blood.

"Terry?"

Sweat dripped off his forehead. No, not sweat—flesh. He screamed, pushing up at the skin, holding back his cheeks.

"Stop it!" Gordon cried. Something pricked the bottom of his ears and pulled down. He dropped to the floor, his flesh wet and slick. A thousand pricks tickled his face and pulled, like the twists of a taffy machine. Gordon struggled for the door, crawling slowly, slipping on his own skin. "Terry?" He could barely say it. He shouted her name a last time, but only managed to spit blood on the floor. Somewhere was laughter. From Terry? From himself?

Terry fired one shot at his head. Gordon dropped to the deck.

Chris looked at her.

"I wasn't done with him yet."

Terry faced him, filled with terror. "I don't want this," she said.

"You belong to me now," Chris said. He took a step toward her. "You want me. You know you do. We need each other."

"I *don't.*"

He reached out a hand.

"No!"

Chris was close enough now to smell her fear. He touched her cheek. Terry flinched but couldn't pull away.

His fingers traced a path across her skin, brushing each of her lips.

Terry screamed. Her voice burst upon the room, throwing Chris and the furniture into a far corner. She ran out the door, scrambling onto the deck and across the icy gangplank.

Chris recovered from his surprise and crawled free of the bar stools. "You've got it!" he shouted after her. He was immensely pleased. *"PK."*

Terry ran off the dock and slipped onto the icy parking lot. Chris followed and stood on the plank of the yacht. He watched Terry search for a place to hide. He stood absolutely still, letting the night air chill his skin, looking up at the storm. The wind ripped at his clothes. Snow clouded his sight.

Terry, he called.

She evaded him, thinking only of the snow.

Terry.

His voice caught her for a moment, but she forced herself forward.

Terry, Terry, Terry . . . He called her name over and over in a patient, nagging voice, as familiar as her heartbeat.

There was no escape. He wanted her soul.

The wind snapped through her clothes, chilling her as

if she were naked. It blew Chris Easton back into the night air.

She ran west on Twenty-fifth Street and looked for a telephone, wishing that for once she could count on Bill Reed and Gordon. No, not Gordon. She had put a bullet through his head. Oh, Christ, Gordon! It would never have happened if she had shot Chris Easton when he came through the door. She hadn't even tried. After all, she had the *power*, too. She could resist him.

Terry pulled her coat tighter. The snow brushed her face—a touch that reminded her of Chris Easton's fingers.

Third Avenue and Thirty-fourth Street. Movie theaters on either side of the street, with small crowds huddled against the cold. It was a new game—Terry running hard, Chris hunting, waiting for her to tire. She caught her breath and looked up at a theater marquee. She walked to an usher collecting tickets. "Do you have a phone?" she asked.

The usher pointed into the lobby. Terry ran inside. She wondered if she should call Bill Reed, then decided he wasn't enough. She dialed 911—police emergency.

"Please state your problem," answered an operator.

Terry talked quickly; identifying herself, giving her location, requesting immediate backup, demanding—

"This is the New York Police Department," the operator insisted calmly. "Please state your emergency."

Terry paused, starting again. "My name is Teresa Cooke. I am a detective with the Police Intelligence Division. My badge number is—"

The line went dead.

Terry turned and glanced at a young woman waiting patiently for the phone. Terry tried dialing the operator.

"May I help you?" asked a thin voice.

Terry requested the police, again identifying herself, telling the operator that 911 wasn't working.

"May I help you?" the operator repeated.

Terry hung up. Behind her, the young woman gave a sympathetic curse. "I tried two phones on the corner already," the woman said. "Must be the storm."

Terry knew better. She walked back toward the cinema entrance, aware of the usher's steady gaze. Chris was nearby, tracking her, probably using the usher. Indeed, Terry realized every passing stranger was a potential enemy, a snitch for Chris Easton.

"Can I use your restrooms?" she asked the usher. He shrugged, and Terry walked behind a barrier to the restroom and watched him discreetly. He had to be distracted.

Terry saw an elderly man standing by the ticket booth. She slipped into his thoughts and gave him an idea.

The elderly man bought his ticket and plodded into the lobby, leaning heavily on a cane. He stood before the usher, ticket extended. The usher tore the ticket. "Waiting room's downstairs," he said.

The old man thanked him, started across the lobby, then stopped.

Terry watched. It had been such a simple suggestion.

The old man walked back to the usher. "You," he said. The usher ignored him. The old man wacked him across the crotch with the cane. "Keep away from Mildred, you hot young pecker!" He reeled back for another swing and the usher dropped on his knees. . . .

Terry slipped out of the restroom and into the theater.

It was exactly what she needed. Dark, warm, and crowded. She walked to the end of an aisle and slipped into the front row, glancing back as a rear door to the theater opened. Was it the usher, or was it Chris Easton?

She looked to her sides. The audience stared up at the screen, engrossed in a war film. She looked at the movie. A Vietnam documentary. The violence of the action had set a mood in the audience. When an explosion flashed on the screen, Terry felt the fear rise in the people around her. She felt it rise in herself, too.

264

She was suddenly certain Chris Easton was in the theater.

Terry, he called.

He was walking forward, searching the seats with his mind, just as an usher might use a flashlight. Terry gently pushed his thoughts away. She wondered how much longer she'd be able to evade him. Perhaps he had missed her. Escape was possible, after all. She had done it once; she could do it again.

Chris stood in the middle of the theater, looking around the audience, losing his patience. "Terry?" he called aloud. Machine guns flashed on the screen and a mortar exploded, throwing up a body. "I know you're in here."

"Shut up!" someone shouted.

He's guessing, she thought. He doesn't know where I am. Not for certain. She could slip by him, and he'd be left alone in the movie theater. He *could* be beaten. She had proved it.

Chris frowned. He looked around the audience, then gazed up at the chandelier.

The house lights came on.

The audience let out a long, loud groan. They shouted at the projectionist, telling him to dim the lights. Chris continued his walk down the aisle.

He saw her and smiled pleasantly.

Terry.

Terry turned around, looking at Chris, glancing quickly at the ceiling.

The lights on the chandelier exploded.

The audience rushed to evade the breaking glass. The screen went black, and the entire theater became lost to a complete darkness. Terry could feel Easton groping for a hold, slipping away, coming back. She became part of the crowd and pushed out an emergency exit.

Which way now? she thought.

But he was on to her again. She ran past Lexington

Avenue, then headed south on Park. He was also running. They shared the same breaths, the same heartbeats. When she plunged into the subway, Terry wondered how many seconds would go by before Chris joined her on the platform. Thank God there was a train in the station. She threw open an exit gate and went straight into the front car. She showed the motorman her badge and ordered him to leave the station.

The doors closed and the train jerked forward. Terry held onto a hand strap. Chris arrived on the platform and glared at the train. It moved into the tunnel, picking up speed.

"Faster," Terry said.

"Got to wait for the lights," said the motorman.

"*Fuck* the lights."

The motorman pressed the horn and pulled back on the stick. In less than a minute, the train was at the Twenty-third Street stop.

Terry gripped his shoulder. "Pass it," she said.

"I got to stop at the station," he said.

"This is a police emergency," Terry insisted. "Keep going."

The motorman blared the horn, cursing as they approached and then passed the Twenty-third Street station. He cursed again when the wheels locked and the train screeched to a halt.

The force of the brakes threw him against the front windshield. Terry lost her grip on the hand strap and hit the storm door. Throughout the train, passengers were flung forward.

The motorman fell back on his seat and signaled the conductor. He turned the key on his control box. The light by the stick flicked off.

"Someone's pulled the emergency brake," he said.

"Turn it off and let's go," said Terry.

"First we gotta find which brake was pulled," he said.

"I gotta search the cars." He closed the cab door and started walking toward the rear of the train. Terry waited, anxious for the search to end. The motorman stopped before he left the car.

"Jesus!"

He walked quickly to the front, opening the cab and climbing back on his seat.

"What's the matter?" Terry asked.

The motorman glanced at her. "We're slipping." Terry pressed her face to the front glass. They were moving backward. "Must be the brakes," he said.

Terry squeezed into the cab and checked the air gauge. "The brakes are fine."

He again signaled the conductor and pulled slowly back on his stick. He held onto the doorway, expecting the train to lurch forward.

Nothing happened.

Terry looked out the window. The rusted beams of the subway tunnel slipped past them, reappearing from the sides of the train.

"We're picking up speed," said the motorman.

The conductor pushed Terry aside and stuck his head in the cab. "What the fuck you doin', man?"

"I'm doing nothing," said the motorman. "Stick's dead."

"What you mean, the stick's dead?"

The motorman leaned heavily on the stick.

"How'd you fuck it up?" the conductor asked.

"I didn't do a fucking thing."

"Then *stop* it!"

"He can't," said Terry. Both men looked at her, but she didn't know what else to say. How could she explain that Chris Easton was grabbing hold of a ten-car train, wrenching it to a halt, and then reeling it in like a fish?

"What about the emergency brakes?" the conductor suggested.

"Ain't you got no eyes? They're down."

"You're gonna fucking kill us!" shouted the conductor.

Terry watched the tunnel slip past them. They were going at a steady pace—fast for a train running backward, but not too fast for jumping out of the train. If only she could be certain of where she'd land.

"Hit the brakes hard," she said.

The motorman pressed down on the brake switch, while Terry ran to the end of the car. She opened the rear storm door, wrapped her coat tightly around her, then straddled the platforms of two cars. A safety gate kept passengers from falling off the train and down to the tracks.

Terry lifted the gate and grabbed hold of the conductor's grips.

The Twenty-third Street station slipped back into view, its steel girders flickering past like the frames of a slow-motion film. Terry climbed onto the edge of the panagraph gates and set her feet on a chain that kept them from swinging apart. She intended to use it as a springboard if she could just find the proper footing. The gates, like the rest of the subway car, were weak with age, and her weight made them swing out toward the passing girders. If she swung too far, she would hit a girder and be knocked under the wheels.

Terry held tightly to the vibrating metal. The girders kept flickering past, each one a barrier that could easily crush her. She flexed her grip and looked down the platform. They were near the end. Soon the train would disappear into the tunnel, and then he would be waiting for her at Thirty-third Street. She had a mere second to decide. Terry flicked her head, whipping the hair out of her eyes. Then she launched herself from the gates. She clipped painfully against one of the girders on the platform and crashed into a man in a business suit. Both tumbled heavily to the ground.

Terry held on to the man and watched the train disappear into the tunnel.

"I'm sorry," she gasped.

The man didn't reply. Terry struggled, trying to free herself, but she was locked in his arms.

"No," she moaned.

The eyes. Chris Easton's eyes.

Terry jabbed her palm under the man's chin, pushing free and rolling away. He didn't chase her. He simply sat on the platform, staring after her—a remote camera for Chris Easton, watching Terry limp out the subway exit to Twenty-third Street.

No place to go, Terry. No place to hide.

She hurried up the steps.

Chris walked down Lexington Avenue and stopped at a Sabrett hot dog stand. He gave Terry a long leash—five blocks at the moment. It really didn't matter. Sooner or later, Chris would tire of their game and bring her to heel.

"Cold one tonight, eh?" asked the vendor. "Nice night for a warm woman."

"You got that right," Chris said with a smile.

A long leash; but he knew her every move. She was a woman without mystery, without secrets. Whenever she did momentarily escape him, all he had to do was make the world his watchdog until he found her once again. So simple, so silly. Still, one did silly things for love.

Chris paid the vendor for his cigarettes and followed Terry downtown. It was a mistake to lead Chris to her headquarters—Chris could demolish the place. The same idea occurred to Terry and she changed direction, heading west.

Chris was pleased. He and Terry were thinking alike. Only one thing bothered him—her ability to push him away. If Chris didn't catch her soon, her blocks might become a real problem.

He closed his eyes and again tried to establish contact. He wanted to mimic her thoughts. One suggestion, that was all he wanted to give. A place to hide; a place where Chris wouldn't look for her.

"Go back to the marina," he whispered.

Terry kept walking west. Chris concentrated harder. He imagined the rocking masts of the boats.

The marina. That's where it's safe.

Terry was now heading toward Chelsea—limping, hurrying, looking for help. Chris tried something else.

"Gordon's alive," he said aloud. He imagined the body on the floor of the *Ambrosia*, moving slightly.

Terry stopped. Chris heard her thinking. She had shot Gordon, hadn't she? Damm it! Gordon was dead on the floor with a bullet through the head. He *couldn't* be alive.

But what if he is? Chris insisted.

Terry needed someone who knew the truth, someone who could help her finish Chris Easton. Gordon understood. Could he really be alive?

Yes, Chris told her. *Help Gordon, Terry. He needs you. And what about the bombs, Terry? Stop him. Stop Chris Easton.*

Terry ignored the thoughts, continuing west.

Chris jogged after her. She wasn't taking the bait.

Terry was on Fourteenth Street, stopped at a crosswalk and waiting impatiently for the light to change. Chris turned a corner, less than three blocks behind his prey. He expected her to block him immediately, or at least to deflect his thoughts into the night. This time, he pushed with the force he had used to stop the subway.

When the light turned green, she didn't move.

Chris ran down Seventh Avenue, certain of victory. He could see Terry standing at the street corner, her back to him.

Don't move, he commanded. She had let Chris into her

thoughts once too often. He put a lock on her mind to make certain she couldn't lunge free and escape.

Drop on your knees, Terry.

Chris stopped running. The snow obscured his vision, but he could see her on the sidewalk. huddled over a grating, buried deep within the folds of a fur coat. She was bowing to a streetlight as if it were an altar.

Something was not right.

Chris ran up behind her, grabbed a shoulder, and pulled her around. The glazed eyes looked through Chris. Instead of Terry Cooke, Chris was faced with a bluff—a stranger, implanted with reflections of Terry's thoughts. A clever trick to escape him. *But where had she gone?*

Anywhere, bugger it; he had lost her. She could be in the thick of Manhattan by now, or on a subway to Brooklyn, or huddled in a crowded nightclub. Eight million people, all of them eyes and ears for Chris—and shields for Terry Cooke.

Unless she *did* take the bait.

He had told her Gordon was alive. Had the thought reached her?

Chris Easton headed east, back toward the marina.

Terry Cooke, he called. *No one's ever done that to me before. Let's trade secrets. I'll show you mine if you show me yours.*

Chris was soon at the river. Terry was there somewhere. Had to be. If she wasn't, he'd have to start looking all over again, and that would take time and a lot of effort.

No. She was there; he was certain.

Chris closed his eyes and joined the darkness. He recalled his days in Nicaragua. walking up trails, using his power to sweep the jungle for snipers. But Chris wasn't interested in jungles anymore. He was in the snow, searching, looking for—

Terry cried out. It was a soft sound, but he heard it. A crack in her psychic wall.

Chris turned away from the *Ambrosia* and moved toward a second yacht, docked against a nearby cement embankment. He followed a set of tracks that led up to the deck.

"I'm going to clean your mind, Terry," he said. "That's the only way, love. Can't have you fussing every time someone dies."

He swung open the cabin door. The interior was broader than Murray's yacht, and the darkness seemed fuller. Chris stopped, listening and waiting.

"Terry?" he called.

He felt his way to another door. It was locked. With a brief thought, Chris unlocked the door.

He heard the shuffle of footsteps. Terry was ducking down a hallway, hiding somewhere in the stern.

"Come out *now*, Terry. Come out, or I'll explode the bombs."

He smiled, sensing her hesitation. Chris walked down the steps to the lower cabins. "You or your kids." She was almost straight ahead, down the hall. "What's it going to be?"

Then he saw her—a dark figure, just in front of him. "It's time, Terry," he whispered. "Time to make your mind all nice and tidy."

Chris stared at the shadow, reached in, and began digging. It was extraordinarily easy. *And* fascinating. Her mind was a treasury of thoughts and images. As good as those of any killer he had absorbed. But what did he expect from a cop? He had been right all along. Terry and he were alike. What moved her, moved him. He drained her power, sucking it dry. All her pain and misery and nightmares. It was so much like his own. Well, why not—Chris had seen it all, hadn't he? He was doing to Terry what the world had done to him, and what he would do to the world.

A memory passed through him. Was that Moira? Impossible! Who was Moira? Chris already had forgotten. The memory was gone. And so was the memory of . . . That cop bitch. She was making him forget. Where was she? Where were the bombs? Time to— What? He couldn't remember.

Emptiness.

He looked about, searching for escape.

Where am I?

A sense of wonder. Dark, hollow life. Nothing but the sound of a beating heart.

What am I?

It felt as if a shell had enclosed him. Limbo.

Who am I?

No answer. Only the darkness and the throbbing pulse.

Who am I?

Terry huddled behind the door, waiting for Chris Easton to take her mind and her soul. There was no escape; she realized that now. A part of her was in him, and he was now a part of her.

Yet he didn't come.

He's waiting for me, she thought. He was just outside the door. She could feel his power battering at her. Terry struggled against it, but it swept her along. She saw her daughter, Jennifer, sitting up in bed screaming. Here was Chris, spinning around the stranger on the street corner, surprise on his face after certain victory. Terry violently scrubbing her home. A dusty African village exploding around her. A gondola disappearing under a stone bridge. A whirlpool, drawing her into Murray Hunt's death. *Her* vivid memories, but no longer in her mind. Reflections of her thoughts, now a part of *him*.

Yet he didn't come.

Terry forced herself to touch the door. It opened silently, and she peered down the dark hallway. She needed light. She needed to see herself and Chris and all the other ghouls. She moved forward hesitantly, her palm rubbing a light switch. Her eyes moved constantly, searching the darkness, finding nothing. Finally, she turned on the light.

"Jesus!" she screamed, jumping back. She had frightened herself. In front of her was a mirror, the length of an open closet door.

Terry turned around. There he was, on his knees, staring at her.

"Chris," she murmured.

He didn't move. When she approached him and touched his shoulder, he continued staring straight ahead—not at her, but at the mirror.

The boat rocked as a wave caught it broadside.

"Damn you," she said.

With a cry of anger, she kicked him. He crumpled to the floor.

He was only Chris Easton now. Chris locked inside Chris. Trapped in a limbo of his own making—unable to resurface. Terry kicked him as he lay on the floor. She moved through the hallway, looking for the galley. She found the stove and ignited a gas burner. Then she tore down the curtains and dropped them on the flames. The curtains caught fire.

Terry hobbled off the yacht and watched the flames grow. Then she limped through the snow to the *Ambrosia*. She stopped at the gangplank, struggling for the nerve to walk back inside and face what was left of Gordon Weiss. She couldn't do it.

PK, she thought. She closed her eyes and concentrated.

The *Ambrosia*'s stove exploded.

Within minutes the two yachts began to drift away, as their moorings snapped and the current caught them. Terry made an "Officer in Need of Assistance" call from the radio in Gordon's car, then switched it off.

In the river, flames wrapped the outside of the hulls. Both yachts were lost to raging fires. There was a loud explosion, and the first yacht sank quickly. The *Ambrosia*'s bow reared, and its stern settled lower in the water.

By the time the police arrived, the *Ambrosia* had disappeared beneath the surface.

Twenty-two

During the next few weeks, most of Bill Reed's problems came to a convenient end.

The D.L.P. was finally gone, after nearly two years of tracking its most-wanted members. Meagan Donnely and Easton were dead; Lawrence Kruger, Griffin, and Walter Beal were guaranteed jail sentences. And Mark Schneider? Well, he could spend the rest of his days in Central America. That was C.I.A. territory. Bill Reed had other things to worry about, not the least of which was another bombing at Penn Station. This one was the work of an F.A.L.N. splinter group calling itself the Puerto Rican Resistance Alliance. P.R.R.A., he thought, already sick of the acronym.

Emily Goldin was out of the hospital, her mind in working order, if at times a little forgetful. She had no memory of what had happened to her. In fact, she had no memory of the institute. The hospital had scheduled some outpatient rehabilitation, which Becker reckoned would bring her back to normal.

Then there were the bombs. Terry's last interview with Walter Beal had helped with that. Beal was still babbling demands that made no sense to anyone. He was being cared for in a maximum-security mental hospital in upstate New York. If he was ever declared sane, he would stand trial. Reed thought it unlikely.

Finally, Reed's thoughts returned to the Englishman, Chris Easton. Reed was still unclear as to how he fit into the picture. Reed had read Terry's report a dozen times and still couldn't quite make sense of it. Easton had apparently spent most of his time outside England, in the Middle East.

The Intelligence Division hadn't discovered a link between the P.L.O. and the D.L.P., or any of the other urban terrorist groups they were currently tracking. What bothered Bill Reed most was the possibility that the Libyans might be involved. And the anthrax gambit? Another strong indication of an international connection. Easton to New York, Hunt to London—correction, Hunt to *Gruinard*. The last Reed had heard, an anonymous British House of Commons subcommitte responsible for state security was in the hasty process of preparing a report on the Gruinard Island incident for the First Minister, a copy of which was going to the C.I.A.

England, Israel, Lebanon, and maybe Libya, too? Reed would need more men, more authority, and better coordination between the I.D. and the F.B.I.

He glanced down at Gordon Weiss's obituary and Terry Cooke's resignation.

First, more men.

The cold followed Terry everywhere, whether outside or inside.

At least there was no more snow on the ground. A month had passed since she had finished her investigation. Sun and rock salt had turned the powder into slush puddles, leaving behind a grid of white-stained streets. On the yards and rooftops, the snow slowly crusted, crystallized, and dropped. Boot season, Terry reminded Artie. Don't let the kids go anywhere without wrapping up warm.

Artie didn't say a word. He stood by the bedroom door, watching Terry pack, wishing he could make her stay.

"Mom?" shouted Sean. "Jenny's hogging the TV!"

Terry folded the last of her clothes, then closed the suitcases.

"Mom!"

Terry smiled. "You go down," she told Artie.

He shook his head. Terry touched his hand. "Stop worrying. It's only a vacation."

"I'm jealous."

Terry smiled at him.

Artie opened his arms and hugged her. Terry was uncertain what to do. Her arms hung lamely by her sides. She let Artie free himself.

"You're not coming back, are you?" he asked.

"Of course I am," she whispered. "This is my family." Terry turned away and picked up the suitcases, carrying them downstairs. Sean and Jennifer were at her feet as soon as they heard her on the stairs.

"Give me a hug," she said. She crouched and took them in her arms. Terry stared at Sean, looking into his eyes, trying to see if the secret had been passed along to him. God, she hoped not. It was too dangerous—too addictive.

Candy in my pocket, Sean. Candy in my left pocket.

Sean hadn't heard her. He leaned in and hugged his mother's neck. Jennifer pushed her way in close, kissing Terry, then digging deep into Terry's coat. The little girl came up with the two chocolate bars and grinned shyly.

I love you so much, Terry thought.

Jennifer kissed her mother again.

I'll be back, Terry promised. *I swear it.*

"Take care," Artie said.

Terry and he hugged again. When they kissed, Terry felt a powerful urge to stay, but she wouldn't. She picked up her suitcases and walked outside to the waiting taxi.

"J.F.K.," she told the driver.

Terry waved good-bye to her children. She felt like crying.

But the tears were gone, and now there was just the long trip to the airport. Terry had often thought about why she couldn't stay. It always came down to Chris Easton. *He* was still alive. A part of him was embedded deep within her. What she was about to do was dangerous. Yet the power trembled within her. *His* power—blending with hers and demanding more. She felt it just beneath the surface and barely under control. Gordon's death had been a beginning for her, not an ending.

"Which terminal?" asked the driver.

Terry hesitated. The driver glanced in the mirror.

She opened her purse and examined her Pan Am ticket to Italy. Artie had surprised her with it. Terry supposed it was a demonstration of support.

"It doesn't matter," she said.

The driver took her to Terminal Five. He weaved through the traffic and parked in a No Standing zone. The meter read $31.90.

"I'll help you with your bags," he offered.

"Don't bother," she said.

She walked into the terminal and dropped her suitcases. Above her head was a departure monitor, its destinations momentarily blank. Terry stared at her reflection on the monitor, seeing two people instead of one.

And, in a sense, there were two people. Chris Easton was dead, but there was so much of him still alive in her. At night she dreamed his dreams. During the day, she remembered his past. And when she thought of Artie and the children . . .

Nothing. In their place was a hunger.

A passion for destruction, with all the consequences. The same passion that had killed him, Terry thought. A passion that could kill her. But it was in her now, barely under control.

She looked a last time at the ticket to Italy, then tore it in half. Italy belonged to a husband, a wife, and their family. Terry was alone now.

Instead, she stared down at the baggage carousel.

Suitcases, duffel bags, knapsacks, foot lockers . . . They possessed more than clothes; they held identities. And if Terry wished, she could break through the wall of anxious passengers and not only claim a suitcase, but also a new life. She could be another mother, or a businesswoman, or a grandparent. It was all so random and all so tempting— but not here, she thought. Somewhere else. *Anywhere* else.

Above her, a departure monitor was starting methodically to fill with cities. London, Paris, Mexico City, Amsterdam . . . There was only one flight missing.

She reached down and lifted her bags, ready to take the next flight that appeared on the monitor, wherever it went. It was the simplest way to choose her destiny, for it didn't really matter where the plane took her; north, east, south, west . . . any direction promised home. The power guaranteed it.

She waited patiently, resisting the urge to push the machine. There was absolutely no rush now. Time was all hers. The world was hers.

Then the last city appeared on the monitor.

Terry stared for a moment at the name on the screen.

She smiled and walked toward the gate.